Deadly Ambitions

A Novel

Alvin Wander

iUniverse LLC
Bloomington

DEADLY AMBITIONS

iUniverse books may be ordered through booksellers or by contacting:

iUniverse
1663 Liberty Drive
Bloomington, IN 47403
www.iuniverse.com
1-800-Authors (1-800-288-4677)

ISBN: 978-1-4917-0054-9 (sc)
ISBN: 978-1-4917-0053-2 (hc)
ISBN: 978-1-4917-0052-5 (e)

Library of Congress Control Number: 2013913276

Printed in the United States of America.

iUniverse rev. date: 8/19/2013

For my daughter Rachel

The courage you show each day of your life is like a shining light that brings the harsh reality into focus.

Introduction

A wonderful fact to reflect upon, that every human creature is constituted to be that profound secret and mystery to every other. A solemn consideration, when I enter a great city by night, that every one of those darkly clustered houses encloses its own secret; that every room in every one of them encloses its own secret; that every beating heart in the hundreds of thousands of breasts there, is, in some of its imaginings, a secret to the heart nearest it!

Charles Dickens

Prologue

Phillip Courtney was a forty-year old executive working for Black Technologies, Inc., a high-end technology company. He grew up in a small town in northern California, just outside of Silicon Valley. His mother and father, Aiden and Maeve, arrived in California from Ireland to join other Irish families that came to this Garden of Eden with the goal of raising their families in America. They dreamed of something they could call their own. Like other immigrants, they wanted to put control into their otherwise chaotic lives. They found homes and soon villages emerged, bustling with excitement. But the town was suspicious of these strangers who landed in their paradise; hard looking men and women with their undernourished, dirty looking offspring. Banks were unwilling to finance those whom they considered a risky underclass.

After unsuccessfully searching for capital to fulfill his dream, Aidan settled for a job driving a forklift truck in the warehouse of a company that manufactured products that he knew nothing about. The few times that he drifted into the production area, he could not understand the burgeoning growth of these small, odd-looking pieces of silicon that were being shipped all over the world. He had no idea of what the future would be like; the new semiconductor industry was just beginning to develop all across these sleepy little villages.

Aiden and Maeve brought Michael into the world, and Phillip was not far behind. Aidan needed to be content with his factory job. After all, it paid decent wages and he became content providing for his wife and two sons. He soon joined the other immigrants on most nights at the local pubs enjoying Irish whiskey in their new country. Working long hours and extra days in this business did not bother Aiden. After a time, he was able to afford the down payment on a small cottage, and life for the Courtney family settled in to a sense of comfortable orderliness.

Tragedy did not happen to the Courtneys until Michael was nine and developed a nasty cough and low-grade fever. It was not. After a few days of fighting what seemed to be a worsening cough, his fever raced upwards and by the time the local hospital was willing to admit the boy and ran tests, he was too far gone; the pneumonia resisted any medication. On a sunny summer day before he reached his tenth birthday, Michael Nicholas Courtney was laid to rest in the small cemetery reserved for the local immigrant population. This blow changed the Courtney family forever. They were never quite the same after Michael's death. Aidan began to drink more than ever, and the distance between Maeve and him became more pronounced. They blamed each other for not recognizing how sick the child really was. The only time they were close was when Aiden struggled home in a drunken stupor and forced himself on hapless Maeve. Seeking any assistance was not part of their culture, even from the local priest. The family ate together and watched television together when Aiden was not at the local pub, but rarely held any conversation.

But then times changed; the small villages became towns and cities. New families, educated people were moving in, and the communities bustled with new ideas, new ways of communicating. Phillip Courtney did not flourish in this environment. He stayed to himself and never mentioned where his father worked or what he did. The memory of losing his brother stayed etched in his memory throughout his childhood. He was a quiet boy, preferring to read and write, and he took great pleasure in inventing imaginary games.

As the Courtney family drifted into complete dysfunction, Phillip's relationship with Aiden and Maeve became more distant. As a teenager he grew tall and lanky, almost spindly. Despite his gangly physique, he was a good-looking boy with a shock of black hair that scattered wildly over his forehead.

Phillip began to develop a keen interest in science and engineering at which he excelled. To the Courtney's amazement, he won prizes in school science projects, inventing new applications that consistently won him accolades from his teachers. One evening, as his graduation neared, Phillip turned the sound down on the *telly* and delivered a message to the

Courtney's that would tear apart whatever remaining thread held them together.

Just before his high school graduation, Phillip announced that he had been offered and accepted a scholarship to attend the California Institute of Technology. It never occurred to him to discuss this with them during the application process; he believed that they would be able to comprehend little of the enormity and challenge that this would pose. As he suspected, the thought of moving away from his home to a school in the "Wild West" was a heavy cross for them to bear. As was true in many immigrant cultures, grown children did not move away from home; they just resettled in the town where they were born, near the family. But Aiden and Maeve knew that when their "grand boy," their super-smart, strong-willed young man made up his mind, trying to contain or compel him otherwise would be useless. He was becoming a young man with a strong Irish spirit. So, with their blessing and lists of sinful activities that he should avoid, he went into the Wild.

At Caltech, his interests broadened; his spindly physique grew into a well-developed body. What emerged from that frame was a tall young man with a striking appearance accented by a thick dark beard, who was well liked by everyone he made contact with at the university. Phillip's social life revolved around anyone he met with shared interests in science, male or female. Women who met him at Caltech found this good-looking, studious young man appealing. Sexual relationships with women on campus became a pleasant diversion for Phillip, but were a distraction from his academic pursuits. Joining a fraternity held no attraction, but as with most students at Caltech, Phillip lived on campus in the residential college, a housing structure similar to Oxford in England. He would have preferred staying off-campus; he still longed for the solitude of the small town, but the Caltech system strongly encouraged students to build close, working relationships.

Four years later, while Phillip was preparing to graduate, he was determined to seek an opportunity to work near the university despite his parents' desire to have him home. He visualized working at a small tech company that was developing new scientific and technological applications and where he could have the freedom to create and invent. It was not difficult for him to find work in an industry that was growing rapidly, especially in northern California.

After graduation, he began his career at a small techno-sphere company in Pasadena, whose workplace was in a converted garage; he loved it from the start. Going to work in jeans, a tee shirt, and flops was perfect. He rented a small apartment nearby and happily bicycled to work with his North Face strapped on his back. His company was developing software designed for automating measuring instruments in an industry that was still labor-intensive.

During the next few years, while the company prospered, Phillip diligently dove into more complex applications and developed highly sought-after skills in software development. When he spent some holidays at home, Aidan and Maeve stared in wonder at what they remembered him to be: a quiet lad. What descended on their household was a sparkling, handsome, outgoing man who often brought friends home with him.

He began to bring recognition in his workplace and in technology land. He now led a small staff of programmers and design people, but this new administrative role never deterred him from his desire to create. As the company grew and broadened its client base, his specialty shifted to the development of software applications in the fast-growing medical technology field. Working with a group of local surgical physicians and engineers, he began to study the use of automation in surgical procedures that, at that time, were performed manually by surgeons. Phillip became convinced that hardware and software design could be developed that would allow retraining of a surgeon's skills using powerful lasers. However, after a few years at this activity, he tired of the slow pace of acceptance in this field and he began to take interest in the development of space age applications.

He was soon being courted by companies seeking his skills in device development; this was where he believed he could put his expertise to work. His interest began to turn to the latest in these newly developing industries. He made a prodigious effort to learn everything about the use of scientific applications in this new field. After short stints at companies whose commitment to development seemed painfully slow, he began a search for a position in a large, well organized company with highly developed strategic goals where he could put his expertise to work.

While attending a technical conference, he learned of strategies being developed by a large organization headquartered outside of Detroit, called Black Technologies. At the conference, he learned more and was impressed with their size and the massive futuristic projects that they were working on. For the next few days, he immersed himself in information about the company and its research in weapons development. He read everything he could lay his hands on concerning high-speed data transmission for use in laser weaponry; this was going to be his *cacoethes*. Phillip engaged the executives of Black in conversation, and so impressed the members of the company attending that they arranged for him to meet Edgar Black, the founder and CEO.

The two shared a lunch at a local café; Phillip found Edgar Black easy to talk to and Black seemed genuinely interested in Phillip's ideas. Later, they exchanged small talk at a cocktail party and arranged to meet the following next day. "I know that the laser will become the ultimate battlefield weapon, and I know I can help develop it," Phillip bombastically opined. Black was immediately taken with this brash, outgoing man with whom he was able to discuss some of his strategic plans.

After Edgar Black had Phillip quickly vetted, he became convinced that this young man was just who he needed to propel his company into the rarified air used by the people who were responsible for new ways to destroy the enemy: the United States Military. Edgar and his staff had several long meetings with Phillip over the next two days, and Edgar invited him to visit the headquarters of his company. Phillip, at twenty-five, was about to enter the world of Corporate America. Edgar talked about the possibility of heading up technical development for the company, which could lead to a top corporate role a Black Tech.

Phillip was impressed with Edgar and the dream of helping develop large-scale projects, but shared a concern. "I know I can do the job but it has to be as the top technologist. I know how to turn ideas into action but I wouldn't be satisfied with anything less than becoming the chief 'techie' for the company." The thought of moving from the sun-drenched world of the Valley to Detroit was clearly not what Phillip would have selected for his career location.

Speaking to his friends, he said, "I think the company's aggressive strategic plans are tops in the industry and Edgar Black is committed to implementing them, but I'd only take the job as the top guy, and he knows it. We'll see how it turns out."

Black saw Phillip as the skilled, young tiger that could spearhead his adventure and quests and quickly made his decision. After days of negotiation, during which Phillip excelled, Edgar agreed to select him to be Black's first Vice-President for Technical Development. A very special young man had finally arrived at the dawn of his new career.

Chapter 1

Just before Christmas on a late Saturday afternoon, after snow had fallen most of last week, the bright winter sun masked a blistering Arctic wind that was blowing unfrozen icy residue like a summer dust storm. Phillip Courtney had worked all day at corporate headquarters, located a distance from the northern suburbs of Detroit. In stark contrast to the modern glass and burnished steel structure dotting the landscape that has been his home for the past fifteen years, neighborhoods just north of the city of Detroit sit in decay; trash littered boulevards, shuttered stores and empty homes in desperate disrepair sit in silence. Once thriving factories up and down busy streets in this white, middle-class community hummed with the blurring sound of machines turning out parts for most of the automobile makers; all day and into the night the smokestacks belched out smoke-filled fumes.

During the 1940s when the country required the construction of massive quantities of war-related machinery and equipment to fight World War II, the factory assembly lines were refitted to manufacture truck, tank, and cargo parts for the war effort. That was a time when men and women, tired from long hours and backbreaking shifts, exited in the early morning or in late afternoon and into the middle of night, heading to the local joints up and down the factory strip to drown their bored and weary spirits. That was a time when smoke-filled union halls once stood, filled with men and women talking about too many hours or too few hours, too little pay and too much work. But that was then.

Now, few of them still work for their companies. The closed factories stand like tall angry ghosts; the parking lots appear like huge empty football fields with weeds springing life between cracks in the pavement; graveyards, they seem.

From Phillip Courtney's top-floor window, he could make out in the distance the solemn streets and closed storefronts that littered like old, shabby safes crammed with the tarnished valuables of a bankrupt middle-class.

Empty factories and homes sat where lamps once burned day and night, under the shadows of facades and dirty plaster frontages that lay embossed with aging scrollwork. The nearly all-white suburban community abutted the city line of Detroit, and inside these imaginary lines, the population immediately changed to black.

Eight Mile Road, the dividing line between the city of Detroit and the burbs, was more than a street. It divided the city, blacks from whites, poverty from a decayed middle class.

It had been an emblem of the hostility and social ills that long ago beset the city and still lingered along much of the wide and hemorrhaged artery. Deep inside Eight Mile Road, abandoned warehouses, fire-gutted businesses, and crime-ridden neighborhoods teeming with broken homes ruled the city.

Once you crossed the boundary out of Detroit, you entered a different world. However, much of suburbia just north of the line was no longer infused with middle class. Many of the neighborhoods along the border had suffered the same fate that plagued Detroit. Crime and poverty festered in these neighborhoods close to the empty, rusted factories that once were part of the fabric of middle-class America. Once poverty ruled inside Eight Mile Road; now the empty factories to the north suffered the technological backlash, and its citizens suffered along with it.

But as one moved farther north, new neighborhoods with gleaming monolithic structures dotted the landscape. Among the outer edges of this blight stood corporations that moved in from the war-torn city after riots chased even the bold and built their monuments. Here among the monuments stood the corporate headquarters of Black Technologies, producing cutting-edge hardware, principally for the Department of Defense, and specifically the U.S. military.

When Phillip Courtney, fifteen years ago, made his first trip to corporate headquarters, the sight of the structure sent chills to his already excited gut. Passing the dreariness of the nearby empty lots and shuttered homes did not lessen his verve. Today, as he stepped into the glass-enclosed entry, suspicious looks from the office crew rattled him a bit, but once the formalities and intros were done, he settled comfortably into his corner office.

Phillip contained his emotions until his office door closed, then put his size twelve Doc Martins up on the fine wooden desk with his hands clasped behind his head, and said, "I made it. This is what I always wanted." He closed his eyes and enjoyed the intensity of the mood that overtook him.

Moments later, Phillip was startled by the sounds of an ambulance and two fire trucks racing to a tragedy that was occurring near the city. As he watched the event unfolding, his thoughts turned from the ebullience of the moment, with its promise of success, to a city, dead now, filled with tragedies, desolation, and emptiness. This stayed with him as he started his journey.

Chapter 2

IN LATE DECEMBER of his first Christmas, as was traditional at Black Tech, the top corporate executives and the members of the Board of Directors and influential corporate insiders received an invitation to a holiday black tie gala. It was typical of a company festivity--waiters passing champagne and hors d'oeuvres, a discreet corner bar for those interested in getting slammed quickly, a huge tree emblazoned perfectly with balls and gold and silver strands, and, of course, the corporate wives. Not a single gray hair or un-manicured finger or toenail was in evidence, and all were attired in gowns and dresses with enough cleavage to prove that there was ample substance beneath.

The men all dressed like penguins, told droll tales of politics, football, and the latest bit of gossip. Phillip clearly was ill at ease in these surroundings. He just wanted to stop in to his new favorite tavern in Greektown, kick off his shoes, and down a schooner and a few gyros.

As he daydreamed, a skill acquired during his less interesting college courses, he noticed a woman his age standing with a group of older women; she clearly seemed out of place. She was tall and had a great body. Her blonde, streaked hair was shoulder length and was combed perfectly framing her oval face. She wore a fabulous gown, cut low exposing most of her back down to the waist and with a side slit exposing some thigh. Her shoes were black straps, high and open for her darkly painted toenails to peek out. He found himself staring at her during the early part of the evening and she smiled and returned the glances. When Phillip could no longer stand the boredom, he introduced himself.

She was Emma Kovacs, a design consultant frequently used by the corporation. This was Phillip's first social interaction since he relocated to Michigan. Emma was single; it was cocktails, a sumptuous buffet dinner, and off the two flew for an amorous evening of drinks and talks followed by the excitement of first sex. Weeks later, after several dinners, a few movies, and some pleasant sex, Emma was developing a continuing interest in Phillip, but it was just a casual interlude for him.

After time, Phillip's social life moved into high gear, consisting of discrete, short-term relationships, often with women in the company. Though this new social life appealed to Phillip, he still realized that his dedicated focus must be on his work at Black Tech, and he would allow nothing to get in the way.

Chapter 3

MANUEL KORMAN WAS a senior associate with a large law firm headquartered in downtown San Francisco. As a child, he was abandoned by his mother, who became a member of the vast homeless, drug-infested population in Los Angeles. He never knew his father: he was left to fend for himself and at ten was picked from the street while fruitlessly searching for his mother. An organization in Los Angeles called "The Center Against Violence to Children," headed by a man named Victor Vasquez, took him to a shelter temporarily where he underwent a complete evaluation.

During the time that the shelter staff spent with the tall, intense, painfully thin Manuel, they noticed his remarkable reading aptitude that included books far beyond his age level. In total amazement, the staff recognized that he was able to intelligently discuss what he had read with clarity and an almost complete recall of the material. After testing, they concluded that despite the social problems that he faced, Manuel was an extremely intelligent child with great potential.

Vasquez and his subordinates deliberated long and hard about the direction to take Manuel. He needed a home, and they made a concerted but futile effort to place him. One day when Vasquez was at lunch with a friend, he was introduced to a businessman named David Korman. Korman became interested in the wonderful work done by Vasquez, and when he was invited to visit the facility, he agreed. During the visit where he saw children who had been discarded as society's refuse, David was told about this strange little Hispanic boy they found in the streets and who had such enormous potential. When David met Manuel, something of another world occurred. The childless David, who had spent almost his entire life without parents or siblings, immediately felt an attachment that stayed with him.

David continued to visit Manuel, and they began to spend increasing amounts of time together. He realized that Manuel needed a home, and Korman badly needed and wanted to provide that to him. After several months of bonding with Manuel and forming an attachment that David believed would never diminish, he went through a financial evaluation and was given temporary custody; from that time on they were never separated.

David financed the boy's education at schools that specialized in children with advanced learning capabilities, and later at college, and finally at Stanford Law School, where Manny graduated near the top of his class. He then joined a prominent law firm in the San Francisco area where he continued to head towards partnership.

The circumstances behind the adopted children, including Manuel, were another part of the extraordinary life of David Korman. He grew up with no parents and no place that he could call home beyond the orphanage. Although the concept of family was foreign to him, living in a kibbutz and seeing the dynamics of Israeli families there, he believed that somehow he would be able to have a family of his own, and he did by adopting three children.

Years before, his lunch with Vasquez led to the eventual adoption of Manuel. Several years later, Vasquez once more invited David to visit the shelter to meet a pixie-faced ten- or eleven eleven-year year-old Asian child who had extraordinary intellect, far beyond her years. David fell in love with her, and after spending precious time with this waif, David became the proud parent of two gifted children. He enrolled and bankrolled their future in special schools, and Susan, as she wanted to be called, went on to become a physician, first in Los Angeles, and then as a successful internist at Children's Hospital in Boston.

Later, David was told about a pedophile ring operating in the New England area in which boys, aged seven to twelve, had been sodomized and tortured by members of an Internet ring selling photos and advertising for men interested in photo ops with the children. Victor Vasquez told David about one of the homeless children, a seven seven-year year-old boy they named Oliver, who, after some time at the shelter, demonstrated enormous potential and easily read, digested, and memorized advanced classical literature. David initially was initially not tempted by the prospect of adding to his family, but spending time with Oliver convinced him that he could not let this child spend his life in temporary situations with no parents to provide the kind of love that David himself never received.

Chapter 4

ON A SUNNY morning in April, when Manuel was in his mid-twenties, he was reviewing a brief prepared by one of the seven attorneys who reported to him at the firm. His assistant buzzed and told him that Jim Jameson was on the line. Jim was a close friend of Manuel's from law school, who was now the senior vice president and house counsel for GEN21, a software development firm. He told Manuel that he had a serious problem and wanted to meet with him as soon as possible.

That evening, Jim began talking even before drinks were served. "Manny, about a month ago, GEN21 interviewed and subsequently hired an individual whose background perfectly suited our style and needs for solid technological control of the projects that we had on the drawing board. Strong design skills and experience with a much larger organization was what we required at this stage in our super-heated growth. We were certain that we found the perfect guy. He joined the company several weeks ago and dug right in with terrific enthusiasm. We knew that his background included run-ins with his CEO, but with that CEO's reputation in the industry, we discounted those issues. Anyone we contacted had high praise for him and he came to us with a positive attitude and fit in beautifully. Manny, it looked like a good fit and he certainly showed it."

"So what's the problem?" Manual asked. "Looks like you guys made the right choice."

"Manny, two days ago, he didn't show up for work, so Ed Morgan, our security guy, tried calling him with no luck. He had someone go over to his apartment but they got no response; with no other recourse, Ed had the police check his place and, Manny.... they found Phillip Courtney dead, hanging from a light fixture in the living room. There was a lot of meds opened and scattered around the bathroom; most were anti-depressants and sleeping pills filled months before from a pharmacy in Detroit. There was a note on his desk talking about how down he had been and how he couldn't see another way out. It was a straight out suicide note. So with all that, the cops called it a suicide. Autopsy prelims surmised that he had taken some pills, stood on a chair, tied the heavy rope around his neck and kicked the chair away, so they closed the case."

Jim continued, "Here's the problem, Manny, it makes no sense at all. Phillip was starting a new part of his life as upbeat as anyone I've seen. Good job, money was OK with him, and the future with us was all positive. Why would he do this? I just don't buy this suicide stuff, but the police feel they have enough to support their position, and since he just started with us and did not seem to have any problems with anyone here in town, there was nowhere else for them to go with it."

Drinks came and there were a few moments of silence. Manny thought for a bit and said, "It sure sounds crazy, Jim. But what can you do about it, and, more importantly, what do you want me to do about it?"

"Manny, I know that your father has spent his life in the military dealing with security issues and later on in a special role with the State of Israel dealing with bad guys around the world. You told me that he has more experience in tracking down these types than most federal intelligence people. I remember that you also told me that he is no longer involved officially in any security matters. But if you asked him, would he take a look at what happened to Courtney? I helped bring the guy out to our company and I think something is not right with his death."

"Hold on, Jim. My dad is sixty-five years old and has spent a lot of years risking his life. I'm not going to ask him to get involved in what could be risky business. That's aside from the fact that my mother would kill me if I asked him to get involved. The last mission he was involved in nearly got him and my mother killed in a rat-hole in Africa. I think he's paid his dues to this country and Israel. They are finally learning how to enjoy life together."

Jim thought for a moment and said, "How about just talking on the phone with him and filling him in on our conversation. Maybe he'd just take a trip and ask some questions. No deep involvement. I would just trust his judgment long before I would a private detective and certainly more than San Francisco's finest." At this, despite his discomfort, Manuel agreed to speak to his father.

The next night, after putting their son Harry to bed, Manny and his wife Cecelia enjoyed a nice Sonoma Valley pinot noir with their dinner. But after husband and wife daily updates, Manuel was visibly disturbed by what he had agreed to do. His wife became upset with his decision and told him in no uncertain terms that he was not to ask David to investigate.

Cecelia explained, "The authorities have done their homework and, who knows, maybe Courtney was depressed and didn't show it or reveal it to anyone at GEN21. Just because Jim Jameson thinks it doesn't smell right, that's not reason enough to involve your father. We both know what that man has done and gone through in his life."

Manuel knew this was true and he spent a sleepless night struggling between Jim's request and his deep respect for the man who gave him his life. By early morning, he reached his decision.

Chapter 5

AT TEN THE next morning, Manuel Korman placed a call to his father's home in Manhattan. David and Dianne Korman lived in an eastside apartment looking south and east to the river. Their luxurious apartment afforded the couple a stupendous view of the city through a living room wall of glass and a balcony on which they were now spending precious time together.

David had been orphaned at the age of five when his mother and father were killed in an automobile accident while visiting family in New York. He was brought up in Jewish orphanages until the age of ten when Rivkah Stein, the senior social worker at an orphanage in Milwaukee, immigrated to Israel and took David with her to a kibbutz where he grew up. She was the closest thing to a mother Dove, as she referred to him, had ever known. There he learned about the violence between Jews and Arabs first hand. After a successful university experience in the States, compliments of the state of Israel, David joined the Israeli army as an officer where he distinguished himself in battle during the celebrated Six Day War.

After several years in service, he opted for an unusual role with a secret organization within the military. He was set up in a career building a business relationship with an Amsterdam-based merchandise brokerage company, and as part of the arrangement, he agreed to take on clandestine missions for the security agency. These tasks ranged from simple information tracking to being a part-time assassin, eradicating foreign plotters and taking on missions that frequently threatened his life. The most recent occurred several years earlier and involved his wife, Dianne. When people he considered his friends engaged in a plot to kill David, it was foiled in an African escapade that cost the lives of several people.

Early in his career in Amsterdam, David formed his own brokerage organization and enjoyed a lucrative career for many years. After successfully operating the business alone, he recently took in a partner and began successfully brokering large quantities of merchandise in China for mid-sized companies that preferred selling through a broker rather than incurring the enormous cost of setting up a sales facility. This new business plan blossomed and the profits grew substantially. Having a partner gave David the opportunity to spend more leisure time and to finally plan a new strategy for Dianne and him.

Dianne was employed as vice president and general manager of the Manhattan branch of a national department-store chain headquartered in St. Louis. Some time ago, she gave up the opportunity to be chief operating officer for the parent company in St. Louis so she could spend time with David and become the "mother" of his three adopted children.

For the rest of his children's teenage years, David was a single parent. As a younger man, before adopting the children, he met someone with whom he could share his life but as the relationship grew, tragedy struck. While dining with his love, Leyla, at a little café in the heart of Tel Aviv, David faced horror as a suicide bomber detonated himself and murdered many, including Leyla, and severely injuring David. He was emotionally destroyed, but during recuperation on a Caribbean island, he met Dianne Westerman, and they soon realized that they were meant to be together. They married that year, and David fulfilled his need for a complete family that he had never believed he would see, and Dianne became the wife of a secret agent and the immediate mother of three grown children.

That morning, while enjoying his coffee, the *Times,* and a toasted sesame bagel, David answered his mobile and greeted his son Manuel cheerfully. After inquiring of the health of Cecelia and their grandchild, Manuel dropped the bomb by asking his father to get involved in the death of Phillip Courtney. "If you could just ask some questions and snoop a bit, that would satisfy Jim. It probably was a suicide but it would be a real favor if you could look into it."

David thought for some time before answering. "You know your mother will hate you for this. I promised her after the last mission that there was an end to the spy business. But let me speak to her and I'll get back." David ended the conversation and a sense of gloom overtook his mood at having to get involved in any type of investigation and having to argue with Dianne over accepting the request.

When Dianne came home and he delivered the news to her, she was fuming. She stared at him coldly, before saying, "You made a promise to me, David. Do you remember? I know you're going to do it for Manuel so go do it, but if it gets to be something, you're going to the police, you hear me?"

David thought she took it well, probably because she believed that it was nothing more than a good friend wanting to believe that he knew how Phillip Courtney died. Secretly, Dianne was worried about the impact of David's decision.

Chapter 6

THE NEXT DAY, David booked a flight for the Detroit headquarters of Black Technologies and by afternoon had checked into a motel not far from their executive offices. His plan was to gain a perspective on Phillip Courtney: where he lived and where he worked for the past fifteen years. From his room that afternoon, he searched for information using his laptop and, in a short time, he knew a lot about Phillip's early life, scholastic record, and work experience; it appeared that Courtney led a clean lifestyle.

After he lunched on salad at a neighborhood cafe, he called Edgar Black's office to arrange an appointment. When Black's assistant wanted to know the nature of the business, David said he was privately investigating the death of Phillip Courtney. It was apparent to David from her reaction that she knew of Courtney's death. She left him waiting for several minutes, and then returned and cleared the meeting for the next day.

David decided to drive his rented car out to the offices late that afternoon. He parked in an empty executive parking spot near the front entrance and sat watching employees begin to empty from the building. At about six, a limo with darkened windows pulled up to the front of the building; David was expecting Edgar Black to emerge; he had a recent photo of Black and could identify him, but instead a woman--tall and attractive, wearing dark glasses and a fur hat over a luxurious looking, baby alpaca coat and knee-high boots--emerged from the main office and stepped into the limo. Several minutes later, true to the description, Edgar Black exited the offices and stepped into the limo. He was shorter than the woman, tanned and dressed in what looked like a camel hair coat.

For some improbable reason, David decided to follow the car. He knew that Black was married and, based on his experience, the woman who stepped into the car did not look like a wife, so he stayed far enough behind until the limo pulled into a small, suburban Italian grotto. When they got out, Black had his arm around the woman's shoulder. To David's impression, they were clearly not husband and wife. David retraced his route and then headed back to the motel where he ordered dinner in and dutifully checked in with Dianne.

The next day, David arrived at Black headquarters and was ushered into a small foyer next to Edgar Black's office. He decided to walk about the area, and, to his surprise, walking towards him was the woman David thought he saw getting into the limo--a tall, attractive woman in a dark business suit covering a white blouse and black patent heels sending her four inches above her already tall figure. She smiled as she passed, and David extended his hand, which she took in a hard, mechanical motion that exuded power. "Nicole Lawrence, executive vice president, finance," was her greeting and she inquired whether he was being taken care of in a timely manner.

At that moment, the heavy oak door opened and Edgar Black emerged, just as David had visualized him, tanned and immaculately dressed in what David took to be a Paul Stuart suit, pale blue shirt with gold cufflinks peeking out of the suit sleeves, along with just a glimpse of a Cartier Ballon Bleu; his feet were encased in Ferragamo black slip-ons. Although Black was at least in his fifties, he was still classically handsome. With serious dark eyes, a careful smile, and a firm handshake, he exuded an air of supreme confidence. He invited David into his office and Nicole followed.

Impressive modern art objects adorned the walls and a massive glass-topped desk sat at an angle in a huge space. After turning down an invitation for coffee, Black inquired of David's interest in Courtney's suicide. David told him what he knew, which was next to nothing, and merely added that a friend of Courtney's wanted David to be sure it was suicide. So he was just asking some questions about Courtney's frame of mind when he left the company. Black opened with an over-the-top elegiac of the terrible tragedy Phillip's death had been. He added that they had been close for all of the fifteen years that he was employed with the company. "He was an extremely talented executive who worked long hours, really tirelessly, both here at the office and at home, to stay on top of his responsibilities."

He quickly confided that Courtney left because he was totally depressed and unable to continue in his crucial role. Black said that he suggested therapy, but Courtney dismissed his mood as temporary depression due to his work overload and they saw little of each other once he left the company.

David turned to Nicole and asked if she had known Courtney and received a sugarcoated response that they knew each other professionally but nothing beyond that. Small talk ensued for about fifteen minutes about the specifics of Courtney's position with the company and his relationship with his peers and subordinates and any other friends that he might have had. Finally David rose to leave, and Edgar proffered his business card, offering any assistance that David might require.

Chapter 7

Black Technologies had started out as Black-Turion Medical Technologies over thirty years ago, a private venture by two young scientists, Edgar Black and Michael Turion. Edgar was born in Detroit, the only child of Edna and Arthur Black. He grew up on a tree-lined street in a quiet community before the riots began to destroy the city. Arthur was a sales rep for Bulova Watches, which required a great deal of travel throughout the Midwest. When he was home, life was always a party at the Black residence, filled with family and friends. In this environment, Edgar inherited his father's boisterous optimism.

However, this left Edna to set the rules of the house; however, she was much too busy with her local charities, mahjong with the ladies, and seeing to family obligations to pay much attention to her handsome son. Rules in the Black household were there to be broken, and Edgar made the most of his youth. During the nights that Arthur was home, he grinned from ear to ear seeing Edgar come home with lipstick on his shirt and his zipper half zipped.

Being smart, good looking and gregarious made him the choice of many Detroit teenage girls and he denied few of them. At first it was on the grassy hill behind the school, and later on in the back seat of his ancient Dodge Dart. His manual dexterity was legend; he could unhook the brassiere of a sweet young thing whose virginity was soon to end using one hand in seconds. His buddies in the neighborhood thought of trying for a Guinness World's Record in "Bra Opening," but thought the better of it when Edgar took more than twenty seconds to unhook a three-hook bra of a young girl endowed with more than ample breasts. School came easy for him; math and science were his favorites. When the time came to select a university, there was no hesitation--Ann Arbor, with all its goofy charm and hippiness answered his call. During his first year while living in a dorm, he shared a room with a likeable young man who shared his passionate interest in science, Michael Turion.

Michael was born in Hattiesburg, Mississippi, a town of about forty thousand. He was the youngest of four children born to a Methodist minister and his homeworker wife. It was made clear at an early age that the minister wore the pants in the family. They rarely argued; peace and serenity were the family watchwords. Dinners were quiet, beginning with the necessary prayers--the only conversation at the table was their father's questioning of the boys' progress in school. Sundays were formal and subsequent luncheons after church always featured a country ham or roast turkey and the usual assortment of sides. Freshly baked pies were always on the dessert menu and only after the Sunday meal did the Turion children have the opportunity to play or go fishing. This was the life for the four children in the Turion family.

Michael and his three older brothers were well grounded in religious training. Michael was small for his age and despite the constant urging of his older brothers, he resisted participating in athletics of any sort. During neighborhood antics, Michael often found himself being tossed upside down in a garbage can by his prank-loving brothers. The other boys played football and basketball in school and later developed interests under the hoods of cars. Michael's idea of fun was dreaming of things like taking space flights and exploring the mysteries of the undersea.

School was more of a pastime than a chore for him, and in the small town school that he attended he found that he could teach himself as well. He excelled in anything that caught his interest, which made him the high school nerd. Few females were attracted to him and those who expressed an interest quickly found that he offered them very little physical satisfaction; his idea of sex was spending his time courting his penis in the bathroom reading his mother's ubiquitous collection of homemaker magazines.

His interest in computer science grew, and with the minister's approval, he applied and was offered a scholarship in the science program at the University of Michigan. The first in his family to attend college, he was the minister's pride. With Michael, there was never a question of whether he would go to college; but the minister would have preferred a local college and had misgivings about sending his boy to a northern city with all its distractions and widely known off-beat activities. After pledging to keep his faith and attend Sunday services, Michael was allowed to go to Michigan. Always shy and quiet, going to a hip town like Ann Arbor from a small backwater town in Mississippi was all the thrill and excitement about which Michael dreamed. He always remained shy and withdrawn, but it never diminished his passion; he was in happiness heaven.

His assigned roommate, Edgar, was his age but with a personality that Michael secretly awed. Outgoing, personable, and always vocal, he was well liked by his peers and the faculty--Edgar Black was Michael's hero. Edgar had to drag Michael to parties, and though Edgar had no difficulty in finding female companionship, Michael was a loner and had great difficulty socializing. After his first sexual experience with a nerdish young woman whom he knew from classes, Edgar had to carry his pal, heavily loaded with alcohol but in a glorious state of euphoria, back to his room.

They felt as close as brothers, these two totally unlike young men, and they shared something important: their love of science and computer technology and the desire to do something great together after graduation. Michael, the quiet scholar, and Edgar, the boisterous entrepreneur, shared the same passion for success developing new real-world applications. Eddie and Mike, *scientific superstars* as they called themselves, were determined to make some astounding discoveries together once they graduated.

Chapter 8

BY HIS FINAL year, Edgar's outgoing personality—along with his dark hair pulled tight into a ponytail; a strong, masculine face; and a powerful, bull-like body--often attracted and was in relationships with more than one woman at the same time. On the other hand, Mike was a small, thin, pale, young man with a conservative, almost painfully quiet personality, a loner who saw Eddie as his only real friend. But whatever personality differences they may have had, their minds worked in sync as they dreamed of success.

One sunny day in May just before graduation, Eddie and Mike were lazing on the grass at the Quad smoking weed, a commonplace activity in Ann Arbor. They had been brainstorming for weeks about the next step in their lives. Eddie kept up a steady barrage of conversation about moving to the West Coast, close to the wave of technological change taking place. Mike felt they should stay in Michigan and use the growing interest in technology in Ann Arbor. But in the end, as usual, Eddie ruled the day. This was the way these two brainy guys dealt with crucial decisions. Mike made the logical, head-trip arguments, and Eddie countered with the broad strokes that Mike could not compete with, and so he gracefully complied.

Not long after that, they dumped their meager possessions into an old Ford and moved to the heart of technology in northern California. They found a boarded-up Sunoco gas station near Berkeley, a community on the east shore of San Francisco Bay, and began working and living out of the small rented garage behind the pumps. They lived above the garage in a space just big enough for them to share two small beds and a tiny kitchen.

Eddie, however, could sense that success would be more easily achievable in an area that supported new start-up businesses. Mike was nervous about such a drastic move, but he had complete faith in his friend. And so there they were, two young men with brains spilling over with ideas about the future.

Before many California sunsets dipped into the western sky, they began to pull together some of the thoughts that they dreamed of in school. They set up a small lab in the garage and began studying something that had intrigued them at Michigan: the application of Einstein's theory called *optical pumping,* which called for a beam of light that potentially could be focused into a high energy source.

Often, late nights found them at local pubs located near a university frequented by graduate science and technology students. It was there they met a professor who introduced them to colleagues who were doing graduate work. In the late 1950s scientists theorized about the possibility of being able to develop a visible laser, a beam of light that they believed had enormous potential. As Eddie and Mike became involved in these discussions and read the subject matter that these scientists were producing, they grew excited about using lasers for practical applications.

One night, long into these discussions, with enough Milwaukee's Best sloshing around, they agreed to put aside the other work they were involved in to attempt to construct a rudimentary prototype of a laser. The shop that they worked in was totally inadequate for what they had in mind, but with the help of those scientists whom they befriended, they began working nights at one of the university's labs.

The first attempt consisted of a cylinder with reflective mirrors at each end. They used a high intensity lamp that provided a flash of white light that bounced light back and forth between the mirrors, the light source growing stronger until it left the cylinder as a powerful beam of light. They worked for months on this theory, assisted and guided by some of the brainiest scientists in the country. All of them were convinced that not only could a practical form of laser be developed, but that there were unlimited potential applications that were waiting for such a device to be built.

At first, Mike theorized the use of a laser as an extremely sharp scalpel that could be used in medical surgeries. In his calculations, his work showed that lasers could be used to make incisions half a micron wide, compared to the eighty-micron width of a single human hair.

Eddie and Mike begin searching for commercial applications for the newly found laser technology. They worked nights and weekends trying to answer questions about the commercial value of the utilization of this powerful tool. Weeks turned into months, but they continued to believe that they would somehow find success. It seemed to them that having a tool with such immense sharpness would be commercially viable.

They continued to survive now by taking programming and software design jobs at small tech companies during the day and working on their precious but elusive project at night. They were never discouraged. Through Edgar's buoyancy and Michael's cool and steady disposition, they finally produced something tangible.

It happened one night at their regular watering hole that had become home for them. Mike sat silently with a brew in hand when Eddie arrived and bear-hugged his friend. "Mikey, I think it works; I tested the laser today and it works!"

Michael smiled with a broad southern shine and grabbed Edgar's head and kissed it. They had just completed the development of a simplified laser that had the seemingly unlimited potential to be used in surgical procedures.

Their connections had put them in touch with some medical residents in the area, and together they expanded a theory that surgical removal of human tissue with a laser is a process in which the lasers could burn away diseased tissue. After presenting their plans to the faculty at the university's medical school, they first outlined procedures to deal with detached retinas. With preliminary approvals, in their first successful test, the beam as small as one micrometer penetrated a patient's eye and welded a detached retina back in place. The ebullience of these men and women rose to new heights.

At times, their workplace resembled Frankenstein's laboratory with surgeons practicing the necessary manual skills. Mike and Eddie watched in awe as their first laser destroyed abnormal blood cells that spread across the retina in patients suffering from diabetes, a procedure which they knew would help to delay more serious effects often associated with the disease.

After securing patents on all of their applications, they found the medical profession eager to buy in to this new, exciting treatment source. Suddenly, they had a company with a mission. Information about the growing uses of lasers was being published across the country in medical journals. Their laser training was soon sought by hospitals and clinics.

Success after success in developing new, approved medical treatments using lasers propelled Eddie and Mike's company to become an extremely profitable private company. They were both dizzy with the success and were able to build a national sales and marketing organization.

It was during this time frame that they began to talk about moving back to Michigan. They no longer needed Silicon Valley for research and support efforts, and they considered returning to where it all started, moving their laboratories and administrative facilities near the university in Ann Arbor. Edgar approached the State of Michigan's Development Corporation, which was eager to offer generous tax and relocation incentives to build a new facility in the area. So off went the boys, awash with money, relocating all their labs to Dexter, a small town outside of Ann Arbor.

Michael was in heaven, virtually living inside his laboratory, rarely socializing other than attending some of the scientific programs offered at the university. Clearly, he was still socially ill at ease in settings involving large groups. Papers that he wrote describing his theories for new laser medical applications appeared regularly in science and medical journals and Michael soon published a volume entitled *The Journey of the Laser.* He later published a volume about the use of lasers outside of the medical profession. In this book, called *Lasers: The Next Generation*, Michael described how lasers could be used for welding in auto assembly lines and for surveying in field operations, and even gave a glimpse of the vast potential in using lasers in space exploration to provide pinpoint astronomical measurements. He truly had found his niche in life and enjoyed it to the fullest.

Edgar, with his affluence, intelligence, and good looks, made himself a popular figure in Michigan society. With his new role managing the company, he was developing a keen interest in finance. As his social circle widened, he became extremely popular. At one of the many societal functions that he attended, he met Virginia Stanton, the daughter of the ex-senator from Michigan, John Stanton. Edgar felt that she was the perfect choice for him: intelligent, wealthy, with strong familial ties in government. Virginia's brother was a state congressman already with higher aspirations.

Despite his affluence, Virginia's family viewed Edgar with some reservations. His exploits with women were widely known, and he did not always use perspicacity in setting his priorities. Nevertheless, Virginia was deeply attracted to him and believed him when he told her his playboy days were over. Within the year, they were married, and for a period of time, Edgar fulfilled his vows faithfully. Two years later, Kate was born, with Leon following in another two years.

Edgar was a devoted father, but his spirit of adventure in developing new business strategies kept him from home many evenings. In addition to his huge financial assets, his physical energies were legendary. Women loved his power and he was a sexual lion. In his defense, he had a strict penchant for discretion, and Virginia, knowing of his bedroom skills, was able to come to terms with the exploits of this exciting man.

And so it was that the two brainy kids, Mike and Eddie, full of love and respect for each other would return to the place where they met, seeking new challenges.

Chapter 9

By the 1980s, Black-Turion's work produced lasers that were used in hospitals for a wide range of surgical procedures. Lasers were being developed that could be used in cataract, glaucoma, and corneal surgery. But this was not enough for the two wealthy entrepreneurs.

Once they were able to produce large numbers of workable laser programs, raising new sources of funds was not a problem. They were able to raise large amounts of private capital from wealthy investors and entrepreneurial firms that saw not only huge profits being generated but the future potential as well. However, Edgar Black and Michael Turion never gave up control of their company. They lived far beyond the life that they both dreamed of, but their dreams never dimmed.

By the early nineties, their investment bankers convinced them to expand by selling stock to the public. The advantage was the vast amounts of capital that could be raised once the story and success of Black-Turion was told to the financial community. Eddie and Mike insisted that they maintain control of the new entity, and now they learned about things like staggered board elections and multi-classes of stock with unequal voting rights to protect against sharks lurking in hidden locations, all new and strange to them.

By going public, they would be subject to rules imposed by both federal and state regulatory agencies, as well as new obligations to their soon-to-be owners of the stock to continually publish information about the company's financial affairs. Edgar was eager to pursue this plan. His thirst for economic wealth and his spirit of adventure could not be quenched. Michael, however, could not be initially convinced to go public. He had accumulated all the wealth he needed and would be content to spend the rest of his life in his lab developing new applications, as in the past.

Eventually, with the assistance of their new investment bankers, they formed a public corporation, and when the story of these two entrepreneurs and their accomplishments was told to the investing public, the initial sale of stock was issued at a stunning price, making both entrepreneurs and their investors even wealthier.

Edgar took the role of chief executive officer and Michael became the president and chief operating officer. It was not long after the public offering of stock, which produced a mountain of cash for the company, that they realized the need to develop a long-term strategy that would define clearly where their energy and capital should be devoted.

What surfaced from this planning effort were strong differences of opinion between the two partners in terms of where to take the company. Edgar wanted to pursue the use of laser technology in new directions and for different purposes other than fighting competition in the newly crowding medical field. He challenged his corporate planners in the company to search for new opportunities for laser applications, much against Michael's arguments.

The rift was becoming severe. They rarely lunched together and the meetings that they both attended were becoming contentious. Executives in the company were taking sides in the battle. Finally, at a strategic planning meeting with all the top executives present, a black book detailing proposed strategies for the highest profit potential opportunities was presented by Edgar. Curiously, it pointed out that, because of competitive pressures and limited opportunities in the now overcrowded medical equipment field and with much larger firms spending huge research dollars to develop new applications, there was a belief that the company must invest in new strategies and new directions to maintain its high-growth perception.

This strategic black book identified a special field where very little progress had been made in laser applications, and where Edgar strategized that profit potential was enormous. Their study indicated that the use of laser technology in the development of weaponry by the U.S. military was rarely being used, and large-scale research was not being done either by the military or by private contractors. It was felt that the military needed more sophisticated weaponry than was presently in use on the battlefields that the United States was engaged in around the world. Beyond that, the sale of this technology to friendly foreign countries would add a bonus to the potential profit opportunities.

The précis of the report stated that "a new type of weapon" could be developed that could be used by troops in the battlefield and fired from fixed and movable installations based on the use of lasers, a weapons system that did not rely on conventional explosive materials. If such a system could be developed, and the technology was presently available, the profits would be enormous with greater long-term potential than the laser medical technology business.

Michael argued vociferously against the conclusions being presented, claiming that the risk of entering a new field with largely untested results was too great. He deeply believed that the appropriate course for the company was to continue refining lasers for hospital and medical facilities. He also was skeptical of doing business with the government and the military. His argument raised questions about the reliability and political ramifications of dealing with U.S. governmental agencies.

Edgar listened quietly as Michael carefully made his case, and when he finished, Edgar did not attempt to convince him to follow, as he had done so many times in their past. He simply stated that he respected Michael's views, but he had already philosophically accepted this new strategy and was ready to implement a plan supporting it.

At this point, Michael shuffled uncomfortably in his chair for a moment, then rose and quietly left the conference room. Their relationship was never the same after that meeting.

Unhealthy, divisive factions about the company's future festered within the company, and finally on April 10th, 1995, after ongoing, bitter internal battles, Edgar Black, with the approval of the Board of Directors, agreed to accept Michael Turion's resignation and to purchase his stock in the company for five hundred million dollars.

By day's end, Michael sadly emptied the personal contents from his office and lab and took his final long, lonely walk to the farthest parking space in the garage. He always refused to park in his designated, preferred executive location. Turion never forgave Edgar for his required departure, and they never spoke to one another again.

The board gave Edgar Black its complete support and approval to carefully but decisively shift the company's research effort into highly technological weaponry. The corporate name was changed, eliminating the words "Turion" and "Medical," and with the help of some members of the board who knew how to gain influence in Washington, the new Black Technologies, Inc. was born.

Chapter 10

THE HUGE TASK of restructuring fell to the most trusted members of the organization. Teams were formed and executives who had specific knowledge in the bidding process and in obtaining large-scale government contracts were brought on board. Strategic engineering departments were built whose principal task was to develop ideas for consideration in this new business: the development of military weaponry based on the significant laser knowledge and capabilities that the corporation had built. It quickly became clear to Edgar that the task of moving the majority of the corporate effort from laser technology used in medical applications to military weapons was going to be a huge undertaking, but he loved the challenge.

Once the legal separation from Michael Turion was complete and the necessary settlement with him was board-approved, the company's continuing research in the development and production of lasers targeted for medical use still provided the profitability and cash flow for the company.

But Edgar quickly began the restructure. The new strategy foresaw the growing military interest in laser technology. The perceived long-term strategy of the U.S. military was to develop high technology weapons systems. Edgar's initial strategy was to hire engineers and technology specialists familiar with the future needs of the military and to begin research into the development of military applications of lasers.

Board members were carefully chosen. Among them was a retired Army general whose expertise was in weapons procurement as well as an aide who had served a congressman who was the ex-chairman of the technology and innovation committee of the House of Representatives. Through contacts provided by these key members of the board who were able to put Edgar into key congressional offices specializing in defense, he was soon pitching the idea of *a bulletless* laser-driven weapon.

This direction attracted a great deal of attention, and soon important lobby groups were ringing the bell at corporate headquarters. Once an influential lobbying firm with experience in military affairs was secured, instructions followed concerning required donations that needed to be made through multi-sourced contributions to key political committees and Super PACs. Now, at a huge price, Edgar hired powerful special interest firms based in Washington that would support and encourage appropriate government officials to develop an interest in his ideas. Surprisingly to Edgar, this became a relatively easy task. Despite huge national deficits, the Republican "hawks" in Washington were eager to spend on new technology.

Having incurred the cost of acquiring insider support, Edgar learned quickly what the military was searching for. Its hot button was to be called *a directed-energy weapon*, a type of weapon that could emit energy at a target from a platform on land, in the sea, or from air without the use of a projectile hurled at the target. Other major competitors had been testing systems since the 1970s but were limited by their weapon's ability to maintain its energy sources.

Edgar Black conceptualized laser beams that would travel at the speed of light and would eliminate a target via a hand-held device as the trigger for a weapon on a fixed or moveable platform or mounted on a pilotless aircraft. During strategic sessions that Edgar presided over, he described the theoretical advantages of a weapons system whose speed and location would be undetectable, whose pin-point accuracy would be unparalleled, and which would run on a power source without the need for ammunition.

Fears that larger companies like Boeing, Lockheed Martin, and Northrop Grumman had the manpower and clout in Washington necessary to bid on a project this large were realistic, but Edgar had the one chip that gave him an advantage. His experience in developing the first commercial use of lasers that his team built years ago gave Black Tech a major advantage over their competitors. Edgar knew that the profit potential would be theirs if technical obstacles could be overcome.

Like a true huckster, Edgar Black built a fantasy world for every employee and all signed on for the adventure of their lives. To pull these technological and organizational issues together, Phillip Courtney, a rising superstar from the West Coast, was brought in as vice president for technical development. His challenge was overseeing the team of young techie geniuses who he was to bring on board to become the key systems developers.

Edgar and Phillip worked as closely as any two senior officers could. They constantly shared ideas and visions and there was hardly a day when they would not sit together, sometimes for hours, in deep discussion. In addition to long hours at his office, Phillip synchronized the computer system at his apartment at which he worked most weekends. A seventy-hour workweek was routine for him; it was a delirium that he relished at home each evening. The sensation of iced vodka landing with a burning thud into his stomach enabled him to envision the completion of the project.

The security department at the company tried to discourage Phillip from having vital information at his laptop computer outside of secured facilities, but Phillip resisted, preferring to have a sophisticated, security-protected system available to him at all hours, wherever he worked.

It quickly became clear to Edgar that using large amounts of funds to lobby key members of congressional committees and the Pentagon's headquarters of the Department of Defense with the magic of a bulletless weapon of destruction would require the negotiation of a multibillion dollar, long-term contract. Months later, after lengthy negotiations, contracts were signed with the appropriate government agencies and Black Technologies emerged as the principal contractor, along with a highly classified branch of the military, to develop a fully operational, fixed-platform laser weapons system. The contract's revenue base, assuming the delivery of a battle-ready weapon, was budgeted to be in the billions and was far and away the largest single project ever attempted by the company.

The Department of Defense, rubber-stamped by the key congressional committees, approved the initial phase of the contract to build a prototype mounted on a platform that could be moved from location to location by a small military vehicle. This was Black Tech's opportunity and the development began.

Chapter 11

AFTER THE FIRST year came to a close, a series of diverse but serious problems began to arise. For one, Phillip noticed that despite the continual large advances from the government, the company was continuously running into periods where large cash shortfalls occurred. Although he speculated that this was probably based on the government's erratic payment cycle, it fueled an already high stress level.

Adding to these internal problems, rumors in the industry surfaced that a foreign competitor was in an advanced stage of a high energy, radio-frequency weapon, which, although not based on Black's laser approach and not nearly as sophisticated as Black's, could upstage Black's strategy for a line of laser-based weaponry. Therefore, Edgar Black was determined to fast track the production of a prototype to become the world's leading source for advanced weaponry.

In addition, Phillip recently noticed what appeared to be a flaw in the design of the most important part of the weapon, the high-resolution, infrared sensor, whose fragility had been a key development problem from day one. The sensor was to be constructed of an alloy that had shown propensity to crack under high-volume use, and Phillip insisted that a more stable, less fragile element must be found and implemented. This meant going outside to find a company that had experience in the development of exotic materials, which caused a significant time delay.

When confronted with these problems, Edgar sought to place blame as his first course of action. Phillip's insistence on continuous retesting slowed the progress against the demands of Edgar for a fast-track prototype. The engineers and production people in the company believed that it was not uncommon in early phases of such a new system to encounter *bugs* in the system that would be dealt with later; they also believed Phillip's constant vigilance was severely delaying progress and causing escalating production costs.

The overriding positive development thus far was the progress made on the most significant component of the weapons system, the guidance technology. It was in this advanced part of the system that Edgar expected to lead the industry. In the weapons industry, this laser-directed system was beginning to be widely heralded as a breakthrough in new technology, and security of this phase was extremely tight throughout the organization.

Within the organization, Phillip had been close to Edgar Black for most of the fifteen years that he worked at Black Tech--they met almost every day on business matters. But as Black Tech grew, difficulties began to emerge between the entrepreneur, who would have his way on every major issue, and his development chief, who seemed to be slowing the project's progress.

Recently, however, the relationship between Edgar and Phillip had begun to deteriorate even further. During the last year, the company's ability to effectively control its growth had weakened. New facilities needed to support the growth were delayed, costs were skyrocketing out of control, and it was becoming clear to the outside world that corporate earnings would suffer, at least in the near term.

Edgar, in his usual approach, searched for a scapegoat, and many times it was Phillip. In Edgar's mind, Phillip's penchant for setting super-high standards for work product, adhering almost religiously to production quality, and refusing to allow substandard work to pass had an impact on Black Tech's timely delivery of pieces of the system. It seemed impossible for Phillip to build a bridge over these troubled waters, and the distance between them became chasmal.

At the company, having the complete confidence of the CEO is critical for success, and Phillip seemed to be heading for a confrontation with Edgar that could mean his departure from the firm. Edgar became more reliant on some of Phillip's subordinates for advice and Phillip believed that his tenure with the firm was in jeopardy. They no longer talked about new strategies and their almost daily lunches no longer happened. Phillip believed that this state of affairs would soon change the world for himself, Edgar, and the company.

A conference call with the financial community and the key investors, mainly technology-based mutual funds and pension funds, took place in January to review the status of the company's financial performance and to update them on the status of the new system. Edgar despised the financial community's demand for continuous profit updates, perceiving the media requests as an intrusion into his privacy. He was barely able to deal with the necessary meetings with institutional shareholders, and forecasting future results to the public was a nightmare.

Phillip had worked over Christmas to put together the technical portion of the information necessary for the meeting, which would be chaired by Edgar. The financial officer was to deal with the numbers, and other key executives would be on hand to answer questions, if needed. Phillip was having difficulty deciding how much of the systems' development problems should be described; a negative reading, even an unintentional innuendo about their search for a new alloy, might be construed as a negative factor and would allow rumors to go viral through the financial community, within the industry, and in the government.

The public relations department had been working itself into a frenzy to put a spin on the financial portion of the release that would indicate that earnings were down for the last quarter and forecasts for the year would be lower than expected by the Street. Edgar had put out the word that he wanted to focus on the potential for the new guidance system and downplay the earnings problems. Profits in the quarter were being hit hard by costs of the weapons project. All the talking heads at company headquarters were desperate to put a positive spin on declining profits.

Chapter 12

Along with business stressors, Phillip Courtney was depressed at his inability to hide the gossip over an affair he had had with a woman in the company. He had been seeing the woman, Nicole Lawrence, vice president of finance for the company, for several months. Nicole, an ambitious woman, visualized the relationship with Phillip as a way to improve her position in the company.

Phillip met Nicole at an industry conference; at that time she was the controller of a small tech company. Phillip, tall, handsome, and well dressed, was feeling full of his self-image. Nicole knew whom he was and was attracted to him at once. Tall and wearing heels, she was almost as tall as Phillip's six-foot frame. With exquisite shoulder-length dark hair with blonde streaks, she wore a conservative, black business suit with a cocoa V-neck shell. Her skirt hung just above the knee, set off by black, four–inch, closed-heeled pumps. Phillip was taken with her face, her body, and her smarts as soon as they met.

After an industry dinner that night that they both yawned their way through, they enjoyed a drink together at the cocktail party and later decided to take a walk into the chilly night air. After circling the hotel grounds, she suggested continuing the walk through city streets.

They talked about the business, economics, and just getting to know one another. Nicole saw an opportunity to talk about her future and her plans to join a larger organization. She was aware that the financial officer at Black Tech had recently moved up to a higher position and the company was interviewing candidates, but she did not mention this. At an intersection, Phillip turned towards her and she turned away for the moment brushing her hair too obviously close to his face. At that moment, under a harsh yellow streetlight, they shared a brief but lustful kiss.

Later that evening, in Phillip's suite at the hotel, they began to know each other's bodies. She was athletically built with strong, muscular arms and thighs. She ran regularly and worked out at a local gym every day. She used her physical prowess to pull Phillip into bed, and during this athletic event, she wrapped her taut, muscular legs tightly around Phillip's body. Phillip took advantage of this by penetrating deeply into her; she gasped in what seemed to him to be total delight. He artfully lengthened the session as long as possible until this sporting event came to an explosive conclusion with Phillip bursting into a groaning, throbbing orgasm.

Nicole was pleased with the event and believed that he now belonged to her. Phillip knew the dangers of mixing business such as this, but he betrayed his judgment, and before the conference ended two days later, he agreed to have Edgar interview her for the open position. This was the start of a relationship that continued until Phillip's problems made her look elsewhere in the company for a wagon to hitch herself to.

Chapter 13

THERE WERE FEW employees working one late December day. Most of top management and much of the population of Detroit, it seemed, had exited the city like a diaspora headed for warm strips of sand or ski slopes. Phillip had neither the mood nor temperament to vacation. In the solitude of the almost-empty offices, he was finally able to concentrate, a painful recent activity. As he began to formulate the technology portion for the upcoming meeting, he tried to put the business development problems in as constructive a light as possible, but he struggled with articulating them.

After working most of the day, Phillip's head was spinning and he left the modern structure that had been home to him for the past fifteen years. The weather was cold, not a numbing cold but a chill hanging over the weak, sinking sun. The residue of day-old snow lined his path as he trudged to the sound of his shoes crunching on the icy parking lot. As usual, when he worked in a deserted office, he dressed conservatively; his long, lean body encased in his off-duty uniform of a soft turtleneck sweater under a navy blazer and jeans topped by a tan cashmere coat and a plaid scarf that he had received as a holiday gift from his assistant.

For a fleeting moment, Phillip mused about her--a stout Jewish woman in her fifties carefully selecting the holiday gifts for the technology group as if she were celebrating a national festivity.

Phillip sat for a while in the warming interior of his German luxury car. It was almost five now and the cyano-colored, late afternoon sky mirrored his mood, a sense somehow of unfulfilled dreams in a life that might have been different. Late December spawned an icy slick to the already cracked cement streets as he guided his car through a once vital neighborhood.

Phillip felt a depression hanging over his head worsened by the weather, the winter's early darkness, and the burden of the problems facing him. He felt lately as if he has nothing more to say, nothing more to give, that much of what happened in his life had already occurred, and it frightened him.

A sense of hunger tugged at him as he eased his car into a small, rundown shopping center near the office. As he walked the short distance to Dave's Deli, he felt the icy chill on his face. Dave's could reasonably be called a greasy spoon but for the sunny countenance of Dave, its elderly owner who walked him to a tired leatherette booth as if there were crowds waiting to be seated in the restaurant. In fact, there were only a few diners. Dave Edelstein, the owner and operator of the deli for some twenty years, handed Phillip a worn-out menu and smiled warmly as he shuffled along.

Phillip sat staring at the menu that he knew almost by heart. "It's all behind me," he thought, "a career once energized and now disintegrating." He sensed the prospect of leaving the company that provided creature comforts that he had enjoyed for many years. They all seemed like mileposts marking stations in the road and now… alone. He sorted through his memories and the ambition that once drove his life; visions remembered now seemed all behind him.

He ordered quickly and began eating methodically. After he partially consumed an overstuffed corned beef sandwich and a Dr. Brown's, he glanced up and in the dimly lit restaurant caught the vision of a woman, fiftyish, seated across from him, deeply engaged in what appeared to be a dinner of several steaming plates that looked like corn, mashed potatoes, and a deep plate of something floating in shimmering liquid. She sat alone at a table, legs crossed at an odd, masculine angle exposing too much of her heavy thighs. She wore a red sweater, and Phillip's eyes drifted first to a tired, heavily lined face and then downward to her large breasts sagging under too loose a harness. She was deeply engaged in the contents of the plates before her, and after a few minutes her eyes lifted from her task and her gaze met Phillip's unemotionally. As she paused, her fingers were delicately poised momentarily above the residue on her plates as if in a magical ballet sequence. Soon, both Phillip and the woman in red, each recognizing the emptiness in the other, were back at their food.

He left after paying and Dave wishing him a happy holiday season. He drove now through near empty lamp-lit streets as his thoughts exploded into his consciousness, drifting back and forward to scenes of past conquests of women during empty sex and then the shallow, thin-surfaced relationships. Those indelible, now-enshrined moments seemed to be merely like bites of a morsel of food.

Phillip's top-floor apartment in a high rise in nearby Birmingham was dark and empty as he entered from the garage below. He lit the rooms and exposed a neat, well-furnished pad. The living space showed expensive taste, which had been developed by a local design consultant. A few modern, abstract paintings hung purposefully around the room, and a large, flat-screen Sony television hung against the far wall. Lighting was subdued and gave the impression of good taste but not much extravagance. His makeshift office in the corner of the living area was stacked with papers surrounding his laptop. He quickly filled a glass with a recently opened bottle of red wine and settled into a well-tufted leather chair. He picked up the book he was reading, which described changes in society that would impact the future role of technology. It had recently interested him but now he struggled. His mind drifted to the complex of issues that faced him and what would shortly rise to the top surface of his life.

It was unclear how long Phillip had been asleep. He awoke suddenly feeling a sense of movement in the room as if there was the presence of some form, but it was just her. He described Nicole as "her" because he perceived their relationship now as one of convenience--two people now comfortable with each other, but without significant emotional attachment. Nicole solved complex financial and legal problems and screwed with the same methodical accuracy.

She was a skilled professional woman who took great pride in her physical condition and appearance, who believed that she understood exactly what men wanted, and, from years of experience, who gave it only when she understood the "quid pro quo."

Their relationship had changed as Nicole now understood the downdraft from Phillip's problems, and she had already begun to search for a new *mentor.* Her fashionably streaked hair was tied back that night exposing the fullness of her face. Phillip noticed the small lines appearing around her eyes and mouth but still found her a genuinely beautiful woman. She had just returned freshly showered from a fitness class and was still wearing her warm-ups, white and red Nikes, and a t-shirt that was small enough to accent her ample breasts. After a perfunctory kiss, she slid into a leather Eames chair across from him under too harsh a light from a table lamp. The light exposed the beginning of small shadows of age; he was certain that they would be eliminated in a few years. Nicole was not a woman to countenance imperfection.

She poured the wine for herself and put her now-bare feet onto a small, antique coffee table in front of her. They chatted for a bit about the daily events in their lives and after finishing the wine, Nicole left the room momentarily. When she returned, she stood naked before Phillip. It was clear that Nicole wasted no time in getting what she wanted or perceiving what her partner wanted. Familiar warmth rushed to his insides. He was moved by too much wine and perhaps the mood he was in, and he welcomed her touch to the already hard bulge as he pulled her down to his lap.

From the lamp in his bedroom, the motion of Phillip inside her cast moving shadows against the wall. Bodies thrashing in unison, the dull slapping of skin on skin, and the moans and throaty sounds of hard breathing gave way to the final, gasping thrust. Then they quietly drifted into a special place where only soft, grey shadows lived.

This delicious state of near sleep allowed Phillip's mind to be free, to be unencumbered by all the fears and sadness that plagued his waking hours. When he was fully awake, for some reason he was flooded with emotions--he felt tears on his cheeks. He realized that he had been replaying happy days with his career flying high and his hopeless infatuation with his own self-image. Well, he thought, the price has been paid. For some reason, he was alone. Nicole had left, as she often did when they finished, and he went off to his own private place. He showered and listened to the silence of an empty home. Phillip understood all that had brought him to this place, and time and the fear of what was to come faced his consciousness. He realized that he must somehow change everything if he was to search for meaning in his life; essentially, he needed a detour to another place and another path. He pulled up the soft sheets around him and drifted into sleep.

Chapter 14

EDGAR, IN HIS fifties, now began to see his power-hungry son, Leon, in a major corporate role. Leon, schooled at Michigan State University, majored in civil engineering. He also had a particular interest in finance. As a boy he had dreamed of becoming an astronaut. He was never one for obedience, taking orders, or sucking up a lot. Leon refused to go down the path Edgar was pushing him towards, a career in science. Leon wanted to build things in a visceral way and never got it out of his system, even though his father was always pushing scientific journals at him.

But one thing was certain; nothing diminished Leon's need for power. He believed that his role was to be the successor in his father's company. Throughout Leon's life, Edgar preached his own *golden rule* that Leon needed to hear over and over again: *never allow someone riding over the horizon to steal your family's crops and burn your fucking hut to the ground. That's what you fight for your entire life.*

Leon resembled his father in physical appearance and personality. He was handsome with an air of confidence and a swagger that led to many a conquest of women, some even in the company. After much consternation, he eventually started in a junior role at Black Tech, where he diligently worked at learning everything he could about his company. That suited Edgar's vision of Leon's future as chief executive officer once Edgar stepped down. Although Leon's background was not in finance, he was perfectly suited to the fast-moving pace of this new tech-based company.

Working at Black Tech offered Leon, like his father before him, the opportunity to socialize with Detroit's finest. At a social gathering at Black Tech headquarters, Leon met the daughter of a socialite family, and within six months they were planning their wedding. Genny Bryant--tall, blonde, and rich--was used to a style of living envied by most of her college sisters, and as soon as she met Leon, she was totally entranced with his looks and charm. They met at a party and Genny, who was an attorney for a large Chicago law firm at the time and had been invited to the party by mutual friends, learned a lot more about Leon later in the evening.

After meeting and sharing too many *jacks-on-ice*, he invited her to see the office complex, especially Edgar's massive office. Soon, the large, heavy plate-glass table that served as Edgar's workstation provided a perfect *get-to-know-you* device. Genny was immediately enchanted by Leon's prescience and gave herself to him enthusiastically. All that she learned in the basic training of her life about being cautious and conservative was abandoned abruptly with the excitement of the super-star in action.

There was little foreplay; sex consisted of clothes flying in all directions, Leon's large, hard organ entering her, a few gasping moments as he thrust mechanically, and then… breathless as they held on to each other. After reconnecting her bra and pulling up the silk thong that had offered little resistance and did not hinder Leon from his entry, Genny was sure that he was the man whom she would marry.

Genny's family, old-moneyed Gross Pointers, had reservations about the probability of success in a marriage with this flamboyant stud. They knew, however, that when Genny made up her mind, she could not be easily dissuaded. The engagement was short and the marriage brought two extremely successful families together, the merger of old money and nouveau riche. As quickly as Genny became pregnant with their first-born, she stopped working and never again practiced as an attorney. It was as if this had been her long-term plan; marry a hunk with money, have a bunch of kids, and enjoy the life of an East Side socialite. Planning charitable events was her specialty, and it allowed Leon to pursue his interests, both business and social, always ready to brandish his large organ when the right woman approached. And there was an ample supply of *right* women in his circle. Whether Genny was aware at the start is a curiosity, but she played the faithful wife routine to perfection, and they prospered in their own dysfunctional way.

Chapter 15

In early January, corporate offices were abuzz with activity. Discussions about what everyone did during the holidays consumed much of the morning, but Phillip was already putting together the final touches to his talking points that he had prepared for the meeting that morning. He had already met with Jason Thomas, vice president of Public Affairs, about the tone of the meeting. Nicole presented the financial data to Edgar Black. At about ten, Phillip, Jason, Nicole, and Laura San Juan, corporate attorney and house counsel, entered Black's office.

Phillip already sensed the theme of the meeting. Whatever they came up with was going to be torn into shreds by a chief executive who could not tolerate anything that varied from his perception of reality. Edgar had announced in financial meetings during the prior year that this year would be a record for sales and earnings, and the project development would move along on schedule. Anything less would be considered blasphemy and Black would not tolerate it.

Arguments started quickly and Phillip watched helplessly as Edgar vented at everyone and everything. After an hour of relentlessly calling for a positive slant on everything, there was a consensus that emerged. A bombastic tone was muted, but the initial financial forecasts would be reiterated. When Phillip raised concerns about the project problems and advised cautionary statements about being on target, Edgar dismissed everyone from the meeting but Phillip; he knew this was going to be a rough time.

Edgar sat on the edge of his desk, his soft Italian leather-clad feet dangling over the side, and with a serious look he said, "You know, Phil, we have had a relationship based on the confidence we've had in each other, and I have to say that I think it has eroded. I need someone who can get the job done, and it seems as if you are distracted and no longer able to do it."

Without waiting for him to finish, Phillip replied, "Edgar, let's cut to the chase. I'll submit my resignation and be out of here today, if that's all right with you. All I want is the company car and for you to unfreeze the restrictions on my options and I'll be history." Leon, listening on the intercom, smiled softly.

When Phillip left Edgar's office, he felt a sense of relief in his body and mind as he began to sort through his personal belongings and pack up the necessities. The head of security met with him, and several people who had known Phillip over the years stopped in to say goodbyes, but at last he was separating and disassociating. Kisses, hugs, teary goodbyes, and vague promises to have lunch were finally over. As he walked out into the frigid January air, he felt like a free man with a deep sense of elation.

Days later, after several unreturned calls to Nicole, Phillip began to realize that this was the chance he had been dreaming about. Starting something new in a new place, feeling energized again, learning more about himself -- these were the thoughts that ran through his brain. There was a flurry of activity in his apartment as Phillip set up an office where he could think and dream. This activity, however, lasted only several weeks. Once the excitement of starting anew wore off and the phone was noticeably silent, he realized that he must begin to reinvent himself in a way that he could not yet determine. He walked, he read, and he dreamed a great deal, but one thing was certain; it was clear that Nicole no longer wanted anything from him nor was she able to give anything to him. It was clear that he no longer held her attention, so eventually keys were returned, the *let's stay friends* scenario was played, and Nicole Lawrence was already hitching her wagon elsewhere.

One day in early February, as Phillip poured over the details of some possible technology deals that he might put together, he received a call from Ann Reilly, an investigative reporter for the *Free Press,* whom he had known socially for some time. They had lunch together from time to time and Phillip liked her wit and sarcastic view of the world. She told him she was running some pieces about Black Tech and its strategic importance in weapons technology, and she wanted to lunch with him to discuss some rumors she heard. She insisted on meeting at a small suburban restaurant some distance from town. She was younger than Phillip and an attractive brunette who was almost pretty. Her oval-shaped head was topped by a wonderful mop of thick and super messy dark hair. She had amazing, huge, deep-set eyes. Her nose was a little button job, and she exhibited an intense look that was captivating. A short woman, she dressed in her usual jeans, t-shirt, backless tennis shoes, and a rain jacket two sizes too big for her.

After ordering vodkas and club sandwiches, she hit him with what seemed like a *two by four* by telling him that she had heard that someone at Black Tech had leaked sensitive details of the system to foreign interests, probably for large money, details that were dangerous to the country's security. She also implied that she knew that the project had serious flaws and they were deliberately done. He was cautious of what he told Ann. It seemed fine to talk about Edgar's lunatic personality, but he gave her little information about the project. He certainly knew nothing of the rumors that she shared. Of course, she would not tell him the source of the information, but she felt it was reliable. Phillip surmised that she must be talking to someone inside the company, but could not even guess whom it might be.

After a second round of drinks and lunch, Phillip agreed to relay anything to her he learned concerning her story. He sensed that she was vigorously approaching her leads, and he knew Ann would get to the bottom of it--she had that kind of bulldog mentality. Neither of them noticed the dark-windowed SUV parked near her car during lunch. As Phillip drove home, the content of her message and what he knew of the system floated restlessly in his mind.

As weeks went by, Phillip became concerned that nothing he read or thought about generated any interest; his activities dwindled down to taking long walks by himself and staring at inane images on the tube. One sleepless night Phillip, deeply troubled, awoke from sleep with an epiphany, a momentous decision. He needed to leave his apartment and this city and search for the meaning of his life in a totally new environment.

In early March, Phillip received a call from an old college friend who was an executive with a new, privately financed technology company.

He was told that the company, run by the founder, a Caltech grad, was funded by a group of venture capitalists with offices in suburban San Francisco who planned to take the company public. They were looking for an executive with solid technology background in a larger company who could bring some organizational skills to their venture; it seemed like a perfect fit to Phillip.

A series of phone calls and a trip to San Francisco convinced Phillip that this was just what he needed, a new city and a position that would allow him to generate ideas in an environment that fostered new development.

Gabriel Kozlov, a Russian émigré who was the founder of GEN21, Inc., would be the kind of boss whom he would like to work with--smart with a fresh view of technology and the future. At GEN21, they knew of his work at Black Tech and had vetted him completely by the time he arrived. By the end of the interview, Phillip knew he was going to accept the offer made to him, a smaller salary than he was accustomed to, but a generous stock plan that could make him wealthy if the company continued its outstanding performance and went public. He spent enough time in San Francisco to lease an apartment, open a bank account, and take care of mundane details before he returned home. He never paid attention to the black Chevy van parked at his new apartment or the cars that followed his rented car as he familiarized himself with his new city.

Within two weeks after returning home, Phillip had subleased his apartment, had the Salvation Army collect his furniture, and readied himself for a journey to somewhere.

On a frigid day in mid-March, Phillip Courtney began his new life. His Mercedes, given to him when he left the organization, hummed quietly as he drove west. The drive cheered him and he took his time driving the southwestern route, avoiding the cruel winters that he had known. His spirits soared as he contemplated his future. Moving in and setting up his apartment was a total turn-on, and starting work at GEN21 was just what he needed. All thoughts of Edgar Black, Nicole Lawrence, and Ann's confidential information were filed away in a dark cabinet inside his brain. Just a bucket of ashes.

Chapter 16

MICHELINA AILLON WAS born in a small town outside of Odessa, Texas, the daughter and only child of Hernan and Lavenia Aillon, both naturalized citizens of Mexican heritage. Her father was a field supervisor for an agricultural cooperative and her mother taught pre-school in the local community school. Michelina, as she was then named, never seemed fit in to a life in a dusty, Texas town. She had few friends and in the steamy, Texas summers spent hours in the library looking at celebrity magazines and reading Houston and Dallas newspapers. Her body was maturing at a faster rate than her mind, and fending off the ineligibles in high school still left her with a bevy of the *in guys* to share a squeeze or two. Michelina always enjoyed the control she had over the boys who weren't satisfied with the sight and feel of her breasts. When they got too rough, she excelled at a kick in the right place, disarming the explorer.

She managed to finish high school still a virgin although she enjoyed her mouth on a young man's organ as he diligently squirted creamy fluids over her face. It was never sexual excitement for Michelina. It was merely the recognition of the fundamental right of the male to take control and the absolute control she had in these situations. Sexual feelings were distant, confusing, and so she put them away, safe for another time. Desire to her was only reaching for the next rung on the ladder.

One could say that she grew up without a sense of herself, unsure of whom she was and what she was meant to do. In a way, this was self-defense against what an empty conscience brings. Michelina often thought of the lengths she would go to achieve an objective. These thoughts never caused her to take stock, to look at what she would or would not do to achieve her private definition of success. She always dreamed of leaving the area, and when she had the opportunity to go to college, she enrolled at the University of Texas.

Michelina was a bright student and majored in finance with a minor in accounting. An extremely attractive young woman, labeled super-hot by the fraternity set, she was so popular that she won the Miss Photogenic beauty pageant at the university. The men she dated were the college all-stars in one activity or another; nothing less would do for this young siren. Her dreams were not about picket fences; they were always about getting to a big city and working for an investment banking firm. Her head was filled with ideas about financing and investing, but after graduation, modeling offered her the opportunity to earn enough money to see what the world outside of Texas looked like.

She changed her name to Nicole Lawrence; *Nicole* always had a special foreign sound and *Lawrence* was such an American-sounding name. It also allowed her to escape from everything about Michelina Aillon. Nicole always visualized the next steps. After a few years, now a more mature version, she became determined more than ever to get to her real love, working in finance in a major money-market center so that success would be hers.

Although she never quite made it to New York, she did land a finance position with a small technology company located in Philadelphia. At 5'10" with long shapely legs sitting on an equally attractive torso, she made progress quickly in her firm. While working at this company, she entered Temple University, and within two years had her MBA. Her focus was on financial derivatives and their use in structuring new types of transactions. Her supervisor at work, a finance manager at the company, took an interest in her, and she was comfortable allowing him to show off his self-acclaimed, super-sized appendage. Although she was not interested in him or what seemed to her to be just about normal-sized genitals, this affair did give her the opportunity to learn the art of moving ahead quickly in an organization.

Within a few years, she was named a manager of finance, and then, finally, she was offered and accepted the key financial position with the company: corporate controller and chief financial officer. She loved being an executive with this organization, and she built her network of acquaintances at higher levels. Nicole was smart and had strong street sense. This ability allowed her to absorb new financial techniques, and by working as long as it took to get the job done, she was considered a shining star bound to rise to higher positions.

She was very careful about who made it to her social network, and when she met someone who she believed could further her career, she always satisfied him in any way that was required. She never enjoyed having sex--it was always more important to her to be able to provide pleasure rather than accept sexual intercourse openly and completely. After having sex, Nicole would think about her inability to feel any sexuality; but at these times she would quickly move her focus to how she could use it to her advantage.

Moving to a larger, more complex organization offered her the opportunity to attend corporate meetings and conferences; she was even invited to headquarters several times to help make presentations. Her new company was a U.S. division of a German conglomerate. Despite her thirst for success, Nicole had no desire to leave the States for a promotion.

Lady Luck shone once more on this Texas lovely; she was invited to attend an industry-wide conference in New York. At last, being with industry execs in conferences and at dinner tables in the city of her dreams was paradise. On the afternoon of the second day of the conference, she signed up for a small group meeting to discuss the key issues within the industry and was seated at a table of eight male executives. From her table position, she could clearly see only three of the men; but each time she turned aside to hear the others, there was always one particular set of eyes on her.

At the break, he came up and introduced himself. He was Phillip Courtney, vice president of Black Technologies, Inc., a large corporate organization specializing in the development of high-tech weapon systems, mainly for the U.S. military. After some small talk, Nicole agreed to have cocktails with him. She immediately liked Phillip; he was handsome and taller than her, even in the heels that she always wore in her business career. Courtney exuded an air of confidence and Nicole was taken with him both for his looks and demeanor. She knew from gossip at the conference that the chief financial officer position was open at Phillip's company.

This would be a major step up for her and she knew how to go for what she wanted.

That night, she gave him what he wanted; this was what she knew about. After sex with Phillip, during which she carefully plied her skills, the stage was set for her achieving the job of her dreams, the chief financial officer for Black Technologies. Phillip arranged for a series of interviews at the company and with his support and her talents, she easily beat out other candidates.

Of course the position came with some baggage. She needed to begin seeing Phillip on a regular basis. They spent a great deal of time together and she thought he might be getting serious in their relationship. Nicole, however, saw it as a natural law of life; you did what was required to achieve your goals. As long as Phillip maintained his power position within the company, she was comfortable with him. As this began to change, Nicole Lawrence began to look elsewhere.

It was not long after Phillip left Black Tech that she turned her eyes upward to loftier nests in the organizational structure. There was only one place for her to look. As a careful student of life in the wild whose expertise was in seizing opportunities, she soon noticed Leon Black, the CEO's son who was the heir apparent to the throne after his father retired. He was good-looking, powerful, and sexy, and it mattered not to Nicole that he was married with children. She knew that he was always noticing her, watching her move and seeing sex oozing from her pores.

Shortly after Phillip's departure, she dropped into Leon's office, sat in one of his enormous tufted leather chairs, and casually crossed her legs in a seductive manner. A lot of thigh showing, she idly swung her crossed leg, dropping her heeled pump off the back of her foot. She could see Leon hungrily watching. She suggested that, with Phillip gone, it made good business sense they should develop a closer working relationship. Of course Leon quickly agreed with as serious a countenance as he could muster, knowing that he needed to work hard not to drool all over himself.

That evening, in his office, they began discussing some of the unanswered issues raised by Phillip. But it was not long before Leon had his tongue searching the interior of her mouth. Quickly, as his mouth locked with hers, they began humping fiercely through their clothes, and when the sexual athletics became more intense, she realized through a recollection of the past how universal the steps men take to finalize the sex act were, how impersonal.

Once the sex concluded, she pulled away abruptly, knocking over a pile of books and documents from his desk. During the act, Nicole allowed Leon to make all the moves. She knew it was important to this macho man that the seduction was well orchestrated. That venture was the start of a working relationship between the two. They began to meet in the evenings at a posh apartment that Leon rented.

Genny saw that Leon was putting huge efforts in the company that was to be his one day, and she understood and endured the late evenings that he spent readying himself for the task ahead. She spent a great deal of time researching the Bloomfield Hills real estate market for larger, more prestigious digs where she expected to be moving to soon.

It was not long before Leon and Nicole became more closely aligned in the heavens, and she now had the whip in her pretty hand. One evening after a frantic sexual assault that she launched, turning Leon into a giant pool of Jell-O, she broached a serious subject.

"Wouldn't it be wonderful if we could be together, just leave Detroit for some far off paradise?" The pliant student agreed, and the master dropped the first of several colossal ideas.

"If we could put away a lot of money, a real lot of money, we could go anywhere together and start a new life. We both hate Detroit, and Edgar will not give up control of the company until they drop him into the ground, and we both know it. What if there was a way that we could develop a plan to quietly, without any fanfare, move maybe a couple of hundred million into a Swiss account, and with no one knowing where the money went, we take off and live the kind of life that I know we both want."

Leon stared in disbelief at what he just heard. He replied, "First of all, you're asking me to leave my family, Genny and the kids, and then steal a shitload of cash from Black Tech with no one knowing it, and then you and I spend our lives together in some other part of the world? Is that what you are suggesting? You must be totally nuts."

At this, Nicole put her naked body next to his, and said, "I think you heard me clearly and you understand exactly what I mean." She felt his rising tower of manliness begin to harden under her.

"Well, do you want to grow old with Genny and her society cronies? If you do, just forget what I said. Make believe you just dreamt it, and get up and go home to your delightful life, but please, dear Leon, do not look to me for excitement, because I want someone who is willing to take the risk."

At this, she moved off him, allowing his flagpole to wither into a droopy pile of loose flesh. "Leon, I love you for your strength, your boldness--this is why I want you to consider it." Leon stared at her for a bit with the countenance of a puppy dog and then began walking naked around the bedroom in silence, as if warming up for the Boston Marathon. He then quickly dressed and without a farewell salutation left the apartment. Nicole stretched out over the creamy sheets with her face showing the softest glint of a smile on her lips. She thought, *I've got him.*

Chapter 17

IT WAS NOT long after that Leon began to recognize that he was being lured into Nicole's flytrap. She was confident that he would come around to her plan, but she had other parts of the plan to put in place. Several months before, Nicole had attended a finance conference in New York. Listening to the tunes of the big money managers was the loveliest music to her ears.

During the mid-day break on the first day, a fund manager of a small hedge fund located in Boston approached Nicole and invited her to lunch. During casual conversation, he expressed an interest in Black Tech and the weapons project. He seemed, to a suspicious Nicole, to have more knowledge of her company than she would have expected. But all in all, he appeared as just a nice guy with a nice manner about him.

That evening, after the presentations of the day, he buttonholed her and, over cocktails, revealed that one of his company's clients was a large foreign corporation that was trying to develop their own weapons strategy, but didn't yet have the technical smarts. He suggested, in a very casual manner, whether Nicole could help him by entering into a consulting relationship with his client. The agreement, if acceptable, would include having Nicole answer general questions about Black's system and, subject to Nicole's comfort level, allow them to see on a superficial basis Black's development plans for the system, they would reward her generously.

He was very convincing, assuring Nicole that her help in this matter was extremely important and should not materially compromise her. Her brain was moving at supersonic speed, not at the criminality of this, but at the value of the information. When he left the bar, he put a folded *Wall*

Street Journal on the table and told her to think seriously about it. He told her if she was sufficiently comfortable with the arrangement, she could keep the contents; if not, she could just keep it as a gesture of good faith and friendship.

When Nicole got to her room, she opened an envelope and counted one hundred thousand in large bills. She ordered dinner to her room that night and carefully thought about the information transfer, which she believed could be fairly harmless. She already had decided to accept the proposal.

This initiated the first transfer of several computer jump drives containing a lot more than harmless information. The arrangement consisted of Nicole copying documents onto small drives and delivering them to a new contact, who remained nameless. She never knew the identity of the foreign company, if there was ever one. Almost six weeks later, residing in Nicole's apartment safe was almost one million dollars.

Chapter 18

NICOLE BEGAN DELIBERATELY avoiding seeing Leon in the office. If he happened to pass her, she avoided his stare. She made regular lunch plans outside the office and left work promptly at five. She had already begun to set in motion the first part of her plan. When Leon left messages on her answering machine, she did not respond. Finally, after nearly a week, she received a text message that said, "Let's meet at the apartment tonight."

When she arrived after seven, Leon had been waiting for some time. There was no perfunctory kiss; she removed her coat and sat down on the couch. With her matter-of-fact expression, she looked at him and said, "Is there a particular reason we are here?"

He said, "I want you very badly; I really am in love with you, and the vision of spending my life with you, well, overrides any issues I might have. Nicole, I'm yours, through this whole deal, but I must tell you I'm scared shitless. It's not Edgar that's got my head spinning; it's getting caught."

She replied, "Well, my darling, you will just have to assist me, trust me, and know that when we are done here, it's just you and me. Enough for you?"

They kissed briefly and Nicole sat with Leon and began to explain what had to be done. "The first step is carefully moving cash to an account that you and I control. I've been setting the prelims for cash transfers for some time. As of now, it's all legit to outsiders as well as to our auditors, but it will take some time before I finally put all the pieces together. I will explain later how it's done with no one noticing before enough time has elapsed."

She paused now, as if to prepare Leon for a bombshell. "There are some issues that we need to resolve quickly. You know that in my relationship with Phillip, we shared a great deal. Not particularly significant information on my part, but he was lonely and shared a great deal of his concerns about the company and, in particular, the laser weapons project. Some of it was, you know, bullshit about his control issues and problems with the sensors, but he also expressed his concern about temporary shortages in operating cash flows and, more significantly, about leaked classified information about the system. None of it was based on facts, just thoughts, but he documented all his concerns on the laptop that he kept in his apartment."

Leon stared at her in amazement; his brain was moving at lightning speed, trying to comprehend her remarks. After a few minutes, with a confused look on his face, he replied, "Wait a second, just hold on. So Phillip made notes about some bullshit theories, so what? Why is that an issue now?" Leon already knew the answer to his questions.

Nicole took a deep breath and began. "OK, I'm sure you realize that to have enough capital to make our lives secure, I've begun moving cash outside the company, and I don't want anything in writing about the subject." She paused, and then continued, "There is something that you don't know about."

She then confided in him about the arrangement made at the conference in New York. Leon sat with his head buried in his hands, rubbing his eyes as he contemplated what he just heard.

He quickly came back, "If I wasn't prepared to go along with you on the cash plan, would you have told me about this? Who the fuck are these guys? How long do you expect to continue with this crap, Nicole? Is there anything else you have in your bag of tricks? Let me say this, I feel as if I'm being dragged down slowly into a deep pile of shit."

"Just stop it, Leon, just stop it right now," she said firmly. "I have opened up everything to you. A few minutes ago, you were willing to steal a ton of cash, and now you're reading scripture to me? I am sorry I didn't approach you sooner about this, but remember, Phillip was still on the scene, and you and I were not talking a life together."

She continued, "These characters never disclosed exactly who they were, and I really don't want to know, but if I had to guess, I would say they are Russian. But forget who they are. Things are different now and we are going to have a wonderful life. I just have a few more scans to collect maybe a couple of million more, and that's all there is to that. Just swallow a few hundred antacids and digest all of this."

Leon thought and said, "OK, I'm in it, not happy about anything, but it's a go with me. I have one question that you didn't answer. What if Phillip gets sufficiently pissed off at what Edgar did to him and decides to talk to someone? I never trusted that hick from never-never land."

"You're right, Leon, it's an issue. Let me think a bit about it." After a few moments she said, "What if I let my Russian contact know about the problem with Phillip? Let him take care of it."

A t this remark, she rose from the couch and kneeled on the thick Karachi carpet in front of Leon. He tried feebly to push her away, but Nicole was a magician at unzipping, and soon Leon was drifting away on a soft cloud as his Zen master deftly used her tongue to search and her teeth to gently close in on her prey.

They lay together on the couch, close, his arms around her, and their bodies as if molded together. As she rested, her eyes closed, her mind was moving at supersonic speeds, digesting what had taken place earlier, and wondering how to approach Leon with the last bomb.

She abruptly rose and said, "Leon, there is one thing that could cause problems for us. It's your father. If any of this came to his attention, I just don't know what he would do. This company has been his life, and if he even gets just suspicious, I'm afraid of what would happen."

"What do you suggest, my sweet one, bumping him off?" he said in half jest.

She replied, "No, don't be ridiculous. I just think I should stay close to him while we're doing our work. If he knows something, I'll know it. I think you know what I mean."

"Sure, baby, it's all in the family. Let me know if he can still get it up. Now just shut up and spread your legs. Let me into that golden valley."

At long last, Nicole was about to achieve what she had dreamed of since childhood. Fame, fortune, and worldwide success were about to be achieved.

So there was Nicole Lawrence, aka Michelina Aillon of Odessa, Texas, who relied on the only life force she could imagine for herself. Not used to crying, which she believed was a sign of a weak character, she realized that everything she had thus far accomplished had been calculated to foreclose any personal introspection. Nikki could not visualize her life being anything other than a training ground for the grand scheme. And so there she was, self-obedient, totally alone, and devoid of any sincere emotion. She allowed herself to drift away to a place where soft lights dance in the sky. She was really happy.

Chapter 19

Several weeks later, Nicole was frazzled. She had held Leon's shaky hands through this process only because she knew he would be needed at the climax of the project. On top of that, she had been discreetly contacted by the Russians, who hadn't seen any more of the documents in a while. So, on a Wednesday night, Nicole decided to have an early dinner on the west side of town. She always liked the salads at the Stage, and when she arrived, Earl McHugh was already seated.

After ordering, he raised the issue, "Nicole, I enjoy having dinner with you, but seriously, our friends need some additional data to complete the files." After mouthing a forkful of salad, she replied, "I hope you liked the latest issue of the Journal." At this, she moved a folded newspaper to his side of the table, and at that, he smiled.

"Funds will be sent to you shortly. You really ought to do this for a living, my dear, I'm sure I can put in a good word."

Nicole kept a serious look at McHugh. "Earl, I have a couple of problems that need our friend's attention." The conversation became very intense and McHugh made some notes on a small, leather-lined pad. When Nicole emptied her basket of problems, they concluded dinner, and in the now-crowded parking lot, McHugh looked sternly at her and said, "I really hope these are the last of your problems, sweet one. I'm sure they can take care of these issues. Anyway, keep up the good work; see you soon, I hope."

Chapter 20

THAT NIGHT, NICOLE Lawrence drove the short distance it took to get to the Birmingham apartment she knew so well. She pulled into the underground garage and parked headfirst into the space assigned to her. She exited, used a private code, and hit the top button on the camera-monitored, luxuriously appointed elevator. It opened directly into a duplex apartment, exposing a ceiling to floor window overlooking the tony town of Birmingham below.

Stepping out of a bedroom, Leon Black met her with a smile. She dropped her coat and reached out to him, her hands running through his thick, graying hair and kissed him softly.

"Did you take care of Pops tonight," he asked with a sly grin, as if he already knew her response.

"Of course, my darling, and he was especially hard. Your old man sure knows how to keep it going. But he was satisfied, for the time being. So, where does your lovely wife think you are tonight, handsome?"

He said, "She's got her own activities to keep her busy, you know, like the Committee to Keep Garbage off the Streets, or something like that." Nicole laughed sadistically.

They kissed, long and hard, mouths eager to probe the other's, and they drifted slowly into the bedroom for some of their regular athletic activities, two physical beings who expected the pleasures of their bodies and were never disappointed.

After their interlude, Nicole opened an extremely serious conversation. "What do you make of David Korman? After I knew he was coming to see Edgar, I Googled him. You know he has a reputation. He was an officer in the Israeli Special Intelligence and worked on projects for them over a lot of years. He could present a lot of trouble for us. My contacts that took care of Courtney are transparent and difficult to find, but I know Korman intends to investigate. Why is he so interested in Courtney, anyway?"

Leon asked, "Are you sure they totally trashed Courtney's laptop, Nicole? Without it, it would be impossible to connect us to the murder, even if they really are convinced it wasn't suicide. If Korman should come up with something, we are really exposed in both areas."

"First, my sweet man," she spoke, "Don't worry about the movement of cash. I've got that almost completely worked out. No one will ever figure out how we moved almost a billion out of the country. But I am worried about the other part, an information leak. We are relying entirely on the security of the Russians. Now that you're helping me with the scanning, you need to be sure that you scan only the data that they need and have paid for. I'm counting on you to make sure you're up to date on all deposits into our Swiss accounts. Don't be concerned about the problems that we've had with the laser shields--let them figure that out. Those idiots thought they could get the full developmental plans for the weapon from us."

Leon said, "I'm on it, sweetheart, but get back to Korman. We need to get a message to him that he's walking on thin ice. He has to understand how deep he is in."

Nicole said, "Okay, big boy, I'll have my contacts send a really strong message. On another note, we have to take care of the reporter who was sniffing around the whole foreign influence issue. She met with Phillip, and I don't know what he told her about problems inside. We need to take care of her, and, as usual, make it look like something else. I've already spoken to our people and they don't see any problems in dealing with her. With Reilly out of the way and Korman on a tight leash, I think we closed all the holes."

They were silent for minutes, contemplating the steps that were being taken to insure total security, serious steps including murders and the prospect of more violence.

After a while, they made small conversation and soon both left, he to his wife and children and she to her apartment nearby, to plan a series of important steps.

Nicole knew that these steps ultimately would not include her lover, but that was for another day. For now, her thoughts focused on how to keep the public, the Securities and Exchange Commission, and other governmental watchdogs from learning the truth about Black Tech's progress, or lack of it. Nicole was clearly the mastermind. Selling information about the new laser weapon to Russian agents and designing the collection of massive company funds that she collected and invested outside the organization was a full-time job.

She realized that it was only a matter of time before she put the last piece of the puzzle together, and she needed to be prepared for it. Nicole Lawrence thrived on this kind of thought process. Being able to conceptualize a scam free from oversight was better than sex--far, far better.

Chapter 21

AFTER SPENDING MOST of his life assessing the honesty of people from many different parts of the world in stressful circumstances, David Korman was convinced that he had just heard a well-orchestrated litany that probably bore little of the truth about Phillip Courtney, Edgar Black, and Nicole Lawrence. That night, David searched the Internet for everything he could find about the company and its key officers: Phillip, Edgar, Leon, and Nicole.

A recent financial release offered no clue to any problems at the company. Nicole just recently had been promoted to her present position, but seemed to have little experience with an organization of the size and complexity as Black. He read with interest about the new guidance system that the company was working on, but no problems were mentioned of delays or cost problems, only praise in the industry as a promising and extremely profitable contract that had nothing but positive long-range implications for Black Technologies. The stock price reflected this audacious market view of the company.

David closed his laptop, ordered dinner in, and, as was his routine when in a different city, leisurely glanced through the *Free Press*. What caught his eye was a piece about a staff reporter for the paper who was found brutally murdered in her apartment the day before. It appeared to the local police as a robbery gone badly.

Why this piece suddenly attracted his attention was odd, but he carefully read and noted that the reporter, Ann Reilly, had been investigating rumors of problems with the new weapons system at Black Technologies. He searched back to an earlier piece that Reilly had written concerning key design elements of the system supposedly being leaked to foreign interests. She also implied that there were operating issues throughout the company and that the future might be less rosy than portrayed by management. David thought that perhaps there was a connection between Phillip's so-called suicide and Ann Reilly's murder.

Did Phillip know of the problems and had he discussed them with Ann Reilly? Could that be the explanation for both deaths? Enough use of gray matter for the evening, David thought, as he easily drifted off into a sound sleep.

The next morning, after demolishing an order of blueberry pancakes and good, strong coffee from the diner across from the motel, David decided to try for a visit to the managing editor of the local paper. Surprisingly, when David told him that he was helping some friends look into Phillip Courtney's death, he got fifteen minutes with its editor. Ann Reilly was described as a tough investigator, and Mark Samson sounded sincere when he talked of the tragedy. The locals were calling it a bungled robbery, but there were some at the paper who didn't buy it, he noted. She didn't have that much to warrant a break-in, and the fact that she was bludgeoned to death with a heavy object just sounded screwy for a young woman who had little in assets. Furthermore, there had been no sign of sexual assault. Her apartment was torn apart, and some folks at the paper, David was told, believed that it had something to do with the story she was chasing.

David asked whether Ann knew Phillip, but got no response. Apparently she left none of her story notes and sources at her desk or on her computer at the paper. Did she tell anyone where she was going with the Black story, David asked himself, but it seemed that this was clearly a dead end.

As he left the newspaper offices, a raft of questions rattled around in David Korman's head. Did the story that Ann Reilly was trying to put together have any substance and was she murdered because of what she knew? If so, what did she know and how serious was it if connected to the laser weapons system? Could this be some kind of foreign intervention that could impact the United States and its military plans for the system, or was it domestic spying?

In another direction, did Phillip Courtney really commit suicide, or was his death a homicide, and was it somehow connected to Ann Reilly's story? And what about the relationship between Edgar Black and Nicole

Lawrence? Was this just standard company humping, or was it somehow tied to the deaths?

After spending time walking through the depressing downtown streets near Detroit's Renaissance Center and thinking of all the possibilities and questions that came up, David realized he had no experience in this kind of investigation, and this put him in a dour, unpleasant mood.

At the motel, he called Dianne and updated her, the whole nine yards. Before she got a chance to express her concerns, he jumped in, "Why don't you meet me in San Francisco and we'll get a chance to see Manny, Cecelia, and that gorgeous Harry. Then we can poke around a bit together. You should take some time off; it will be good for both of us." David knew despite her reluctance, she would agree.

Chapter 22

THE NEXT EVENING, David and Manuel met Dianne at San Francisco International, and after hugs and kisses, they made their way downtown to the Prescott, an old but tastefully remodeled mid-sized hotel. David had stayed there many times during business trips and when visiting Manuel and Susan over the years, and he always loved the personal service they gave.

After checking in, they made their way to the Sears Restaurant, a popular downtown eatery for lunch where David fully updated them on the developments. "The nagging sense I get," David shared, "is that somehow we're looking at much broader questions than Phillip Courtney's death. Manny, I would like to see Phillip's apartment, which must be empty and still sealed. Although I have no idea what I would be looking for, sometimes you just need to look with a different set of eyes."

Manuel responded, "I think I can get that done. I'm on good terms with a police captain, who owes me one."

After David and Dianne dropped Manny off at his office, they decided to take a long-sought walk through the wonderful hilly streets of San Francisco. "It's been a long time since we did this," she spoke softly. She draped her arm over David's shoulder.

"We need to get acquainted again," joked David, and that they did that day and evening. They had an early dinner at Jardinière's where the seafood was outstanding, and then it was just a matter of time before their bodies meshed in the plush hotel bed.

Dianne was comfortable lying next to David. She stroked his face and played with his hair. "This is so good, but I have bad feelings about this whole situation. When can we turn over what we find out to the police?"

David kissed her softly and tried to assure her, but he too was uncomfortable with the task at hand. "I promise you, my love, as soon as we finish this review, I'm off the case." Dianne soon fell asleep naked in David's arms, but he stayed awake, doing what he has done for decades, the ritual of preparing for tomorrow.

They arose late the next morning. It was good for both of them to be together with no plan but to wait for Manny's response whether they could visit Phillip's apartment. After ordering breakfast in, David's cell phone vibrated. It was Manny and he had good news. He had spoken to his friend at police headquarters, and an officer agreed to meet David and Manny at the apartment at three that afternoon.

When she heard the news, Dianne quickly spoke up. "You really think I would come all the way out here just to get shut out of the action? David, do you really believe that could happen? Do you remember the last mission you were on and the part I played? Do you recall how we were nearly killed in that hellhole in Africa?"

David thought about protesting, but he knew Dianne and loved her tenacity. He also knew that her smarts could be useful in trying to see something in Phillip Courtney's life that everyone might miss.

Later that afternoon, David and Dianne met Manuel and Inspector Ed Mallory outside the apartment complex where Phillip Courtney had lived. Mallory was the investigating officer on the case. They spoke briefly before entering Courtney's apartment. He reviewed the case file and indicated that he had met with Phillip's parents, who were in a state of total shock. All signs pointed to suicide, but they were convinced it couldn't have been possible.

After reviewing the file, they entered the apartment. It was an attractive three-story building that had been tastefully refurbished several years ago. The red brick, attached townhouse in which Phillip rented the entire second floor was located in a well-to-do part of the city. They walked up the two flights of stairs and, pulling away the crime scene tape, they stopped at the door before unlocking it. David enjoyed trying to sense what type of person would live there.

He looked closely at the hallway and imagined Phillip unlocking the door. After passing a small entryway, the layout was essentially a large, expansive living space with a small, updated kitchen to the left, and one bedroom off to the right of the living area. Exposed beams and bricks gave it a warm feel. The floors were of dark, polished wood. In the center of the room hung an ordinary ceiling-light fixture and an overturned straight-back wooden chair that was marked and taped by the crime scene investigators. On the floor below the light fixture, several pieces of flooring had been cut out for analysis.

In the corner of the living area was a desk with a cordless phone, which David assumed had been a workstation. A new leather couch and small glass table were all the furniture that he saw. Off to the right, on the floor, sat a large flat-screen television set with a remote lying on the couch.

The bedroom was equally sparse. A mattress sitting on the floor had been stripped of all linens and pillows. David assumed these had been taken for forensic analysis. A small night table alongside the bed and a bureau that faced the bed were all the furniture there was. Opening the bureau, they found an assortment of shirts, boxer shorts, and socks all neatly folded. On the night table sat a small, digital alarm clock facing the bed. Two tall windows facing the street were covered with dark wooden blinds that were closed and pulled down to the sill. The bathroom was off to one side and a large walk-in closet was next to it, filled with several dark suits, a few sport coats, several pairs of jeans, and four pairs of casual shoes, including a pair of running shoes.

It was clear that Phillip had recently moved in. The walls looked freshly painted and had nothing covering them. The bathroom had been recently remodeled--the black granite washstand was taller than the standard height and was marked with the location of the medicine bottles that had been found scattered by the police.

Although nothing unusual seemed to be there, David took out his camera and began taking shots in each of the rooms. They all walked back to the living area and stood under the ceiling light where Phillip's body had hung. Dianne shuddered at the sight she imagined. The rope had been removed and there was no sign of the tragedy other than the overturned chair.

David stood silently for several minutes, motionless, thinking about what seemed to be a normal apartment. Other than the chair, there was nothing out of place. He always believed in being as thorough as possible in any mission in which he had been involved, and this was no exception. Viewing this scene was like completing a jigsaw puzzle; David always said that if you if you play long enough, you can find the missing pieces. David studied each room and made mental notes of what he saw.

They left the officer securing the crime scene, and Manny hailed a cab to his office. David was unusually silent during the cab ride as Dianne and Manny made plans to see Cecelia and Harry, their first grandchild. The offices were well designed and Manny's space was tastefully furnished. His view overlooked busy California Street, and after ordering coffee from his assistant, David began to pace, his head down, deep in thought.

Suddenly he announced, "I don't believe Phillip Courtney committed suicide." Dianne and Manny were struck by David's forceful announcement.

"Let's look at the circumstances," he continued. "Courtney was leaving a stressful and potentially dangerous situation at Black. We don't know whether he suspected any wrongdoing, but we know that a reporter named Ann Reilly was killed in what was termed a 'robbery gone bad,' and she was investigating the company's activities and problems. So Courtney gets a new life here in San Francisco with his new company – a new city, a promising new job with a different kind of company – and apparently had put all his problems behind him. Then shortly after showing the folks at GEN21 that he is the kind of executive who fits in nicely and has a lot to offer, he takes an overdose of pills and hangs himself."

"Manny, you already know these pieces of the puzzle, but add this one to the menu: Edgar Black told me that Phillip Courtney was a dedicated executive who spent a great deal of time working both at the corporate headquarters and at home. Can you conceive of a tough, hardworking executive with a strong work ethic without a laptop or PC in his home? We didn't find one, and the police did not indicate that there was one in the apartment. I think Phillip Courtney was murdered because of information that he either had knowledge of or had on his computer, or both. Manny, can you check with the folks at GEN21 to see if anyone had any knowledge about Courtney taking work home."

At that point, they all sat back to take in what David sensed was the obvious. Someone wanted Courtney silenced and all information destroyed. There was an uncomfortable silence while Dianne and Manny contemplated the next step.

Manny spoke first. "I should let the police know what our theory is and then step away from this. Dad, it sounds dangerous, and if you're right, there are people out there who would kill to silence anyone, including you. I'm sorry I got you into this, and it's time to exit as quickly as possible."

Dianne was silent because she already knew what David's response was going to be.

"Look Manny, I read the crime reports of that poor girl, Ann Reilly, and of Phillip Courtney. The cops in both Detroit and San Francisco have signed off on the cases as a random robbery gone sour and as a suicide. I can't just go home and hope that the police will reopen this just because of an unproven theory. I have to try and put this together. I agree that this could be dangerous, but I know you understand that I've dealt with dangers most of my life, and no individual on this earth will track this down but me. So you'll just have to trust that I will not take unnecessary risks."

David continued, "For the rest of the day, my dear Manny, let's put this aside and go to your home so I can squeeze little Harry and hug my wonderful Cecelia. Let's enjoy the evening with no more talk about these very disturbing events." There was no rebuttal from Dianne, but her face was clearly a *tell.*

Cecelia had dinner totally under control and left David and Dianne to play with Harry while she prepared a spicy lentil soup and fabulous salmon Wellington with a wilted spinach salad and fingerling potatoes. Manny uncorked a beautiful Sonoma Valley Cabernet Sauvignon. They topped the meal off with a rich tiramisu and coffee. After that, they all sat down in the spacious great-room. As Manny poured after-dinner drinks, the conversation turned to what David and Dianne's plans were. Dianne wanted to spend a few days with Cecelia and Harry, while David needed time to think about his next steps.

David was deep in thought about the events that brought him to this point in his life and privately thought of the potential dangers to his family. As David sat in Manuel's car on the way back to the hotel, he looked out at all darkly clustered houses and thought each contained its own deep secrets, and now he was trying to unravel secrets that lay hidden from view. David could not look into this darkness without contemplating the death of Phillip Courtney and Ann Reilly, as if they were submerged in the darkness of the night.

Even with his beloved Dianne next to him and his son driving, it was as if each of them were mysteries to each other, each with their own secrets. Phillip and Ann, both dead now, also had secrets that they carried to their graves. It was these innermost secrets that David sought now and, with great effort, he knew he must uncover them.

He believed that in some manner, the truth of these murders lay not in San Francisco, but was somehow connected to Black Technologies. He needed to gain greater insight into Edgar Black. The first step, he thought, was to search out Black's ex-partner, Michael Turion. After a little Internet snooping he located Turion's company, a smallish, privately owned software development shop outside of Ann Arbor. He called and Turion agreed to see him the following day. David caught a late night flight and arrived in Detroit early in the morning.

After checking into a local hotel, he shaved and showered and then ordered in breakfast, which gave him an opportunity to prepare for the meeting. Driving a rental car, David took about a half hour to locate the factory building with a small office located at the front.

A receptionist showed him into Michael Turion's office. The large wooden desk was a picture of organized clutter. Thick files occupied most of the desk space and were stacked so high that David needed to position his chair to see over them. Storage boxes and shelves stuffed with files of documents filled most of the room's floor space. Turion sat behind the desk, a small man in his late fifties wearing thick glasses that were tinted a dark shade.

"How can I help you, Mr. Korman? You must know that I haven't seen or spoken to Eddie Black in many years."

David began to unroll the events that he felt were pertinent, leaving out the Ann Reilly murder and his suspicions about Black Technologies. "What I really am trying to put together is some kind of assessment of Edgar Black's character. What sort of a man he is, in your opinion. Could he be involved in any kind of business problem? Would he deliberately hide information that might be detrimental to his company?"

Turion removed his glasses and rubbed his eyes for a moment. Then he spoke quietly and deliberately. "Eddie was the best friend I ever had. From college, working day and night until we solved a problem, we were inseparable. But then he changed. The man he became was a stranger to me. Money became his mantra. Anything else, anyone else, was irrelevant. It wasn't that we disagreed on the course and strategy of the business; that happens. But his maniacal attitude towards achieving, at all costs, turned him into someone I didn't want to know. So I let them buy me out, and I started this little tech shop and have run it for years. As a matter of fact, I'm getting ready to retire next year, probably sell it to my employees if they can put together the financing. But Eddie would do anything, hide anything, and hurt anyone that got in his way. Does that fill you in on my old buddy?"

They chatted for about half an hour and David now had the answer that he expected. Somehow, Edgar Black had a motive to harm Phillip Courtney.

When he arrived back in Detroit, David tried to put the pieces together. He was confident that Phillip Courtney had not committed suicide. But then, who murdered him and why? What was Edgar Black's role in this?

Chapter 23

ON A DREARY, rainy day in early May, after a restless night in the motel that he had stayed in once before, David began preparing a file about all the events that had taken place since Courtney decided to leave Black Tech. He repeated his earlier task of tracking any information he could find on the Internet about the company and its officers and downloaded information about the January investor conference call.

From that call, he reconfirmed the company's previously announced earnings forecast for the year, which indicated that the laser project was proceeding on schedule with no delays. Black vociferously spoke about the future profit potential of this project. He then described the laser project in some detail and turned the call over to Leon, who began to talk about some of the other activities and projects in which the company was involved. Then Nicole spoke of financial details about the upcoming quarter's results and other financial information.

There were some general questions from the participants that were easily handled, until someone asked about the sudden departure of Phillip Courtney and its effect on the company. Edgar fielded this question, describing Phillip as an outstanding and dedicated executive who was burned out and dutifully waited until the end of the year to tell Edgar that he needed to seek other, less stressful opportunities. It was an amicable departure, and Black had the highest praise for Courtney.

After this upbeat meeting, the price of Black Tech stock continued trading at a price earnings multiple far in excess of the competition and the industry as a whole. It became apparent to David that Wall Street was buying into all the incredible growth that was projected by the company and supported by achieved results. This was a company to be taken seriously. It had a backlog of military projects, which would generate huge cash flows and profits, and the company would become a dominating force in the weapons development industry. David found no mention of any complications or potential threats or any negative publicity of any kind.

He knew what the next step needed to be. He would retrace his steps starting with Ann Reilly's employer. Someone at the paper might know more than the scant information he got at the first interview. His call to the newspaper's managing editor was less than satisfying. He was passed off to the editor's secretary, and David asked if he could spend a few minutes with her to talk about Ann Reilly. She very quietly suggested a local restaurant near the paper's office and they agreed to meet at noon.

Rose Mallory was a thirtyish, short brunette who fit the description given to David. They were seated and ordered lunch. Rose looked distressed as she spoke, "I really don't know if I should be speaking to you. When you called, my boss whispered to me to say he was always going to be unavailable. It's like Ann's murder never happened. Nobody talks about it. It's as if everyone expects her to walk through the door one day and continue working for the paper. It's just not right. It seems as if the police spent very little time trying to find out who did that terrible thing to her."

David replied. "Rose, that's one of the reasons I'm here, to try to find the answer. Your editor told me when I met with him that she kept all her notes and files at her home. Did she have any place at work where she might have filed or kept something related to her job? Did she have any friends or relatives whom I might speak to?"

Rose Mallory responded, "I really liked Ann. She was a very private person, and I doubt that she had any friends at the office. I know Mr. Samson didn't like the piece she was working on about Black, but it was, I mean it still is, an important issue. Since she was killed, no one is picking up the story and it just died, just like her. She never spoke about being close with any relatives, but she does have a sister that lives somewhere on the east side of town. She told me once that she speaks to her often. I met her once when she stopped by to have lunch with Ann. I think her name is Sarah."

David asked, "Is there any way that you can help, any thoughts about where her work files might be?" Rose answered. "Samson told me she kept all of her files and story notes either with her or at home."

"Did she ever talk about her work to you?"

Rose hesitated, and then apparently reminded herself of something, "I don't know if this would be helpful, but we were sharing my lunch one day in the office when she dropped her keys near her food. When I said to be careful or someone might accidently eat them, she laughed and held up one key on the ring and told me that all the keys were replaceable except this one. I just let it pass, but I know it looked like a safe deposit box key. You know, the long kind with just a few notches on them. Could that help you?"

In an excited voice, David asked; "Rose, can you tell me where Ann did her banking?"

"Sure, we all bank at the Third Federal office over on Flagler. It's near the office and our paychecks are automatically deposited there. I know she banked there because she always used their ATM and went there to wire money to someone a few months ago."

David said, "Rose, you don't know how helpful you have been. Maybe she kept certain data or files there. I am going to find out, and please, don't discuss our conversation with anyone. Now, let's just enjoy lunch and tell me more about you."

It didn't take much effort for David to find Sarah Reilly living on the east side, just beyond the city of Detroit. He waited until evening to call her, and she answered on the second ring. He asked if she would meet with him concerning the death of her sister. She seemed to jump at that question with an immediate, "Do you know who did this? Do you have any information about the sick bastard who killed Ann?"

Later, David parked in front of a cluster of what appeared to be modest townhomes in a middle-income neighborhood. When Sarah Reilly answered the door, she was dressed in jeans, a brown turtleneck, and flip-flops. She slightly resembled the image of Ann that he saw in the newspaper, but older. Her hair was lighter than Ann's, but her facial features seemed similar. David also noticed dark circles under her unmade-up eyes, obviously signifying the sadness she must still feel at losing her sister.

After some initial conversation about David's connection to Ann's death and a little history of the relationship that Sarah had with her sister,

David got right to his reason for being there. "Sarah, I don't believe Ann was killed in a bungled robbery attempt. I think she was working on an important case and someone needed her silenced. She may have spoken to an executive of Black Technologies while he lived here; he later was found dead in his San Francisco apartment. The two deaths may be related. I don't know a lot more than that because all her files and her laptop are missing. Do you know anything about a safe deposit box that Ann kept?"

Sarah thought for a moment, stroked her chin, and then responded, "Yes, she made me a signatory on the account. I didn't want to be but Ann insisted and, you know, Ann was such a perfectionist. I've never been to the box. I completely forgot about it til this moment. Do you think it could shed some light on what happened to my poor Ann?"

At this point, Sarah began to sob mournfully. It seemed like a gray gloom hung over the small living area. He consoled her, "I don't know, but it's the only lead I have. Can we go together to the bank tomorrow?"

The next day, David picked Sarah up at home, and they drove together into the city to the Third and Federal bank. The bank occupied a building at the corner of a busy downtown thoroughfare. Inside, several glassed-in offices faced the right side of the bank and to the far left was the depository desk. Sarah signed in and they took the box to a private room.

Inside the box was a large, manila envelope folded in two. Sarah opened it. It contained about six sheets of typewritten pages and two sheets of handwritten notes. Sarah handed the pages to David, who noticed that the first typed page was headed *Black Investigation*.

He began excitedly reading what appeared to be a summary of what Ann Reilly had written for the newspaper. It outlined what seemed like a theory about irregular activities at Black, including the leak of some of the key elements of the new laser system that Black was developing. He quickly got to the final page and was beginning to despair. This was information that he already had read.

He turned to the handwritten notes and it hit him like a two-by-four in the face. At the top of the page, Ann boldly wrote the words *Terrorist Suspicion!* There followed a series of notes that appeared to be taken from an interview with someone. It described major problems with the weapons system and the doubts whether they could be overcome. Apparently the system bugs evolved from the mirrors that the lasers utilized to project its beam to the target. Black seemed to be having major problems with a device that would protect the mirror from external damage while not deterring the system from operating on a fixed platform. In addition, Black was not even close to the development of a small version that could be utilized by one or two persons. There were more details, obviously coming from someone who had inside knowledge of the system's design and development.

On the middle of the second sheet, Ann wrote that there was a strong suspicion that the plans were being copied and taken out of the secure part of the facility. There also were theories about some of the technical-section employees' linkage to individuals with Mideastern ties. Some of the next several lines were illegible, but near the bottom was the note that Ann wrote to herself: "Arrange follow-up with Harris Malone."

David put the pages down on the tabletop and smiled. "I think this will let us know why Ann and Phillip were killed, and, if we're lucky, we'll find out who the bad guys are."

Chapter 24

LATE ONE EVENING at the end of May, Edgar Black and Nicole Lawrence were planning a business trip to visit several of the major lenders to the company. At a private meeting, Edgar, Nicole, and Leon were discussing the most pressing matters. The subject of the earnings release was the main topic.

Nicole started the conversation on a serious note, "I hope both of you know what I had to do to prop up the earnings. The reserves that we put aside for a rainy day are gone, and there is more. We also had to adjust the value of the parts inventories of the more exotic materials to create the profit level we needed, and we advanced some of the deposits to income, as well. Things will have to get better fast or we will have big problems. We'll never get this past the auditors at year-end. I don't have a solution at the moment, but I want to be certain that we are all in sync on what was done. Edgar, I know that you needed me to do this, but please understand that this has to be addressed prior to the fiscal year-end. I hope I'm making myself as clear as I have to."

Edgar said, "Nicole, you've done an amazing job. You should know that Leon and I will stand behind you all the way. I'm confident that we'll find a way out of this. It's not the first time I've faced problems in my life and it probably won't be the last, isn't that right, Leon?"

Leon nodded with a smirk on his face that belied his true feelings. It was clear that he didn't want to enter this conversation. "Let's talk about the project, Pop. You know that Courtney wasn't entirely wrong with his gloom and doom theories. We are really having a hell of a time designing the shield for the mirrors, and I'm not sure we'll ever get one to work the way we want. I'm pushing the techies as far and as fast as I can, but so far, no results."

Edgar turned crimson. "Leon, if I wanted excuses, I wouldn't have fired Courtney. Just stop this bullshit and get the job done. If you need more expertise, go out and get it. We risked everything on the success of the laser system. Not just for me. The free world expects the U.S. to succeed and we intend to do it. That's what at stake." There was a silence in the room.

As Leon exited Edgar's office, his mind began to rehash thoughts about what kind of man his father really was like. He began to weave a strange mental soliloquy. "My dad, and it seems that all CEOs like him, must be lunatics and have to lie to protect their reputation. They all lie. Our employees know it. The public knows it. The investors and Wall Street know it. They are all egomaniacs. If they weren't they wouldn't be in that job. They all have total faith in their self-image. In their minds, everything that goes wrong is due to the ignorance or laziness of someone else.

"At stake for them," he mused, "are more than the private jets that whisk them to faraway places, or the young broads who are willing to jump into the sack at their beck and call, or the ability to buy anything they want without having to worry about how it's going to be paid for. It's something else; something so ethereal that it's god-like. When they pick up their phone, someone is always there to do whatever needs to get done. When things are going well, they bask in the sunshine of the accolades showered upon them. When the company is not performing to expectations, they seek out the person who they think has failed.

"To sum it up," he silently realized, "it's power. Knowing they have it is the ultimate orgasm for them. My father has it and needs it to survive. But even having thought this, I know that what he wants right now, what he craves most at this moment in the deepest recesses of his mind and body, is sitting right across from him. She sits across from his oversized desk with her legs crossed and her high-heeled pumps moving ever so slowly back and forth. The dress she is wearing is just short enough to show her legs up to her knees and a little of her thighs, and this is driving Edgar insane."

Edgar finally ends the meeting, and, with his arm around his son, he delivers his message in the most serious tone. "I didn't choose you totally because you're my son. You are enjoying the fruits of the tree because I know you can get it done. Don't disappoint me. You know how I hate to be disappointed."

When they were alone, Edgar took Nicole in his arms and inhaled her exquisite fragrance as his mouth probed and nibbled at the nape of her neck. Before he could make any further advances, Nicole dropped to her knees and unmasked the bulge in Edgar's pants. It did not take her long--she was a professional and knew how to dismiss this older man as quickly as possible. When she completed her task, Nicole reached in her purse for some tissues and gently wiped off what was left until she was satisfied with the results, and then placed his depleted, sagging part back and zipped him up.

She stood and quietly said, "Edgar, I'll meet you at the airport tomorrow. I'll bring all the materials we need for our presentation. Just have security walk me to my car. I'm looking forward to spending some real quality time with you in the next few days."

As soon as Nicole settled into her car, she poked a pre-set number into the Bluetooth on her steering wheel phone, and when the phone answered on the first ring, she said, "I'm on my way. I'll be there in about fifteen minutes."

Chapter 25

On an unseasonably chilly Monday morning in Detroit, David stepped out of his rental car and made his way to the Fleetwood Diner, an eatery about ten miles outside of town. There was a chill in the air and when he opened the well-worn restaurant door, he was greeted with overwhelming smells of bacon, potatoes, and onions frying on a grill while the short order cook was directing waitresses to pick up steaming plates of eggs, pancakes, and meat. Tables were filled and loud conversation echoed in the air. He looked around and saw his soon-to-be breakfast partner.

Seated in a booth looking out on the parking lot was a heavyset man in his late thirties wearing a plaid, woolen shirt. A reddish beard flecked with brown hung over a round face, and he looked nervous as he glanced up from a mug of coffee and caught David's eye. David neared him and asked, "Are you Harris?" Harris Malone nodded and David sat across from him.

A thin, blonde waitress with hair dangling around her face and beads of sweat on her forehead asked with reverence, "Regular or decaf," and poured coffee for David from one of two carafes that she carried from table to table.

After a touch of cream and a Sweet'n Low, David spoke, "I read Ann Reilly's notes about your conversation."

Before he could say another word, Harris nervously responded. "I'm sorry I ever talked to her. I think that got her killed. I shouldn't be here except she was killed putting together the story and no one has picked up the ball. The police seem to be satisfied that it was a robbery and she just happened to be home at the time, but I don't believe it for a second.

These people at Black are evil people. They lie and are ruthless and I can't let Annie's murder just go away. I am an assistant in the planning and technical section at Black, and I know what they are doing."

"Why don't we start at the beginning, Harris? I think you know why I'm here. I started helping with an investigation of Phillip Courtney's death in San Francisco that was ruled a suicide, but it doesn't look like that to me. During the course of my investigation, I learned of Ann Reilly's murder and the story she was working on, and I think somehow they are tied together. What exactly do you know, and how did Ann reach out to you?"

Harris Malone shifted nervously in his seat and began to tell David the entire story. "Annie and me have been friends since high school. I've always really liked her. We would have a meal together or a couple of drinks from time to time, and I was so proud when she got the job at the paper. A few months ago…. no, it was in January that she called me and wanted to have dinner. Of course I said yes. She asked me whether anything going on at Black was peculiar. Apparently she was doing a story on the success of Black Technologies and the future outlook for the company. She was especially interested in the laser system under development. When she asked for a meeting with Edgar Black, she was told that the high level of security prevented him from meeting with the press. She insisted that the interview would not deal with any classified matters, but Edgar's whore, Nicole Lawrence, told her not to bother anyone at Black.

"Everyone knows Edgar is fucking Lawrence," Harris continued. "She is there only because she's in tight with him. Annie got very suspicious of the way they dealt with her. The request for an interview seemed reasonable to Ann. So, she called me. I have been very nervous about what goes on at the plant, so I told Annie what I knew."

"And what was it that you told her?" questioned David.

"Well, Mr. Korman, my job is really just a clerical one. I make copies of all the plans that are drawn, the test results, and the meeting notes from the tech team, and I receive and send faxes to and from all the subcontractors. It's not much of a job, but it's steady and it beats working in the auto factories, which is where I used to work. Not long ago, I noticed something very strange. When there was a meeting where the team was to discuss the progress on what seemed to be an important part of the system,

I never saw the meeting notes. When I asked if they needed copying, I was told there were no notes, but I knew that couldn't be true. Also, when I was to fax some documents about the specs for some part that was being manufactured by an outside company, they told me that someone else would do the job. But, I know no one else did because I keep the log of ordinary faxes sent by the machines in my area."

Harris continued, "Lately everyone seems so nervous. It wasn't that way when Courtney headed the area. Then, security was tight, but I always knew what I was to do and why. Now, Black's son, Leon, is in charge of the technical area and things have really changed. Annie asked me whether there was any evidence of outside influence in the company's affairs, but I told her I really didn't know of any. She seemed very interested in what I had to say, and she said she would try to contact Phillip to see if he could shed some light on this."

"Do you know whether she ever got to speak to Phillip?" asked David.

"I think she did because she called me a week later and said she had some interesting information to bounce off me. We were supposed to meet when I found out that she had been killed."

"Have you told anyone about this, Harris? If you have, you may be in danger. Someone seems to want to keep whatever is going on at the company a secret, and if they think you talked to someone other than me, you could have a real problem. You should be careful about everything you do at the plant; this could be very serious."

David and Harris talked for more than an hour. David was so intent on learning as much as he could that he didn't notice the large, black Lincoln Navigator with dark-shaded windows parked in the rear of the parking lot. When they stood and headed for the door of the diner, the SUV pulled away.

David sat in his car for a long time trying to decide what the next step should be when a creeping fear began to overtake him--fear that he had not felt for several years. It reminded him of some of the missions he had undertaken in defense of Israel where the unknown always seem to lurk close by, deep in the shadows, waiting for his next move. In years past, while he waited for final orders to assassinate the president of the terrorist African state of Malumba, he had sat motionless, rethinking all his moves and wondering if this was to be the last night of his life. That was how he felt now, as if some major stressor was going to impact his life.

When he returned to his hotel, he called Dianne and updated her on his meeting. She had returned home to New York and was planning on having their children Susan and Oliver down for the upcoming weekend. The next day, she was to handle all the food preparation, and she was especially excited to see Oliver's serious girlfriend. He had made such personal progress in the last few years, and being in a serious relationship was especially heartening.

Chapter 26

DAVID WAS PLANNING the next steps in his strategy to learn the truth about Phillip and Ann. Foremost in his mind was learning more about this mysterious, top-secret project that Black was developing. He realized that until he could understand what they were doing and why they were hiding information, he was headed up a blind street. The next day, he was at the main branch of the Detroit library, researching the field of directed energy sources.

He immediately discovered the *Journal of Directed Energy*, a peer-reviewed publication by a group called the Directed Energy Professional Society, whose goals were to address the many aspects of directed energy and the exchange of information about this complex subject. From this, David learned that some of the largest corporations in the field were doing their own research. Boeing had recently test-fired a laser from the air and hit a moving vehicle on the ground.

Black had somehow become the prime contractor for the government's high-energy laser, outbidding Boeing, Raytheon, Northrop Grumman, and a large number of foreign entities anxious to enter this new world of destructive weaponry. The edge that Black had was that the competition was still working in a laboratory laser environment and not yet in a field-testing mode.

Black had recently demonstrated the capability of building the extremely high-energy portion of the weapon that the Department of Defense was funding under a fast timetable. Apparently, David learned, the major obstacle for all companies was the miniaturization of the weapon, and Black had recently announced that it achieved some startling success in mounting a laser to a military Humvee and successfully test-firing it at an unmanned aircraft.

After reading for most of the day, David became convinced of the importance to the nation of directed-energy weapons. He returned the next day, continuing his research into Black's claims of high success rates in what was purported to be the final test phases for a deliverable laser weapon.

After several days in research, he felt that he now knew enough about laser-directed systems. He knew that this field was crowded with companies, each doing research on the viability of a weapons system powered by laser beams. He knew then that he was going to revisit Black Technologies, hopefully for an in-depth discussion of its system. Somewhere in the development of the system lay the secret of the tragedies that had occurred.

He was awakened early the following day by the sound of a terrific thunderstorm. It had been raining for the past two days and the day was grim-looking. Before he could shower, the phone rang from a frantic-sounding Sarah Reilly. "Did you see the Internet this morning? I'm so frightened, David, isn't it horrible?"

"No, please calm down. I haven't even opened my laptop today. What happened?"

She sobbed, "In the local news, they reported that a car skidded off the road last night and the driver was killed. He was on his way home from work, and they found his car overturned outside of town. The car was demolished and they could barely identify him."

"That's terrible, but why call me with it," questioned David.

"David, David," cried Sarah, "it was Harris, do you understand? This can't be an accident. They knew about Harris, and they must know about us."

As soon as David heard these words, a series of flashes burned through his brain. It meant that whoever was responsible for Phillip Courtney and Ann Reilly's murders realized where the information was coming from and had that person eliminated. They also must know about his visit with Harris. David's mind was paralyzed by another earthshaking fact; that whoever was behind this also knew that Sarah had access to information about Ann's research.

His thoughts drifted to Manuel and Dianne, who had spent time with him investigating Courtney's death. They must be told where David's investigation was going, as well as his talk with Mike Turion. David realized that someone must be close by, and this terrified him. His next move needed to be a bold one. He must meet with Edgar and try to get to the truth.

That evening he updated Manuel of the events that had taken place. David's son pleaded with him to drop the investigation and head home to New York before the scope of the tragedies widened, but David was resolute. "You know, Manuel, there are three murders that no one is chasing, and I think that there is even more at stake that we don't know about. I need you to do something for me."

"Sure, dad, what do you need?"

"Speak to your friend Jim Jameson over at GEN21. See if he can fill in any of the blanks regarding Black's contract with the government. See if he has heard anything about something wrong with the project. You told me he's close with Kozlov, the CEO at Jim's company. Maybe we can find out why it seems that someone doesn't want any information about the system leaked."

"I'll meet with Jim tomorrow and let you know what I find, but until then, you have to be careful, we all do. Because whoever is involved knows you are on the trail. Dad, this is not like your old Israeli missions. We know nothing about whoever is involved or why they are involved, so please be safe."

Chapter 27

On an unusually warm Boston morning in June, Dr. Susan Korman was just getting dressed for work. After completing her residency, she had received an appointment to the staff at Children's Hospital. Spending a lot of money on clothes or dressing in a current style was just not important to her. Jeans and Gap polos were her standard work outfit. She was tall and thin, with a pale Asian complexion and long, dark hair pulled tight into a ponytail. Enthusiasm and vivaciousness gave her an attractive aura that made her well liked by her colleagues.

As she finished in the bathroom, she kicked the bed and laughingly said, "Hey, lazy one, it's seven and time to rise." There was no movement at all from any part of the bed. A large pillow covered any sign of human life. Susan sneaked closer and grabbed the blanket and pulled it completely from the bed, leaving a naked body with arms pulling the pillow down. When Susan's antics finally had an effect, the body turned and pulled her down to the bed.

"You're not going to get away with that so fast," said Patty as she pulled Susan down onto her naked body, wrapping her legs around her body. They kissed deeply and Patty softly spoke. "Sue, I love you so much, I hope you know that."

Susan smiled and held her face in her hands and very quietly spoke. "I've never known love like this. I'm going to tell my mother this weekend about us. I know she'll love you as much as I do. Then we'll figure how to break it to dad. Oliver says dad be all right with it. He's such a great guy."

Patty rolled over and said, "I'm going to sleep in today. I'll call in to tell them I have the flu. That always works."

"OK. My sweet one, I need to be at the hospital by 7:30, so I'm off. Let's do pasta tonight. See ya."

About an hour later, the doorbell of their apartment buzzed and when Patty threw on a robe and looked through the peephole, a deliveryman stood with a bouquet of roses and said, "Flowers for Susan Korman."

She unlatched the door excitedly wondering who would have sent Sue flowers. When the door opened, she did not see the flowers. All she saw was a short man in a dark jacket with the collar pulled up and a gun pointed at her. His eyes were pale, his expression grim, almost detached, like a surgeon preparing for major surgery. His light-colored hair was thick and spiked in a style unfamiliar in America.

Before she could cry out, he hit her three times across her face and on her forehead with the butt of his weapon. He then began hitting her again until she dropped to the floor, blood flowing freely from the wounds to her head. As she cried out, he began systematically tearing up the apartment until he was satisfied. When he was finished with his work he gathered the flowers into a bag and before he closed the door behind him, he quietly said, "Tell Daddy to go home and take a long rest. If he doesn't, I'll be back and treat you to some real excitement."

That evening, when Susan turned the key in the door and found it unlocked, fear began to throb in her temples. As she opened the door and called out for Patty, she saw the blood throughout the foyer carpet. She began to tremble and turned her eyes on a barely distinguishable face lying on the couch. Both eyes were closed and already blackened. An icepack lay on her forehead. At first, Susan didn't scream out--she couldn't utter a sound. She merely stared at the beaten body in a transfixed state.

Through bloated lips, Patty struggled to say, "They came for you." It was a supreme effort for Susan to reach the phone and call 911.

Then came the call to Dianne, which brought Susan to the reality of the situation; she barely was able to breathe through her hysterics. She thought, it's odd to think that when we are faced with tragedies, we can deal with such horrid visions by forcing them to other parts of the brain and focusing on mundane or unimportant issues.

After witnessing Patty's condition, Susan's first words to Dianne were, "Mom, I'm gay."

What happened then was an emotional response only familiar to a mother and daughter struck by the horror of what Susan saw in that apartment. Dianne told her sharply to lock the door and go to another room and stay there until the police arrived. She uttered words that a mother delivers to calm a daughter. She would be on the next shuttle to Boston, and her father would follow as quickly as possible.

Chapter 28

LATER IN THE week, Manuel Korman finally caught up with Jim Jameson. They reviewed David's call about the tragedies of Ann Reilly being killed while she was investigating some leaks at Black Technologies, and Harris Malone being involved in a fatal auto accident after talking to David.

"Jim, I need for you to talk to Gabe. He's really close with a lot of tech execs and maybe he's heard something. I'm scared for my dad. It's obvious that whoever is responsible knows he's investigating. And you don't know my dad, but he's like a bulldog when he is on a mission. He's done this kind of stuff all his life and he won't let go until he figures it out, so help me out, will you?"

"I'll get back to you as soon as I can get to the boss, and thanks for getting involved. Phillip didn't deserve what happened to him and from what you're telling me, neither did the Reilly girl or the guy at Black."

Chapter 29

LATE THAT NIGHT in San Francisco, in a suburban hilltop home, Gabriel Kozlov sat in his den nursing a neat vodka, grimly looking at the glass and thinking about the call he was about to make. The children were asleep and his wife was in her office, editing an article that she wrote on dietary issues for pre-school children in inner city locations for a magazine for which she free-lanced.

He closed the heavy, oak door to the den, used his quad band cell phone and dialed an international number. When the voice answered in a foreign language, Kozlov said, "Speak English, I am not in Grozny."

Kozlov began to relate the events of the day, including the meeting he had had with Jim Jameson and the events uncovered by someone named David Korman. He spoke in English to this foreign person.

"We need to find out more about this Korman and why he is so interested in Black Tech. Those idiots in Detroit could screw up all our operations. On the surface, he is trying to find the killers of three people connected to Black's business. But it's clear to me that he is a professional. He must be looking at Black for laser system problems. See what you can find out about Korman, and make it fast. Remember, we are subcontracting a small piece of that system. This cannot compromise our objectives. I put out the word for Korman to come see me; my guess is he'll call me tomorrow. Maybe I can point him in another direction. That whoremonger who runs that company is always shooting his mouth off and his son is no better."

They spoke for a while about their business activities and then Kozlov abruptly ended the call with a reminder to get back to him as soon as possible. The Russian whom Kozlov was speaking to hung up his mobile phone and sat for a moment before he spoke to an associate with instructions, "Find out all you can about David Korman and put a tail on him at once."

Chapter 30

DAVID GOT THE call from Dianne's cell as she was on her way to LaGuardia. She was scheduled to be on a shuttle to Boston within the hour. She tersely related the call from Susan and urged David to catch the first flight available to Boston. He was silent, listening fearfully, knowing full well that Susan's roommate was not the target of this horrid action, but not willing to disclose this to Dianne until they were face-to-face.

The truth of the situation was finally crystallized--this was a warning to David to stop his intrusive investigation. He knew that Susan started her workday very early, so it would have been a natural mistake for a killer to attack in the early morning, thinking she would still be home. Although the sadness of the incident played on his mind, he was thankful that the victim was not Susan. He was not totally surprised to learn of Susan's sexual preference. She rarely discussed her social life, and men never seemed to come up in conversation. She doggedly dodged the issue of her social life, and she was always much too busy to get involved. He wondered if Manny and Oliver knew. It was a pity that Susan didn't have enough confidence and trust in the love they shared to tell him earlier, but that discussion was for another day. He just wanted to be with her. On his way to Detroit Metro Airport, he decided to call Manny and Oliver. Oliver, living in the Boston metro area, was already on his way to Logan to pick up Dianne.

Hours later, Susan, Dianne, Oliver, and David sat in a suite at the Marriott. Susan's eyes were red and she continued to sob mournfully. Dianne stared at David--she knew that this must be somehow connected to David's investigation. It was a warning, she thought, and her whole family was at risk, especially when the word came from David that it wasn't Susan who was the victim.

David's mind was moving at supersonic speed. His first thought was how to protect his family. The enemy knew he had some knowledge about Black so they were all targets. Dropping the investigating activities was out of the question now, so he would have to provide security for his family, an activity that would take some time. Secondly, he realized that he could no longer continue this alone. He needed help. He carefully assessed who would be the best confederate to deal with the still unresolved issues.

As he pondered his next move, Manny called. He had received a message from Gabriel Kozlov, who wanted to meet with David as soon as possible. Manny felt that Kozlov's tone was very serious, and he indicated that he might be able to offer some assistance.

David acted swiftly. He abruptly left the suite, and in a quiet section of the lobby, he called the highest security office in Tel Aviv. He still knew many of the senior officers in the special security section he reported to while in the service of his mother country. His closest contacts at the very top were gone now. The ex-leader of the section, General Benjamin Hadar, and his second in command, Colonel Hirschel Kiklovitz, were involved in a fraudulent scheme several years ago; Hadar was now dead and Kiklovitz was in prison.

He did have contact some years ago with a younger executive, Adam Handler, now a colonel, whom David knew he could call on. It took David a while to make contact, and when he did, he gave the officer an abbreviated update of his situation. David could still call upon Israeli security for assistance. He had given his entire life to the State, and many in critical branches of government and the military knew this. Handler wanted to know what kind of help he could provide.

"I need security for my family until I can resolve these problems. I also need someone to work with, someone who has been through enough missions and is strong enough to provide some real assistance. The longer it takes to find out what and who is involved, the more dangerous it becomes, not only for my family, but for collateral damage to others close to the information."

Handler responded. "I think we can help out on security as long as it doesn't become protracted. On the other request, do you remember working on a tough mission several years ago with a guy named Danny Merkel? He still works for us, and he had good things to say about you after that escapade you guys had in Iraq. I'm sure if I asked him, he'd help out."

"That would be excellent. He's a great detail guy and we worked well together. How soon can you reach him? Have him call me as soon as possible. Adam, I am grateful for your help. I am terribly worried about my family. Damn it, they came close to killing my daughter!"

"I'll get on it right away, and I'll have him call you quickly, and we'll put some people in the States on security right away."

Chapter 31

When David hung up, it was like a weight had been lifted from his head, and he could now focus on flying out to San Francisco to meet with Gabe Kozlov. Strange that Kozlov would have important information. David would find out what he could about him and his business, GEN21. With luck, Danny Merkel would be able to meet him there.

David lay on his back in his hotel room trying to get a few hours of sleep. He was so tired that he was sure he'd fall asleep quickly. Thirty minutes after he turned off the table lamp, sleep seemed a thousand miles away. He stared at the small strip of light coming from under the hotel door.

Slowly the door lock clicked open and the door opened. Dianne whispered to him as she entered. "The hospital called. Patty's tests following the beating were negative. She will survive. Susan fell asleep as soon as she got back. I think the Klonopin did the trick." David's eyes could just make out her form moving slowly towards him on bare feet.

After she dropped her clothes to the floor, he held out his hand to her, and she slid next to him onto the bed. Her face tilted up to him and their lips met. They held each other for a long time, saying nothing. Her naked flesh shone as dusty gold in the dim light. As total exhaustion took hold of them, their bodies came together and they made love, not of passion, but as a relief from the tragedy and the uncertainty of what was to come.

Several hours later, David was up. He showered, ordered coffee and some breakfast for both of them, and was at the Internet, drawing a portrait of Kozlov and, more importantly, of his family. Kozlov appeared to be the son of a very rich Moscow family who apparently made its money developing oil and natural gas properties in Russia. He went to school in Russia and somehow was able to come to the States on a scholarship to Caltech. Several years after graduating with a degree in information systems, he started his own small business doing software design. Apparently, he was a success story, with U.S. citizenship, ownership of a large-growth company, and married with kids. David thought, "Sounds like he discovered the American dream."

Later, he and Dianne discussed the plans for that day. She would get Susan and Patty to take time off and come back to Manhattan with her. David was making flight arrangements to San Francisco to meet with Kozlov. He spoke to Danny Merkel that day, and after a detailed phone briefing of the situation, they agreed to meet in San Francisco, and then together they would fly to Detroit to confront Edgar Black.

As he hung up the phone, he thought about how he has noticed a change in Dianne--a kind of palpable anger that lay beneath the surface. David guessed where this was coming from. Were it not for his involvement in the events beginning with Courtney's death, Susan would not have had to feel her lover's pain, and the family would not be threatened. When the time was right, he would open this discussion with his wife, but for now he was on full alert.

When David landed the next afternoon in San Francisco, Danny Merkel was waiting to meet him. They had not seen each other since they had partnered on a mission for Israel several years ago. It had been a dangerous one that turned out successfully, and they shared respect for each other. They hugged and made their way to a high-security private car where they could talk as they drove to see Kozlov.

David took his time slowly unraveling the deaths and Black's involvement, as well as his conviction that problems at Black might pose a larger danger. He confided that the deaths all seem to be related to something that Black Tech was hiding.

When David was finally done filling Danny in, Merkel smiled and said, "Boy, Korman, you sure know how to get yourself wound up in crazy situations. For starters, Adam told me to assure you that your family is safe and secure. So now, we can deal with the Black problem. How does this Kozlov guy fit into the picture? You think he has other motives than playing the good guy?"

David responded, "I just don't know, but after speaking to his source who is high up in the GEN21 organization, Manny thinks Kozlov runs a good company."

It took them almost an hour to get to the corporate offices of GEN21, a sprawling group of low-slung campus buildings on a pretty, wooded piece of real estate. The security team guided them on golf carts to a one-story, concrete building completely shaded by some tall spruce trees.

Gabriel met them at the front entrance--a smiling man, stocky, wearing a short-sleeved, maize-colored shirt, khaki pants, and brown penny loafers. He showed them to his office and David detected a very slight northern European accent as Kozlov spoke.

After some general talk, Kozlov spoke, "Jim told me of your interest in Black Technologies, and I may have some information that will help you understand them. Edgar runs the company with an iron hand. No decision of any size is made without his stamp on it. Leon is a tool--Edgar barks and Leon runs. The only other power figure is Nikki Lawrence, and I think she belongs to Edgar. You know, she and Phillip were very close. He brought her into the company, but I guess she had higher sights. I know the gossip is that their laser system is in trouble, but I also know that it is normal to have field-testing problems in a system that complex. If there is one visible problem, it's with Black's operational results. Our guys have studied their numbers and they just don't make sense. Based on the revenue generated, they can't be that good. Our feeling is that they are cooking the books until they get solid field results from the lasers. That should bring in enough cash flow to get the numbers on track."

"Do you do any business with Black?" asked Danny.

Koslov immediately responded, "We are just doing the fabrication of a small part of the mirror assembly. It's small potatoes for them, but it keeps our factory busy. They have extended the payment terms a couple of times, so I know cash is tight. The only other piece of information I can give you is that Black got this contract through their sources in Washington, but they have the big guys in Congress breathing down their necks. If the program goes sour, I don't see how they can stay alive."

When David and Danny left, Danny asked, "I wonder why we needed to come out here for that gossip? Couldn't he have just phoned or emailed the information? Maybe he wanted to meet you face-to-face. Maybe he knows what we are working on and wants to be in the loop, for whatever reason."

As they were driving back to the airport, Danny again asked, "Did Handler say he was going to provide security for you and I as well?"

David shook his head curiously.

"Because since we left the airport, someone has been tailing us, and I can't believe Handler would send an Israeli to cover us." They were silent the rest of the way as they both thought about this potential complication. Did Kozlov have anything to do with the problems at Black? Or did he have his own agenda in this puzzle that was growing darker with each meeting?

Their next step was to fly to Detroit and come down hard on Edgar Black and his mistress. David realized that they must be planning something, but what it could be was still elusive. David sensed that they are getting closer to some recognition of the problem and the danger involved.

Chapter 32

IT HAD BEEN raining in New York for several days. Despite the season, it was the kind of weather that made you wish you could pull the covers over your head and stay until the sun came out.

Dianne had just finished dressing and was putting on makeup when she stopped and looked in the mirror. Nights of restful sleep were few and far between, and her once-firm cheeks seemed hollow. Her eyes needed extra mascara, and it seemed to her that each day more foundation was necessary for her to look human. She looked for shoes that would be gentler on her toes, but none seemed to help. She checked the bedroom where Susan still lay in her bed alongside Patty.

Tip-toeing into the kitchen, she poured from the coffee decanter and sat at the table, wondering where David was and why he didn't call. Anger boiled inside her. She had called him two days ago and then yesterday again and he had not responded.

She felt like screaming at the top of her lungs or just crawling back into bed, but times were difficult at Manson's and she needed to be there. The economy was in the toilet and their sales were down sizeable percentages from last year. Cutbacks were happening throughout the company – full-timers were replaced with part-time employees, inventory levels were reduced, and every expense was scrutinized. She scheduled another meeting that morning with the top merchandising and advertising execs to increase promotions as well as do anything else that would bring business into the store.

Her mind momentarily drifted to the new, smart young men who were all trying to earn their spurs in the merchandising department—eager young men totally willing to spend extra time at the office to be noticed. Yes, she certainly noticed them, but quickly put them out of her mind as she worried about the future of her family.

Later that day, alone in her office, she shook off her shoes and put her feet up on her glass desktop and let her head drop back on the chair. After sweating over idea after idea, the stress was becoming all consuming and each time her phone rang, shivers went through her.

She heard a knock on the open glass door to her office, and Mark, appeared. Tall, and well proportioned, he was wearing a black pinstriped suit, dark blue fitted shirt and gold-striped tie, and tasseled black loafers. She scanned his features--thick black hair neatly parted with an interesting face that always seemed to look like he needed a shave.

"Anything I can help you with, Dianne?" he asked.

"Come in, and let's talk about anything but the business. I've just about had it for today".

"That's a deal. At the risk of getting my butt kicked, why don't we have a drink?"

She hesitated, thinking about David, Susan, the rest of her family, and took a deep swallow and said. "Okay, I'll meet you at Caesar's in about twenty minutes."

The bar was a posh oasis near the Manson offices. It was one of those step-down spots, squeezed into a space in the middle of a street with a long bar and tables for dining scattered in every available square foot. Dark wood walls and a faux fireplace gave it the appearance of a pleasant country inn.

"He is totally charming, this twenty-eight-year-old hottie," she mused about Mark after the waiter delivered her second vodka martini. She learned of his upbringing in a Jewish family from Milwaukee, his schooling, and his way up the corporate ladder to an associate merchandise manager, first at company headquarters in St. Louis and recently to their store in the Big Apple. Listening to Mark, the stress she had been feeling abated for the moment and she was able to relax.

When he suggested dinner, she eagerly accepted. A wonderfully prepared baked flounder stuffed with lobster that followed a small, but tasty salad was just what she needed. With dinner, a bottle of superb Barossa Valley pinot noir, and more good conversation, Dianne felt better than she had been in a long time. After leaving the restaurant, they waited for taxis, hers to the resplendent Upper East Side and his to an apartment just outside of Soho.

When she dropped her purse, they both bent to retrieve it. As she rose, he leaned close to her and hesitatingly kissed her softly. Her head was spinning now from a combination of the alcohol and the stress as she weighed what was certainly going to happen in the next few moments. Against all her better judgment and experience, all that her family meant to her and all that her dear David would think, she leaned close to him and whispered, "Let's go to your place."

As the key turned in the door lock, Dianne trembled with a sense of excitement. Mark's small apartment was minimally but tastefully furnished. After hanging up her coat, he turned to her and asked in a serious tone, "Do you really want to do this, Dianne?"

She could barely get the words past her lips, but finally whispered, "It's wrong, it's denigrating, and it's trouble, Mark, but I need to do this for me."

They kissed for several minutes, first gently, then with a passion, and her entire body throbbed. When he softly caressed her breasts, her nipples were already hard and sensitive to his touch. They undressed quickly, deliberately, and purposefully. His body was firm, not muscular, but taut, with ample hair covering his body. After they engaged in some foreplay, he entered her, and Dianne drifted to a special place where his thrusts aroused strange feelings.

After he came and they laid together, his arm draped over her stomach, she began to cry, softly at first. But then the reality of her actions that night caused tears to flow freely down her reddened cheeks. Despite what Mark said to console Dianne, she continued this tearful sadness. After what seemed to be hours to her, she reached for her cell phone and called Susan. "I'm not coming home tonight, sweetheart. I'll be home at about five in the morning."

Dianne was surprised at Susan's response, "It's okay, mom, whatever you do, I support it. If you can get some relief from the fucking mess we are in, take it. Don't feel any guilt or remorse. I'm on your side. If dad calls, I'll take care of it. I love you so."

That night, Dianne slept fitfully, awakening constantly to see this handsome young man beside her.

The next day went badly for Dianne. She was exhausted and her head was splitting. The guilt factor was in full force and she hoped David would not call today. Although she tried desperately to avoid bumping into Mark at the office, it was unavoidable. Each time she saw him, she trembled. She wavered between guilt, fear of someone seeing Mark's glances, and shame that she had failed David and her children. But, as the next few days crawled by, the image of Mark's mouth on hers and the feeling of his penetration inside her became incredibly strong.

When she finally did speak to David, she felt lost. There had never been anything she withheld from him until now…an impossible situation, and her conversation was distant. He sensed it as well. They spoke haltingly--David so deeply involved in his mission that he pushed everything else away, and Dianne desperately trying to disguise her guilt.

She gave in to her urges several times after that, each one becoming more exciting. She became less fearful and she and Mark fast became close. She rarely thought of the consequences and even left some clothing at Mark's so she need not come home. Susan never questioned her, and Dianne did not allow the situation to become a subject of conversation. Only when she was home and by herself did the worries of how to deal with this affair come to the surface. She felt her entire existence was surreal, leaving her nowhere. When she was finally able to sleep, it was not deeply, but one that gave her some relief from what was to come.

Chapter 33

AFTER DAVID AND Danny Merkel checked into the motel where David had stayed during prior visits, they decided on dinner at a small cafe across the street. As they sat near a window, Danny asked David if he saw the Lincoln Navigator with the dark windows parked at the back of the lot, off to one side, but still visible.

"Sure," David replied. "I think at some point in our dinner, one of us should excuse himself and see who thinks us such interesting people. The problem is I don't have any firepower and walking up to the car and inquiring what their interest is doesn't excite me."

Merkel smiled, opened his attaché case, and discreetly showed him two Glock 9 mms and several ammo clips. "When I knew we were going to be in Detroit, I had our contact drop these off in a box at the motel for me."

David smiled and said, "I knew we were going to work well together."

Their dinner came shortly, and after taking several bites of his meat loaf and mashed potatoes, David reached into the attaché and checked to see if the weapon was fully loaded. He slipped it into his pocket and got up without putting on his coat, ostensibly to use the men's room at the rear of the diner. He was able to slip out the side door without being seen.

David approached the car, first crouching at the left rear door and then reaching the driver's side he noticed that the window was down, exposing the driver. He was a short, ugly man, unshaven, and balding with tufts of unkempt hair at the side of his face. He wore a cheap-looking wool coat, and David could see a dark, V-neck undershirt under the coat, with thick, black chest hair poking its way out of the top of the shirt. He was smoking what appeared to be a small, foul-smelling cigar when and his left arm rested on the open window frame.

It was without difficulty that David was able to lunge at the stranger's arm, pulling it back forcefully as he leaned into the cab and grasped his throat with his other hand. A stifled cry was all that emerged, and seconds later, Merkel, running at full tilt from the diner, opened the passenger-side door and put the nose of the gun barrel against the intruder's face. David jumped into the back seat and Merkel instructed the stranger to drive, shouting out directions for about ten minutes when they got to what appeared to be a quiet street of abandoned warehouses. As they pulled into a broken concrete driveway overgrown with weeds, Merkel ordered the driver to stop.

Merkel said in a menacing voice, "Okay, my friend, tell us a story. Tell us who you are, why you are following us, and who ordered you to tail us. I have no desire to, but if necessary, I will blow your mother-fucking head off." As he began to speak, a northern European accent was clear. David guessed Russian.

"My name is Grunoff and I mean you no harm. I was asked to watch your movements, that is all. Please put the gun down before it goes off."

David reached into Grunoff's coat and extracted a cell phone and a Beretta. "Not good enough, my friend." David reached from behind and wrapped his arm around Grunoff's neck and began to pull back. Grunoff gasped and gagged. As David pulled tighter, Grunoff's face began to turn crimson.

David whispered in his ear, "You have about two minutes before you will begin to lose consciousness. You will reach a critical level in about four minutes and then it's goodbye, Mr. Grunoff."

He struggled to take a breath, but with each attempt, David pulled tighter until Grunoff signaled him to stop. It took almost a minute for him to begin to breathe normally--his eyes were tearing and strands of saliva dripped down his chin, landing onto his coat.

He began to speak haltingly, slowly at first. "Two days ago, I got a call from my contact in Grozny. He named both of you and told me where to find you. I was to follow you, no particular time frame, just stay on top of you and keep a log of everywhere you went, who you talked to. Every day,

I sent the notes to an email address in California. The money is wired into my bank account once a week. That is all that I know, I swear it."

Danny Merkel responded, "I'm sorry, but you must know or have a pretty good idea who hired you. I think I could guess by now, but I'd like you to say it." He shoved the barrel of the gun into Grunoff's mouth and pulled the hammer back. "Damn it, say it," he screamed.

"It was someone named Koslov. I don't know him, I never met him, but I heard his name. My contact used his name once."

They were silent as he drove back to the diner, and as Danny got out of the car, he leaned in to Grunoff and said, "Time to go back where you came from and let Koslov know that we don't appreciate you or him." At that point, Danny slugged Grunoff across the forehead with the butt of his gun. The skin burst like a popped balloon and blood spurted across his face as he clutched his head with both hands and let the deep crimson flow through his fingers, circling his dirty fingernails.

David and Danny were silent as they drove their car back to the motel. Thoughts raced through both their minds as they tried to unravel what seemed to be a puzzle with all the pieces missing. Nothing fit. They were chasing Black Technologies for the murders as well as for the reasons why three innocent people were brutally killed. Now, suddenly, a Russian with no apparent connection appears, *stalking them, trying to learn their every move.* Why? Where are the pieces?

When they got back and sat quietly in the near-empty bar, the melancholy music playing somewhere mirrored their mood. After the second Jack, neat, Danny broke the silence, "I need to go to Tel Aviv. I must speak to the intelligence sources I still know. The Koslov piece doesn't fit. I want to learn all I can about him, and they will provide the answers because, David, I must tell you that there is a sinister plot brewing here. I know it--I can almost smell it. You go to see Edgar Black and get him to tell you what their part is. I'll be back when I have some information, and meanwhile, let's stay in touch."

With that stern declaration, Danny disappeared and David was left with his drink; a splitting headache; and a potpourri of facts, clues, and information roiling through his brain like grey, scudding clouds. A few vodkas later and all was a blur, allowing him to realize that the one person he had totally ignored was the woman in his life. He undressed, showered, and looked in the bathroom mirror at the image of a tired sixty-five-year-old man who had fought wars all his life, and now found himself drawn into a mystery that he could not unravel.

"I'm too old for this shit," he muttered as he reached for his cell phone and called Dianne. It was late, already past midnight, but he needed the voice that had always soothed him.

The person who answered was not whom he expected. It was Susan, sounding asleep, with her voice barely recognizable--sadness, in a tone that he had never heard. She was the spark with the indomitable spirit, always full of the animal juices that made her special, from the street orphan in Los Angeles all the way through medical school. She blandly asked why he was calling so late and he asked for Dianne.

"She isn't home yet. She has been working unbelievable hours at the store. You know, Daddy, that she is terribly angry with you," she retorted with acid dripping. "She warned you not to get involved in this mess more than once and look where it got us. My dearest, sweetest love is broken; the family is threatened, especially Manny and Cecelia; and she hears from you sporadically. What the fuck did you get us into? This should have been turned over to local police and that would have ended it. Mom is a mess, so stressed out that work is the only therapy. Daddy, fix it, please. You always told me that I could count on you, so please find a way to end it."

He could now hear the tears in her voice, and the weight of the unsolved problems at this instant felt like a ton on his shoulders and head. "I'm getting close," he lied, "and I will make it up to all of you when it's over. Please tell your mother to call me when she gets home, whatever the time."

Sleep did not come easily that night, and when it finally did, he slept fitfully, with wild dreams, and then woke up covered in a damp sweat over his body. The clock blinked mercilessly at three A.M. and he knew that sleep was over for the night. He showered, dressed, and left the motel, at once feeling the blistering, cold chill of the dark. He drove the quiet streets of the suburban city searching for some all-night diner.

It took what seemed to be a lifetime until he found an open greasy spoon. He blinked at the bright lights and found two patrons at the counter leaning over mugs of what must have been steaming coffee. A heavy-set, tired-looking, apron-clad woman approached him. Her blonde hair was tied messily into a bun, with loose strands hanging over her face. He ordered coffee and an English muffin, and as he waited, new concerns poured into the already overfilled bucket.

Where was Dianne? Was she safe? What will my next step be? He was not even aware of the waitress standing over him. "You sure have a lot on your mind. Need some company? I get off at five."

When he did not answer, she moved on, and slowly David Korman began to see what he must do next.

In the next hour, over three more mugs of weak, watered coffee, he developed the plan. He would force a meeting with Edgar Black and lay the whole picture out for him--Phillip Courtney, Ann Reilly, Harris Malone, and Susan's love, Patty. This had to stop, and he had to stop it now.

At about six, he decided to call Dianne. She must have forgotten to call or gotten in so late that she decided not to call him. After three rings, Susan answered, and this time she was awake. He knew that there was something unsaid by the awkward tone in her voice when she recognized David and said, "Daddy, she's not home."

"What are you saying? Why didn't you call me when it got so late? What do I not know? Stop the crap and tell me, Susan, where is my wife?"

"Listen, Dad, in the last two weeks, how many times have you spoken to your wife, tell me that? Well, I'll lay it on you. She told me she'd not be home last night and it's not been the first time. Get with it, can't you? You're going to lose her if you don't do something, and soon."

David sat in stunned silence hearing words that he never expected to hear and yet knowing that everything his daughter told him was true. He knew he had to confront Edgar Black with all the events that had taken place, but he also knew that getting involved in these crimes had taken him back to days when he could focus on the problem without any interference, without thinking of anything but what was on his table at that moment.

Now, his dealings with Black Technologies and their suspected involvement in three murders as well as the Koslov connection, for which he totally was in the dark about, seemed to be shuttled to another part of his brain. Instead he thought of Dianne, the beautiful woman who entered late in his life and captured his heart as no one could before, and how she was separating herself from him. David knew her strength of character and realized that he must have sent a dagger through her heart by taking on an assignment that she totally disapproved of from the start. Then he endangered their family and caused so much hurt to Susan. And despite Dianne's insistence that he walk away, he pressed on. Now he knew that their relationship was in danger. He must see her, hold her, and give her some sign of assurance that he would end this voyage into the unknown quickly. His plans to confront Edgar must be postponed. He needed to find where Dianne's heart lay.

These were David's thoughts as the jetliner taxied down the runway heading to LaGuardia. How he would approach her and what he would plead was unknown, and for a few short moments, he put his throbbing head back, closed his eyes, and tried to empty all fears and uncertainties as he waited for the vodka to beckon to him.

Chapter 34

CECELIA WAS AWAKENED at six-thirty on Saturday morning. It was Jim Jameson calling, and his tone of voice frightened her as she handed the phone to Manny. "If you're calling to set a tee time, buddy, you obviously lost your marbles. I have a ton of errands to run and I promised my sweet wife, who's lying next to me and is listening to every word, that I would spend some time at home, for a change."

Jim said, "Manny, what I have to tell you is vitally important and absolutely unbelievable. I had to call you as soon as it happened. I'm at the office now trying to put together some estimates for a really large contract that we are going to bid on this Monday, and I needed some information from a few documents that Gabriel was reviewing. I was poking around in his office in the files that he keeps in a cabinet behind his desk, and what I found scares the shit out of me."

Jim continued, "I was pulling on a file cabinet drawer where I know Gabriel keeps the current data. It wouldn't open, so I pulled real hard and accidently pulled open a small drawer at the very top inside of the cabinet. I was just curious, Manny. I mean that, nothing more. I came across strange-looking files that really had nothing to do with the contract I was looking for, but they caught my eye because in the file folders was a batch of documents sent from Iranian, North Korean, and Russian companies.

"Attached to those invoices were duplicates of those billed on the same day, with the same invoice numbers, but coming from Austria and Poland. Those duplicates were innocent-looking billings for hardware---materials that we use in insulating some of the equipment that needs temperature controls, but the originals were for very strange castings and devices that

I know are used for anchoring really large-sized equipment--equipment that we have never used. One group of documents looks like they cover electronic timing devices. We certainly never would use those.

"Manny, the strangest part is that they were billed to GEN21, but shipped to a location outside of the city. We don't have a facility there. I've been here long enough to know that. Manny, they're building something there, but why dupe the invoices to cover the shipments? And why hide them? Manny, I'm scared to death that something is happening that is real bad.

"And there's something else. Gabe recently hired a fairly large group of interns as trainees over the past six months, and I know they're on the payroll, but after only a few weeks of working in the factory, we never see them anymore. I asked him about them and he told me they were farmed out to some of our suppliers to give them a full grasp of the business...but, Manny, we have still been paying them and no one around here knows where they went. You're a lawyer, what the hell do I do?"

Manny thought for a few minutes, his brain racing with the information he just heard, and then he said. "Jim, close everything up, just as you found it and do it fast. Then get your ass out of there and go home or just go sit somewhere for a while. Then meet me at my office at nine. We'll figure it out from there. If you see someone before you leave, put on a normal face, tell a joke or something, and calmly get out. Do you understand me?"

Jim said, "OK, I got it, thanks so much. There is one last thing. Koslov is due in later and he might want to go over the contract status."

"Are you listening, meathead, just get out now, we'll figure out what to do later."

Jameson carefully put together the files as he remembered them and closed the cabinet drawer. Within fifteen minutes, he rushed to his car, nerves shattered, and sped out of the parking lot. If he had remembered that the entire facility was tightly secured and surveillance cameras recorded all of his movements, he might have tried to better conceal his emotions.

Later, Manny sat in his office doing busy work, anxiously awaiting Jameson. He glanced at the large Ingraham clock staring at him as it reached nine and then ten. He tried Jim's cell several times, but got no answer. He hesitated calling David until he had the opportunity to review the entire situation with Jim, but at eleven, he decided to call David, who was unreachable.

At eleven-thirty, Manny frantically answered his cell phone. It was Debbie Jameson, and he knew as soon as he answered that he would not like the message. "Manny, Manny, I just got a call from the Highway Patrol. Manny, Jim was in an automobile accident. He was taken to the Pacific Medical Center. They said it was critical."

Manny replied, "Don't say another word, Deb; I'll pick you up as fast as I can get to you." Manny's fear hung like a noose around his neck. He just knew what had happened. Either Jim was so distraught when he left his office and made a foolish driving decision or, worse, they found out what Jim had seen and they had to get rid of him as quickly as possible.

On his way to Debbie Jameson's, he finally reached David and tried to fill him in with as much precision as a lawyer like Manny could muster. David was packing to catch an evening flight to New York and was dealing with his own problems. He would get back to Manny as soon as he could.

Chapter 35

NICOLE LAWRENCE WAS working late. It was becoming more and more complex executing the fraud that she had masterminded. It took all her energy to keep a series of transactions in two sets of accounting records so that the financial condition of the company appeared sound and the income statement continued to show steadily growing earnings.

In addition to the financial work that she controlled, she needed to deal with Edgar Black and his son Leon. Edgar had remarkable sexual energy for his age and his appetite for long trysts was becoming time-consuming. Leon was another matter--a chip off the old block. He was in love with her and was now a partner in her plan, but his sexual desires were overpowering. She dreamed of the day when her plan would be realized and she would be able to live anywhere else in the world in grandiose style.

She worked in Edgar's office tonight so she could update his computer with all her transactions. These were hidden from his view in deeply coded files so that at the appropriate time, they could be accessible for the authorities to scrutinize.

When the phone rang, she assumed it was one of the Blacks, and she hoped it was not a call for her body to do its work. The phone screen indicated it was from California, so she answered. "Who is this?"

"This is Gabriel Koslov. I hope I'm not disturbing you, Nicole. I wanted to speak with Edgar, but if he is not there, it's important enough for you can relay a message to him. A few days ago, I received a visit from two men, David Korman and Daniel Merkel. They don't seem to represent anyone, but they wanted to put together some information about Black Technologies, so I thought Edgar would want to know." Dark shadows suddenly appeared on Nicole's face and she reached for the phone-monitoring unit as he continued.

"They were most concerned with your laser project and Phillip Courtney's death. They are convinced it was murder and somehow, for some reason, Black Technologies is involved. They seemed to be intent on following the trail of some other murders that they believe could be connected and also related to something with your company."

"That's just a pile of shit," answered Nicole flatly. "Phillip was terribly depressed when he left to join your outfit, and I know the police were perfectly satisfied that it was suicide. So what, if I may ask, did you tell them about us?"

"Come on, sweetie, I've known Edgar for years, and he would never be involved in anything like that. You guys run a straight ship, as far as I'm concerned. I gave your company a clean bill of health and I told him that. I just think you folks ought to know that they were out here." Nicole calmly thanked him for the information and promised she would relay it to Edgar as soon as she saw him.

"OK, my best to Edgar and Leon," lied Koslov, and he smiled as he hung up the phone. If he knew anything about Black Technologies and the Blacks, they would quickly do something about both Korman and Merkel. This would hopefully take them off looking into his plan, which was moving along at a predictable pace. How he dreamed of the day when his plans would come to fruition and he could go back to his native land a rich man.

As soon as Nicole hung up, she got Leon on the phone and played the Koslov call to him. After it finished, she said, "We need to get a better message to Korman about the impact of his snooping around. I think I will send the crew to New York to pay his wife a visit. They were sloppy last time when they missed the Asian kid, but this time, he will get the message," Nicole said in a vicious tone.

Her call to her contact was brief and concise. "Don't kill her. Just do enough to scare her. Find out where she works, what she does for fun, anything. She needs to get Korman out of our hair, and this time, make it convincing."

The next night Dianne was dressed in a dark wool suit with a silk blouse open at the throat. She had a strong face. Her deep hazel eyes were set wide apart, intelligent, and curved slightly at their outer corners. Her luxurious hair now fell to her shoulders. For a fifty-year-old woman, there was a magical beauty about her, and she knew exactly who she was and why she was on this street.

Dianne Korman left her apartment and walked purposefully on the still-wet city streets. There was an excitement inside her despite the sense of guilt at what she was about to do. She flagged a taxi at the corner. She was dropped off several streets closer to her destination near the Village. She became aware of footsteps some distance behind her; she walked with a measured stride and her heels clicked noisily on the pavement. She had no idea that she was being followed by two men. The first walked a discrete distance behind her to not be suspicious, while the second kept a parallel stride with Dianne on the opposite side of the street.

She was on her way to Mark's apartment where she expected to spend the night. This had been her routine for the past few nights. The guilt of betraying David and her family was pushed into the deep recesses of her mind; all she wanted was to be held by someone who genuinely cared about her. She was in too deep, she knew, and at some point she and David would need to face it, but for now she walked on with purpose. Last night Mark confessed that he was in love with her. While she cared for this younger man, love was not an option for her, at least not yet.

The two men knew exactly where she was going; they had followed her before. The taller man across the street carried a large bag containing a Nikon professional camera, a bag of long-range lenses, and the photography collection they were building, which was growing rapidly. They knew who Mark was and where he lived, and were able to rent an apartment almost directly across from his. They paid six months in advance to get the view they needed.

By now, they had accumulated a remarkably clear collection of photos, and tonight was to be their last surveillance. This was an excellent job for two free-lance photographers. They were paid by a mysterious source, but it mattered not to them. Their job was to develop a complete set of photos detailing Dianne's indiscretions. They did not know who she was or what the photos were to be used for, but they knew what their job was and they were pros.

Dianne now had a key and let herself into Mark's pad. With their camera's lens magnification, the two men were able to see the numerals on the key that Dianne dropped onto the small entry table. She made her way into the living area and poured a double from a large bottle that was evidently vodka, and dropped in three cubes of ice She sat on a large, soft, leather divan and kicked off her black high-heeled shoes. She was alone and she drained the vodka quickly, wanting to blur the bouillabaisse of emotions.

After about fifteen minutes, Mark arrived and she arose from her seat and kissed him softly, her hands stroking his face. They spoke briefly, and when she rose to refill her glass, Mark stood behind her pressing himself against her body. Her eyes were closed as he kissed her neck and ears. The steady clicking sound of the cameras echoed endlessly as the two men madly photographed Dianne's eyes, now closed as Mark reached to the front of Dianne's blouse and caressed her breasts.

After a few minutes Dianne disappeared into what appeared to the two men to be a bathroom. Because it faced the opposite side of the apartment, it was the only room not visible to them. Mark went to the bedroom, which had closed blinds but had thin spaces between the slats that allowed ample entry by the camera lens. He removed all his clothes, carefully hanging them up in a small closet to one side of the room. His penis was already hard. He then opened the drawer to a small table bedside and removed a small red package. They were able to read the name in large letters on one side of a small square section that he tore open and laid on the table. He then lay down on the bed with his hands behind his neck; he seemed relaxed.

The only noise in the room occupied by the watchers was the steady, monotonous clicking of the high-speed camera shutter.

After about ten minutes, Dianne joined him in the bedroom, smiling and wearing a silky looking knee-length garment. She sat by him and they talked for several minutes while her hands slowly moved from the hair on his chest to his taut stomach, rubbing softly. The watchers commented on her body--for a fifty-year-old woman, her breasts, though not large by any means, seemed firm to Mark's touch. Her stomach was flat and her long legs appeared to be of a much younger woman.

In the next moment, the monotony of the night-after-night filming of him on top of her, and then her on top of him, finally paid off. She climbed onto the bed and directly facing the window, put his large, throbbing penis into her mouth, moving her mouth around it in a circular motion. The filming was furious and the close-up shots of Dianne's mouth on Mark's penis were fantastic. One hand held the long, beet-red organ while another began to move up and down on it, slowly at first, and then with increasingly quick movements. Her cheeks throbbed in and out as she bathed his organ with her saliva. The watchers filmed it all and found pleasure themselves, titillated by this *show.*

This continued for several minutes and suddenly Dianne removed her mouth as the throbbing organ suddenly erupted with a silky fluid that caught her on her eyelids, along her cheek, and at the bridge of her nose. They both smiled at this, and after leaving the room for a few moments, she returned and lay down next to Mark.

The watchers had all they needed. They carefully packed all the film, fit the lenses and cameras into the large bag they arrived with, and locked the door of the room they would no longer need. They left the building with full knowledge that the photos they produced at their lab that night were all that their employer would need and that he would be satisfied.

It was late that night when Nicole Lawrence answered the private cell phone on her desk at home and listened carefully to the reenactment of the events of the evening. A small smile, showing just a hint of her white teeth, emerged as she gave them the next instruction, one that was to unalterably change the lives of the Korman family and remind David that he must cease the investigation into Black Technologies affairs, or face whatever she had in store.

Privately, she didn't care which direction David took; her eyes blazed with the knowledge that she would destroy David's life forever.

Chapter 36

When David Korman's flight arrived at LaGuardia, it was almost midnight, and his car was waiting to take him to what he expected to be a confrontation with his wife. As the private limo exited onto the Long Island Expressway, he saw two missed calls on his mobile phone. He decided to speak to Danny Merkel first.

After two rings, Merkel sleepily answered in a shitty mood and began to relate his meetings with Israeli Intelligence and the subsequent involvement with the FBI and the CIA in the U.S. At this point, agents from the U.S., Israel, Europe, and the Mideast were pouring through data on individuals employed by GEN21, as well as materials and supplies shipped to the company from anywhere in the world. A very recent piece of information involved an employee of GEN21 who was killed in what was initially termed an automobile accident. There was no further information concerning that event.

David immediately announced his concern for the safety of Manny and Cecelia and their baby. Danny assured him that they were under the full protection of the Israeli security forces and would be moved, if necessary. Danny planned to meet David after his meeting with Edgar Black in Detroit, but David stressed that this was on hold until he dealt with personal matters at home.

"Dianne upset with the level of your involvement?" asked Danny.

"That is the understatement of the year, my friend. My relationship with my wife is in question and I don't have any idea how it's going to turn out, but I need to deal with it now," responded a noticeably worried Korman.

"OK, pal, my best wishes to you. I'll go to Detroit and snoop around Black Tech until you let me know what the home scene is like."

As quickly as David ended his conversation with Merkel, he dialed back the second missed call; it was from Manny, and a cold sweat formed on David's forehead as he listened to the first three unanswered rings. Finally he answered. "Dad, is that you? Where are you? Why didn't you get right back to me," fired Manuel Korman in staccato.

After David explained the past two days, Manny quickly relayed the news that David was sorry, but not surprised, to hear. "Danny Merkel's sources told me that an employee of GEN21 was killed in an automobile accident and I immediately thought of Jim." Manny then related his terrifying conversation with Jim the morning he was killed, and it became icily clear to David that Jim had found some damaging evidence of a terrorist plot and either the phone was tapped or surveillance picked up his movements.

Quickly David realized, but did not tell Manny, that Jim's call could not have been discovered or Manny would be dead by now as well. David instructed Manny to call Merkel as soon as their call was completed and give him a full rendering of the conversation with Jim Jameson before he was killed. He told Manny that he, Cecelia, and the baby were protected, but to try to stay close to home as much as possible.

As soon as he stepped out of the limo, David sensed the presence of immediate danger. A man in a dark topcoat stepped out of the shadows of the building where David had lived for nearly twenty years. David kept his hands at his side waiting for an aggressive move.

The stranger approached David, opened his coat, and took out a manila folder. He held the folder out in front of David's chest, shoved it against him, and let go of it. David instinctively grabbed it and before anything could be said, the stranger bolted across the street and stepped into a car that had been parked a short distance away from where the limo was parked.

When David entered the lobby of his apartment, he sat down on one of the heavy, padded chairs that were rarely used, opened his coat, and nervously opened the folder. The first sheet was a typewritten note telling David to immediately cease the investigation of Black Technologies. It warned him that if public dissemination of the contents of the envelope was insufficient cause to stop his meddling into affairs that didn't concern him, there were other ways, and harm would come to his family. There was no signature and no indication of anything unusual about the paper or the phrasing of the letter. No indication of a way to contact the writer.

With trembling hands and blood rushing to his head, he pulled away the letter and saw the unspeakable contents. About fifteen, 8-1/2 by 11 photographs appeared, and his shaking became almost palsied. One after one, David saw his wife fucking a younger man in various poses. The last photo depicted Dianne with the man's penis in her mouth and a soft smile on her engorged cheeks.

He sat silently for what seemed to him to be an hour, but was in fact no more than ten minutes. Head bowed down, the folder and its contents sitting on his lap, he sat mindless and thoughtless, engulfed by a sadness that he had never before experienced. He knew at that moment that his life had changed for the worse. It was a while after receiving this photographic message that his brain, tested by conflict over decades, began grinding an initial response and preparing for what was to be the worst face-to-face that he had ever experienced.

The short elevator trip to his apartment allowed David to compose himself and prepare. He turned the key in the door and switched on the lights. The living area and den were empty, and he dutifully hung his coat in the small closet behind him.

When he turned back to the living room, Dianne stood in front of him. She had on a silk robe over a short nightgown, and she stood just outside the hall leading to the bedrooms. Her face was frozen. The lines around her eyes were more pronounced than David remembered, and without makeup, she looked ashen.

David did not say a word. He opened the envelope and slid the photos onto the dining room table, allowing Dianne to see most of them at the same instant. He had removed the poisoned letter--he did not want her to see it now. She looked at them with a horrifying stare, but said nothing. At that moment, Susan, awakened by David's arrival, entered the room and, seeing the photos, put her hands to her mouth as if to silence a scream.

David spoke first; it was directed at Dianne. "What I do, I do for my country. What reason do you have this for?"

Before she could even dream of a response, he continued, "Three people have been killed and none of them were labeled deliberate. The love of Susan's life was brutally beaten, and just the other day, the last murdered man had a family and was close friends with Manny. The initial incidents that we looked into have broadened into what appears to be a worldwide hunt for terrorists who are actively planning some unknown mission here in our country. So I repeat, Dianne, my job is to find and track down these plotters before they create a major tragedy. My question to you is, "Was his cock good enough for you to walk away from me?"

The tears drifted slowly down Dianne's cheeks, but again, before she could reply, David said, "I'll sleep on the couch tonight and clear some of my stuff out tomorrow. Maybe you should consider moving in with this guy. From the look on your face in these photos, you obviously like him."

He then turned, looking angrily at Susan. "As for you, my sweet girl, it is time for you and Patty to get the hell out of here and get back to reality. I will expect you back in Boston by the end of the week. Call Oliver in the morning and tell him both of you need to stay at his place for an indefinite time. Get back to your job, Susan. You trained to be a doctor and now you are a wonderful doctor, so start healing again. Do you have any questions?" Before they could respond, he said, "Good, I didn't think so."

Dianne remained staring at the dining room table, her focus transfixed at the display of the photos. She knew at that moment that her relationship with Mark was over, and she believed that David would never forgive her. But it was hard to believe that David had someone take these photos. If not, then who, and for what purpose? She didn't see a note and right now she did not feel able to ask David if there was a note.

David was pulling together some personal items after which he cut the lights and tried to grab a little sleep, which did not come that night. He expected to return to Detroit and call Danny to meet him there after he had some definitive conversation with his wife. He needed to describe to Dianne his immediate plans and get some direction from her on what she intended to do.

After a sleepless few hours, David awoke to the rich aroma of strong, Sumatran coffee. He sat up slowly from the couch, his aching joints sending electric currents to his back and legs. He saw Dianne, sitting at the small kitchen table, and it looked as if she hadn't slept either. She turned to face him and he saw the swollen eyes, skin sagging under them, and pallid, ashy cheeks. She arose and poured his coffee and moved to the dining room table where the photos had been collected and replaced in the envelope.

David moved to a chair across from her and spoke first. "There was a note included in the envelope that warned me to stop investigating Black, or they threatened to disseminate the photos publicly and also further harm my family. At this point, I don't know what to do."

David then heard the first words spoken by Dianne since he arrived home. "You do what you always know is the right thing to do. These people cannot continue to hurt innocents, and I'm not speaking of myself. I'm a big girl and I know how to accept responsibility. I will resign from Manson's later today and take the girls up to Boston. You're right about them. They need to move on with their lives. As far as the young man in the photos, I will tell him of my decision and I'll end that as well."

She continued, "David, as far as you and I are concerned, based on what I found myself capable of doing, I don't deserve you. When we married five years ago, I hoped I was as strong as you. When I became involved with you during your last mission for Israel and we got through it together, I thought I had everything. You gave me your love, you gave me your family, but your involvement in these terrible crimes and the danger to all of us made me realize my weakness. Not hearing from you, not knowing what was happening…well, I just gave up. Mark was simply someone who made me feel good, and I accepted him. You go get these fucking monsters."

David sipped his coffee and let the strong caffeine bring him to reality. He quietly said, "I'm probably going to Detroit to meet Danny Merkel. We'll confront the Black people who may or may not be behind these photos. When I finish this, we should talk about the future." He arose and showered, dressed, packed some fresh clothes, and dialed Danny at the Detroit motel.

Chapter 37

DIANNE KORMAN AWOKE from a dismal sleep, a few hours of nightmarish drifting that left her with a host of feelings. First and strongest was the anxiety of what was to come after David's exposé of her affair with Mark, those horrid visualizations of their sexual exploits, uncovered and now on display. Then the lamenting of events she perceived was to shape her life from this day forward. And finally, the indelicate shame over what clearly seemed dirty to her, almost putrid to this up-to-now devoted woman of principle; shame that she could share with no one.

Dianne tried to understand the motivation for her actions. She dug deeply into that murky bank of memories that brought her to this place. She remembered her childhood and the special relationship with her father, which abruptly ended with his death due to a sudden and massive heart attack. From that time on, the reality of life took its toll. In her teens, despite academic success, she walked the danger line. Wild years filled with experimentation with drugs, promiscuity, and acting out was her behavioral norm. Her college education was cut short when she ran away from home with a man she met at a rock concert and whom barely knew. That ended quickly and was followed by a series of relationships with men who enjoyed her company briefly but fled after a time to greener pastures. After some years of developing a mistrust of all such relationships, while living in a dusty town in Arizona, she was involved a serious auto accident and was hospitalized for weeks.

Somewhere in the time it took to recuperate, Dianne Westerman woke up and decided it was time to return home to New York and, with help, learn more about the mess she perceived she had made of her life.

Supporting Dianne was her mother, who always believed that Dianne could start anew.

After extensive therapy and a return to college while she interned at Manson's Department Store, Dianne began to recognize her strengths. After years of the slavery endemic to a career in retailing, she rose to an executive position and now was the chief marketing executive for the most popular department store in Manhattan as well as the flagship store for the nationally known Manson chain. But there was still the sense of mistrusting relationships with men that was buried deeply in her; that is until, on a vacation with a friend in the Caribbean one January, she met David Korman.

At first, she wanted nothing to do with this man who seemed to have everything and yet seemed lonely, dispirited. As she spent time with him, she learned about the terrible ordeal that he lived with--the explosion in the Tel Aviv café that killed the love of his life and left shreds of bone and metal in him. As he learned about her, he openly dealt with her mistrust of any serious relationship, and after time he proved to be the one who could make her feel secure, who was willing to understand where she had come from.

And now she returned to the present, believing that he would never forgive her for her actions. Yes, part of her was deeply angry with David. But more than anything, Dianne lost touch with her husband as he was attempting to unravel this mystery. The closeness with David that Dianne had treasured dissipated before her eyes and she needed to scream at him, to smack him, to wake him from his distance. So she did, but in a way that put the entire relationship in peril. And now the price must be paid. Dianne was overcome with the sadness that comes with recognizing the consequences of her actions.

David, who slept on the living room couch that night, was already gone when she finally decided to face him that day; any hope of him soon returning was merely fiction. Strong coffee, two mugs-full, did little to brace her for the activities of the day. Showering, she hoped to somehow wash away the stains that covered her. But as the steaming water slapped at her skin, all she was able to do was sob pitifully. Her head leaned against the shower wall, both hands held flat against the tiled wall in front of her as the water raced down on her body. She dressed slowly, mechanically, donning a black skirt, white blouse, and matching black wool jacket with black, mid-heel, closed pumps, a funereal outfit befitting the tasks ahead.

Eating anything solid was not possible. She looked in the hall mirror and found it hard to recognize herself. The heightened dark circles under her eyes showed, even with the foundation that she liberally applied. Her lips looked twisted, washed out, even though she had used a small line of color.

As she waited for the private car to take her to her office, her mind began to assemble the information she would give Arthur Mester, Manson's CEO. She then thought of what to say to Mark, and that was painful. His career was probably going to be over if the photos were sent to the company, a thought that she totally believed would happen.

When Dianne touched the top-floor button on the executive suite elevator, her heart began to pound in her chest. She made no attempt to settle into her office but went directly to Mester's corner office. He was reviewing some data sprawled over the large, heavy, plate glass that sat on a green marble slab. It was an imposing, even imperial site, but one that Dianne had grown used to putting her legs against as they spent years working together to make the store the highest sales and profit producer in the Manson chain. This time she stood, almost reverential, waiting for Arthur to look up.

"There is something I need to say to you, Arthur." He looked up curiously, smiled and nodded, and waited for her response. "I have done something terrible, so shameful that I can hardly find the words. I took advantage of my position and the trust you gave me over the years that we worked together and ground it into baseless perfidy."

Arthur sat motionless, not believing his close friend.

She continued, "Over the recent weeks I have engaged in a relationship with an employee, a junior executive of our company. Whatever the reasons, it became personal and sordid. I failed my husband, the firm, and you. To make it worse, for reasons that are irrelevant, my activities with this man discovered by people who want to hurt my family, and they photographed our trysts in complete detail. I believe you or someone at the home office will be receiving these photographs. For that reason, I am resigning as of now and completely terminating my employment. I will not discuss the man with whom I was involved in the unlikely situation that the photos are not sent, and I plead that you not ask for his name. He followed my lead and I take complete responsibility for the affair. It is over now and I am going to try to save my marriage, although if I were David, I would throw me to the wolves. That's it, Arthur, short and not too sweet, but I have nothing else to say except that I am sorry, so very sorry."

Arthur just stared, saying nothing for several moments before he stood up and brusquely answered, "So stupid, so very stupid, to throw away twenty years of your life on a young stud with a big dick. I suspected something was happening between you and Mark, but I hoped it would disappear quickly so I just tried to say nothing. I guess I gave you too much credit."

At this point he began raising his voice and his bloodless hands were fisted hard on the glass desktop. "Leave at once and rest assured, Mark will be out of here as soon as you're gone. For Christ sake, Dianne, I only hope for David's sake that you can somehow repair whatever went wrong in your relationship with David. I am totally ashamed of you. Just get the fuck out of my sight as fast as possible."

At the mention of Mark's name and the knowledge that he would be fired, Dianne could not stop the tears. She turned quickly and kept a tissue over her eyes as she left the firm that had allowed her to achieve personal success over the years. It was not until she arrived at the home that she and David shared that her crying became uncontrollable. Susan was not at home, so Dianne was able to submerge herself into the soft calm of the silky bottle of Grey Goose, along with several little yellow helpers. Soon the pain began to subside and Dianne Korman drifted into the land of carefree haze.

Chapter 38

In the perpetually war-torn country of Chechnya, the battle with Russian expansionism has continued for centuries. Wedged between Russia to the north and Georgia to the south and bordering the Caspian Sea, this mountainous region sits aside the Caucasus Mountains, rich with oil, gas, and other valuable minerals, making the conflict with Russia mainly about economics. Major oil pipelines traversing the country have made the Russian attempt to rule an ongoing crisis. After brutal massacres and vilification under Stalin's rule, the legacy of conflict has been radical and anti-Russian for years. Even after the collapse of the Soviet Union in the early 1990s, the newly formed Federation refused independence to Chechnya. In the Russian invasion in the mid-1990s, upwards of 100,000 Chechens were killed. Still they struggled for independence, defeating their enemy.

With the start of the 21st century, Vladimir Putin's Russia once again began a full-scale war with Chechnya. The capital city of Grozny was pounded and much of the city was destroyed. Over one million people of Chechnya were said to have been uprooted and fled the country. It was during this time that the Chechen government began having suspicions about the West. They suspected, with good reason, that the United States wanted a destabilized region in order to continue the conflict that Russia had with this little empire. Russia's continuing military actions received tacit support from the U.S. and Britain.

So it came as no surprise, with the majority of the Chechen population being Muslim and with the suspicion that the U.S. supported the country's destabilization, that the government of Chechnya secretly longed to play an important part on the world terrorism stage. Considered one of the most repressive societies in the world, Chechnya, now called the Chechen Republic, became a fertile territory for Al-Qaeda training and influence.

Amidst this conflict, secret societies began to plan for massive repayment to the West in the form of terrorist attacks against the major powers in the world. As the plan began to take shape, the Chechen government searched for children within their country who, at an early age, evidenced superior intelligence. When officials approached the families of these children, offering to have them educated at a private school and trained for service to their country, few parents could resist. The families would be compensated for the removal of these children from the family unit. The children would be sent to a training center where, as adults, they would become members of the secret organization. Few families could refuse such a generous proposition, though there was little choice.

So it was that Viktor Basayev, born in a ramshackle dwelling in war-torn Grozny, was chosen. At an early age when his superior intelligence was identified, he was chosen to play a part in the newly created battle with the West. His name was changed to a more ethnically Russian one and one that would more easily be accepted in western countries, Gabriel Kozlov. His early education was structured to include American culture, language, and customs. History was slanted to deem Russia as equal with the West. So to him, Russia and America were characterized as predators and the unending enemy of Chechens and Muslims.

In his teens, he received training in military science and the art of guerrilla warfare. Weapons training included two years in an academy that trained him in the use, disposal, transport, and safety of explosive devices. Later he learned about the newly developing application of the use and implementation of small-size, nuclear devices.

During this time, Gabriel, as he was called, had little contact with the outside world. His peers were young men and women receiving the same education and training. He had classes in American humor, cultural preferences in entertainment, and sexual mores appropriate in the West, with the faculty controlling his sexual knowledge and exploration. Physical fitness and interest in all things American made Gabriel a model for the upcoming plan.

At 17, he was sent to America to be schooled in technology and engineering at a university in California. Gabriel found the education fulfilling and even had friends with similar interests. His social skills improved although his relationships with women were frequent and short-lived.

He was given a network of contacts to which he reported regularly. From early in his arrival to America, his mentors were excited at the prospect for success for the project to which Gabriel was to be assigned. He had no foreign accent. The cover story of his background was that he came from an affluent Russian family with interests in oil and gas development. Within years, it was not difficult for this bright young man to obtain American citizenship. At his university he joined a fraternity and was well liked by the faculty who knew him and by the students whom he met.

After graduating, he and a few classmates with similar technological skills started their own business near a Berkeley community outside of San Francisco, with financing from both his family and local sources. With the tech business growing at a fast pace in the U.S. and with some lucky developments, it took just a few years for Gabriel to build his firm into a fast-growing, well-known local company. Gabriel and his supporters developed aspirations of becoming a public corporation.

Soon Gabriel began to use his newly developed political contacts to gain small, computer software business contracts from the state government. With this newfound wealth and success, he became active in local Republican politics and became a generous contributor to state and federal election committees. Once his star began to shine in California politics, his Chechen handlers arranged for Gabriel to meet a woman who came from a family deeply entrenched in California real estate and active in politics.

Gabriel was now known in important California political circles and his relationship with Merrill Halston began to flower. She saw Gabriel as a future Republican gubernatorial candidate, and he fit right in with the San Francisco social set. They were a perfect match. His physical assets and sexual prowess were well developed and honed in Chechnya, and they excited Merrill in a way that she had not experienced before. Merrill's family was delighted with their future son-in-law. His prospects for greater success made a vision of a political career for Gabriel seem realistic to them.

It was not long after they married that their first child was born, and within five years, Gabriel and Merrill and their proud grandparents were blessed with two boys. Though Merrill's parents urged Gabriel to bring his parents to the U.S., he avoided this issue by describing a difficult relationship with them. He also claimed that he had attended boarding schools where he rarely saw them.

By now, Gabriel was part of mainstream America with a successful business, a lavish suburban San Francisco home, an influential family well known within California, and two American children--the perfect American dream. He always kept in close contact with the leaders in his homeland through a series of business intermediaries. Gabriel knew the time grew near for the implementation of the special assignment that would send shock waves around the world.

Chapter 39

DAVID'S FLIGHT TO Detroit was agonizing. He tried to sort out the potpourri of crises that were on his plate. His relationship with Dianne was *blowin' in the wind* and he was not sure if it could be resurrected. He needed to expose whatever scheme Edgar Black was hatching, and he needed to understand what Gabriel Kozlov was plotting that forced the murder of Jim Jameson. Adding to his problems was the nagging question of the message sent to him with the photographs of Dianne and her lover. Lurking in the recesses of David's mind was the notion that Edgar Black was somehow tied in to Kozlov. Any attempt at sleep was useless--dark visions rolled through his brain constantly.

He hoped that Danny Merkel would be able to shed some light on Kozlov. They met at the airport and he clearly saw the desperate look on Danny's face. Without much conversation along the way, they stopped at an all-night diner near Detroit Metro.

Danny commented, "Funny how meatloaf always seems to be the *daily special* on every diner's menu." David settled for a club sandwich and a cup of decaf as Danny slogged through the meatloaf and mashed potatoes.

As soon as they were seated, however, Danny delivered the bad news that Israeli intelligence had not been able to get any closer to the source of Gabriel Kozlov's activities or his background. That created an ominous danger; the Mossad was always able to scrape out information about a background and identity. Their inability now was an affirmation that Koslov had successfully hidden his agenda and that he was undoubtedly part of a Russian plot. Their experience from the KGB days taught them that Russia and its satellites were sophisticated at hiding and exposing identities.

This left David and Danny with absolutely no clues, so Danny suggested that they sleep on it and reconvene the next morning. He was the eternal optimist who believed new ideas emerged in the morning.

After checking into the hotel, David saw the blinking lights on the phone, indicating a voicemail was waiting. Based on the spate of recent events, David was nervous about listening to it. After staring at the red blinking sentinel for about a minute, he realized that he had to listen.

It was from Dianne, and in the softest voice he had ever heard from his wife, David heard Dianne plead for some way for them to come together.

"I know I have no right to ask, and I completely understand if you refuse, but I, I love you so much…It was my utter inability to deal with the loneliness and not hearing from you and…I guess I can't expect it… but if we can start over, just give me a chance to prove that my love for you is real and will last forever. Anyway, my darling David, I will be with Susan in Boston for a while. Please call me. Goodbye."

For David, that was all it took to deprive him of his sleep that night. He finally drifted down to the hotel bar and began to have doubles of his favorite twenty-five-year-old scotch until the throbbing in his brain began to drift silently away. As he sat on a worn leatherette stool in the near empty bar, his mind crisscrossed between contemplating how he would respond to Dianne and where his tracks would take him next.

For him, she represented everything that had been missing in his life before they met. He recalled the day she came into his life—he was sitting at the hotel pool in the Caribbean and saw this tall woman with skin bronzed from the tropical sun, her hair tied back, firm face and jaw, with a small crescent scar etched into the line of her chin. Drop dead gorgeous. David adored her from the beginning and they quickly formed a bond that seemed unbreakable, but now, what? Photos of Dianne and this young stud in bed together flashed into his brain, etched there forever. He forced these images from his brain and tried desperately to focus on any one of the situations that he now faced.

The scenario then switched to the murders and Black Tech's involvement. Somewhere in the deep recesses of his mind, he believed that Edgar Black did not have the balls to mastermind a grand scheme of this magnitude without serious help from someone else at Black Tech, someone close to him.

David knew of at least two possible partners, his son, Leon, and the blonde slut, Nicole Lawrence. There was also the chance that Koslov was somehow involved, although he couldn't visualize Edgar partnering with the Russian. All these theories were blending with his hope that his relationship with Dianne might still be salvaged. That idea stayed with him until the alcohol created an ugly, gray distance from all reality.

Eventually his thoughts all blurred together and he staggered up to his room and collapsed into a near sleep full of wild, dark dreams where packs of wild dogs were attacking what appeared to be a group of innocent men and women. The dogs tore into their human flesh and their blood painted the earth as the innocents screamed in agony. David watched the eyes of the dogs as they continued relentlessly. In the dream he was a bystander watching this disaster from behind a high, chain link fence with barbed wire laced across the top. He struggled to climb to the top of the fence, but as he reached for the barbed wire, he slipped hopelessly back to the ground. As he struggled to get over the fence to help the victims, he cried out for God to help him, all to no avail.

He awoke to a phone call from Danny. "You up yet? Time for breakfast. Meet me in the lobby in a half hour."

David was bathed in sweat. The dream would not leave him as he showered his way through the hangover. As the hot water pounded onto his body, the fog began to clear. He recalled the horror of the thug who threw the envelope of photos of Dianne's affair at him. He visualized getting out of the cab and turning to face the opposite side of the street.

Suddenly, it all came together. It had always been there but he couldn't see it. The local branch of the Apple Bank sat directly across the street from the front doors of his apartment building, its cameras photographing onto permanent imagery the events taking place. He then knew the plan that he must execute to lead him to the perpetrator of these hideous crimes.

Chapter 40

WHILE DAVID AND Danny were putting together their plan, Gabriel Kozlov was relaxing at home on a warm northern California afternoon in July when he received a call from his contact that would change his life forever. A meeting was set later that evening by one of his contacts, Atalo Karamanlis, a self-described Greek businessman in the U.S., on the pretext to discuss some new important piece of business for Gabriel's company. They met under full security and he was ushered into Koslov's office. Glasses with large shots of vodka sat on a table off to one side of his desk.

After a deep slug, Karamanlis spoke. "Gabriel, let me tell you of the project that you will undertake in the name of your homeland. First some background. More than half of the goods shipped into the United States come through the port at Long Beach, California. It is the second busiest seaport in the country and the gateway between America and the Asian trade. Over one hundred billion dollars in trade enters the country through this huge port. Being within twenty-five miles of Los Angeles, over three hundred thousand employees, living in the Greater Los Angeles area, are involved in port activities. Aside from the immense Asian trade, the port handles over four billion cubic feet of liquefied natural gas from Canada each day.

"Gabriel, you have been chosen to put together and implement the plan that leaders in our homeland have been working on for several years: to build and detonate a nuclear device in America. This is the structure of the plan. The parts will be obtained from Pakistan, Iran, and other sources, shipped to friendly Latin American countries, and then transshipped to your facility. Simply stated, your team will assemble the device and detonate it in the port of Long Beach."

Gabriel sat with rapt attention as Karamanlis continued, "We will show the West that we will not tolerate its collaboration with Russia to deprive Chechnya of its freedom. With the port's huge output, such a catastrophe would cripple the U.S. distribution cycle, make the area uninhabitable, and spread fear around the world. Its proximity to Los Angeles makes this a perfect target.

"Of course, in order to orchestrate such a plan, we need a well-respected American to be the linchpin of this project. That is why you were chosen. Someone who will make contact with you shortly, applying for a management position, will assist you. She is highly intelligent and technically qualified in the development of tactical nuclear weapons. The parts of this weapon will begin to be transported at once in small containers, principally from Mexico and other countries friendly to America. You will immediately establish a large storage facility near the port, perhaps an empty warehouse."

He paused briefly, and both men reached for their shot glasses. Karamanlis continued, "We have some suggestions in this regard. As materials are brought in, you will invite a group of young American engineers whom we have selected especially for their skills in nuclear explosive development and assembly to intern in all departments in your company. To avoid suspicion, they will be rotated through all your firm's operations as trainees and then sent to work at the storage facility to begin the process of assembling the device.

"It is our plan to containerize the final nuclear device disguised as a small export shipment, perhaps no bigger than a suitcase. While being loaded on a specific vessel in the port, it will be detonated.

"We have estimated the casualties initially would be 250,000-500,000, with the number increasing as the clouds loaded with nuclear fallout spread out to neighboring Los Angeles and other parts of southern California. The damage to the port itself would destroy major trade facilities including vital natural gas imports. The collateral damage as a result of the detonation would be devastating to the most populated region in this country."

Karamanlis' voice lowered reassuringly as he continued, "Just prior to detonation, when everything is in place, your assistant will take full command of the project. You will take your family on a well-deserved, lengthy vacation, perhaps a cruise. The final destination and your new home will be determined at a later date. I know that your wife is dedicated to you, but if she finds that she is unable to accept her new lifestyle, we will convince her in an appropriate manner. Gabriel, you have been trained all your life for this opportunity; we know that you will execute the plan flawlessly."

As Gabriel processed this information, he strangely felt a sense of mixed emotions swirling in his head. The riches of the capitalist lifestyle had great appeal to him and he loved his family, particularly the children, but he knew that this was what he had been groomed for, and he accepted the challenge. He knew it would be a daunting one; assembling the device immediately raised so many questions that he decided to put it away for the evening.

The two men sipped vodka for a short time, like two friends sharing small talk. Then Karamanlis rose and bid Gabriel luck. They embraced and he left, leaving Gabriel to think about how his life had come to this.

Chapter 41

ABOUT THIS SAME time back in Detroit, Nicole Lawrence was moving forward with a plan that would create unlimited wealth for her, a plan that had been all consuming since she first met Edgar Black. Because the laser missile program was entirely financed by both the military and clandestine governmental agencies, it was believed that the success of this weapon could dramatically tip the balance between the United States and its enemies across the globe. Scheduled payments had been made to the company for the past two years, and although progress was slow and tangible results were not yet realized, the huge cash advances never diminished. This formed the primary focus of Nicole's plan.

After months of research into the U.S. economic disaster, she realized that the country had built a fragile house of cards that was just waiting to be toppled. In her role as chief financial officer, she had complete control of the management of corporate funds. Events were taking place in financial markets globally that were to provide Nikki with enormous opportunities, and she was eager to take advantage.

In addition, the housing market in the U.S. was overheating dramatically. It was evident to her that asset-price bubbles coupled with embarrassingly bad underwriting standards and crazy compensation schemes on Wall Street were soon to be exposed. The subprime mortgage machine was running at full tilt. Wall Street had entered the housing market in ways never seen before. It was not as if loans were not being made to people who couldn't repay them; on the contrary, financial institutions were making loans with little or no down payment, with terms that called for either low-interest rates or no interest payments at all for a predetermined period of time. Many of them carried interest rates that *floated* based on economic conditions but most came with *teaser rates*; for example, a mortgage might have a two-to-three-year fixed rate of five or six percent, after which the fixed rate would jump to eleven or twelve percent, which caused a massive wave of defaults.

But beyond the subprime problem, Nicole became aware that major financial institutions saw opportunities to vastly increase their leverage and profits as well, and she scrutinized this activity in depth. Mortgage loans, many of which should never have been approved, were made and then packaged into a new kind of investment, the sub-prime, mortgage-backed bond; in Wall Street lingo, *collateral debt obligations.* During this time, nearly every major Wall Street investment bank was being run by its bond department, and it was clear to Nicole Lawrence, brilliant student of both sex and finance, that this was a bubble that had to burst.

At this time, she and a relatively small number of investors were beginning to perceive that what was happening to the financial system was happening to society. She spent a great deal of time reading about something called a *credit default swap*. This scheme consisted of simple insurance policies, written against the failure of these bonds, betting against the risk. In effect, these policies were intended to be a protection for investment banks and investors who held large amounts of a corporation's bonds and wanted to protect their investment. So they simply bought an insurance policy to protect them in the event that the corporation could not pay back the bond at maturity or defaulted on the bond during its term. These *swaps* had the effect of closing down the risk of owning large amounts of bonds, and they could be purchased for a fraction of the value of the bonds.

This then became a popular vehicle on Wall Street; if you held a corporate bond, you bought an insurance policy insuring that if the bond defaulted, you would recover the principal. Because the greed on the *Street* had always run deep, these swaps began trading as if they were a security on their own. You could buy or sell the swap for a premium and hold it or sell in a totally unregulated market that was growing exponentially. In essence, the credit default swap was just a financial option. If you bought a swap, you paid a small premium, and if enough subprime borrowers defaulted on their mortgages, you could get enormous gains.

So this is what intrigued Nikki. She was convinced that the housing bubble would soon burst, and when it did, these so-called mortgage-backed bonds, made up of packages of thousands of individual mortgages, many of them essentially worthless, would be worth very little or in many cases, nothing.

She developed her plan in two parts. First, she would divert a portion of the capital of the company in a way that would not raise eyebrows. She had access and as long as she could move the funds quickly and easily, this would succeed. Then she would bet against the market; that is, with the capital generated, she would buy credit default swaps. Since the premiums on these insurance policies were small, the leverage that she could create was enormous.

In her position as the chief financial officer of Black Technologies, she had complete authority over the borrowing and investing of corporate funds. At this time, the corporation had received from the U.S. government almost a billion dollars that were advances funding the contract. As excess cash was wired from government accounts into the company, she carefully and conservatively managed them, primarily using professional outside firms.

But secretly, Nikki began moving some of the excess cash to offshore accounts. The funds in these accounts could be withdrawn only with the signature of the chief financial officer: Nicole Lawrence, Senior Vice President of Finance.

Within a short timeframe, Nikki had the capital that she needed. In the initial phase of her deception, in order to cautiously approach this market, she bought premiums on fifty million dollars of credit default swaps from Goldman Sachs, ten million each on five different mortgage-backed bonds from funds in these accounts. She was buying these *swaps* with premiums in the two to four percent range per year. After reading the prospectus of each, she picked bonds that raised the greatest questions about the viability of the mortgages themselves. They were the junk within the market. Nicole was picking exactly the right homeowners to bet against. She would bet that the mortgages within these bonds would ultimately default, and it was always a good bet.

She carefully began on a test basis to move denominations of five-to-ten million into these swaps. Once she was comfortable in this approach, she moved transfers of up to twenty million dollar increments. She was *investing* from a series of accounts that were opened in several Caribbean banks.

As the plan progressed, the transfers increased. Only she could withdraw the funds in these accounts. By late in the year she had accumulated over five hundred million in credit default swaps made with institutions such as Bank of America, Deutsche Bank, Credit Suisse, and Lehman Brothers. As these transfers increased, Nikki established solid relationships with financial institutions and hedge fund managers that had vast holdings of mortgage-backed bonds and were eager to write the contrary bet.

Pundits across the horizon were assuring investors in these bonds that home prices were not prone to *bubbles* and a housing crash was absolutely beyond reasonable belief. Nicole even received calls from companies like Goldman Sachs, who were willing to tell her off the record which of the *junkier* layers of bonds were in fact the worst risks so she could bet on their demise. She was dealing directly with the directors of private wealth managers who were adept at *chasing yields.* She bought these from the wizards at Bank of America, Lehman Brothers, Morgan Stanley, and a handful of *super-Street* mavens. By this time, the subprime mortgage market worldwide was generating half a trillion dollars' worth of new loans a year.

On a scheduled timetable, she drew out funds from corporate accounts into accounts in Leon Black's and her name. When the company experienced temporary cash shortfalls, she always had excess funds invested in market instruments and was able to move funds back into the company, avoiding any suspicion.

Nicole knew she could escape detection from the outside accounting firm for one annual audit. She expected that during the next annual audit by Hyde and Malone, the certified public accounting firm, questions would be raised about these accounts, but Nicole, who had developed a deep personal relationship with the partner in charge of the Black Tech account, would be able to produce false confirmations of the fund balances that would satisfy him. She knew that he would identify the investments as corporate assets. After all, why would someone with the credentials of Nicole Lawrence, Senior Vice President of Finance involve herself in any nefarious activity? Trust was her middle name, thought the financial world.

So, when her bets were looking golden, Nicole sent a list of the swaps that she owned to the *Big Guns* on the Street. The mortgages underlying the bonds were going bad at a faster rate than expected, but there was no hard evidence as to what these things were worth. By the time she decided that it was time to unwind these swaps, her troubles began, and Nicole feared that her bets on almost two billion dollars of these bonds would not be settled quickly.

She began to negotiate even before the trigger occurred, which was the credit event when the bond would go belly-up. She could not wait until the final determination of the worthless securities would occur, so she began to unwind the swaps at a negotiated, so-called recovery value.

Time was running short in the latter part of the year and the handwriting for disaster was written in both the housing industry and mortgage-backed bonds; catastrophe was just around the corner. Working eighteen-hour days was becoming the norm and by the time the 2007 annual audit was under way in early 2008, she had successfully unwound all the credit default swaps and was sitting on a profit of nearly seven-hundred million.

The world went into total shock as Lehman Brothers was about to declare bankruptcy and the fabled firm of Merrill Lynch was up for grabs, soon to be a part of Bank of America.

The reality was that Nicole Lawrence, financial superstar, originally known as Michelina Aillon of Odessa, Texas, was worth almost one billion dollars, all safely tucked away in Swiss accounts, and was ready to pack her bags and fly the coop, leaving Leon Black, in what the "Godfather" character Sonny Corleone referred to as holding his *dick in his hands.*

The last phase of Nicole's plan would occur when the entire fraud was uncovered and it all would finally hit the fan. She would be long gone and there would just be Leon to explain the whole ball of wax. Nicole was certain that he would fumble his way into a long term in prison.

When Leon Black next found his way into Nicole's boudoir for a late afternoon blow job, he began to talk nervously about their plans together. "Nicole, you need to give me enough lead time so I can settle some affairs before we jump ship. I think we'll never make it past the year-end audit, but I've got to know. My passport is current and I've accumulated enough short-term cash to get us out of the country and make the moves we planned, so put it together soon."

She looked at him and with one hand massaging the back of his neck, she replied. "Hey, baby, stop with this nervous attitude. It's all coming together, but I have to make sure the transfers are all in shape. Just don't worry, sweetheart, it will be a breeze and we have our whole lives together. Just let me handle things."

He closed his eyes as the effect of her sensual massaging relaxed him and all cares vanished as Leon slipped into the soft world of sexual ecstasy.

Chapter 42

DAVID AND DANNY decided on a change in venue for breakfast. Just a few minutes away was a smallish restaurant called Bagel Deli that looked clean and was busy serving plates of steaming *cholesterol.*

When a heavy-set waitress in white with a streak of blond and black roots dished out steaming coffee in large mugs, David began to talk, "Dan, I think I know where to start. The Apple Bank is right across from my building. The bank's cameras must have captured the guy who handed me Dianne's photos that night. I've been banking there since they opened years ago. I'm going to see if the manager will get me a photo of him. I know they date-stamp the film and they probably keep it for some period of time, so maybe I'll get lucky. If I get his photo, I can impose on some good guys at the 27th precinct. Maybe we can find him and, more importantly, find out who he was working with that night. Long shot? Sure, but it's a start.

They both sipped their coffee as David continued, "If I get lucky, I'll be able to confront Edgar Black as soon as possible and tell him what we've got. Let's open the books to him. We've got murders of people connected to his company. Black is obviously trying to cover up something in the business and trying to threaten anyone who gets near the truth. If I can put some muscle on him, he'll talk, or if he's dumb about the whole mess, maybe we can scare him into helping us find out who is behind whatever is going on there. Remember, they're building advanced weapons in that company and I'll bet it's financed by a government contract that's worth billions."

"Sounds like a plan, David, but that still doesn't get us squat on

Koslov. We know he's up to something and it sounds like it's big. From the conversation Manny had with the Jameson guy that mysteriously got him killed, there must be some action in a warehouse near Koslov's headquarters. Let's say I go to the West Coast and start snooping around his place. I also think I need to get back to Israeli Intelligence about Koslov's activities--when I last approached them, I asked the wrong questions. I need a current photo of him to send to the Moscow station. We have to fast track this whole investigation. David, I know that you have a personal stake in this, with Dianne and Susan involved, but from my perspective I would love to turn the Koslov matter over to Israel's Foreign Intelligence Service."

After they finished their bagels and eggs, they agreed to stay in touch as they both headed for Detroit Metro Airport, Danny to the West Coast and David to LaGuardia to get a handle on the thug who delivered the photos.

Chapter 43

THE FEDERAL SECURITY Service, known as the FSB, is the main security agency of Russia, succeeding the infamous KGB. It is involved in all aspects of internal security. Its headquarters is on Lubyanka Square in central Moscow, in the same location as the KGB. From the Tsarist regime to the repressive Stalinists, the arrests, espionage, and persecutions continued as Russia passed from one repressive regime to another.

Regardless of Chechnya's internal conflicts, their conflict with Russia is over two hundred years old. Although gas and oil fuel the conflict, the basis of the conflict always has been about freedom and religion--Chechnya is largely made up of Sunni Islamists.

Real action started in 1991, when the Soviet Union collapsed and the Chechen government decided to recognize itself as a separate republic, part one of a war that had been going on for centuries. But now, of course, when talk of freedom and separateness became an issue, it led to an all-out war with Russia. In the 1990s when Russia decided to end any talk of independence in this mountainous region and invaded the country, the conflict rose to new levels on both sides. After a bloody two years, during which Chechnya actually held off the mighty Russian army, Boris Yeltsin declared peace. This first horrible escapade lasted more than two years during which some estimates of the number of Chechens displaced by the war were in the hundreds of thousands.

This notion of peace between the parties didn't last very long. By 1999, they were fighting again, but this time was different. Now Chechnya took the conflict to Russia; killings and bombings in Moscow and in other Russian cities became commonplace. In one instance, Chechen guerillas took over a theater in Moscow, kidnapping the occupants. Russia dealt with the theater incident in the same manner for which they are notorious. They gassed the entire theater, killing the perpetrators, but in the process killing over one hundred innocent Russian citizens who happened to be attending a performance there. Russia knew precisely how to exact punishment.

In another incident, Anna Politkovskaya, an outstanding writer and defender of peace, was murdered by the Secret Police because she had written about granting freedom and stopping the violence.

The Chechen government has continued its repression against anyone it deems a danger, including Chechens who appeared to be pro-Russia. Kidnapping, torture, and human rights violations in their own country are commonplace. It is a country being ruled without law.

Many Americans have been suspected of being allies of Russia and even more have been supportive of Russia during the two wars. So it was not unreasonable to believe that if they had an opportunity, Chechnya would love to disrupt and spread some of its poison in the States.

Chapter 44

THE SPECIAL COVERT Ops group in Tel Aviv that was responsible for worldwide surveillance, counter-terrorism, and counter-intelligence heard what is known in the trade as *chatter.* They picked up random pieces of information from conversations abroad and when the analysts pieced the information together, they immediately brought the clips to the attention of the Director, Shimon Eskenazi. His senior analysts were brought in to hear talk of a day soon when a disaster was to take place; the code name "Angels" was heard more than once. It was clear that the chatter was coming from somewhere in the outlying regions of Russia, and the thought was that it emanated from Chechnya or from the nearby mountain territories.

Danny Merkel was already on a secure line, raising questions about the possibility of a terrorist plot that could be linked to the West Coast. Israel's Moscow station chief, Moshe Ostrovsky, was video-conferenced into the conversation, which centered on the information that Danny had received from David's son Manny, who had spoken to Jim Jameson just before he was killed.

Ostrovsky spoke up, "Let's use our sources to find someone here in Moscow who knows something. Merkel, we'll send some help to you in San Francisco. See if you can meet with Korman's son about his last conversation with Jameson. Get someone to get a decent photo of this Koslov. He's either the mastermind or a key part of the group. We should move quickly on this."

Shimon asked, "When do we tell the Americans? After all, it seems like it's going to happen on their soil, and you know how Washington gets their nose out of joint when we keep secrets but not yet, we don't know enough. Once we get something from Moscow to authenticate it, I'll make the call to the Pentagon."

Within twenty-four hours, Eli Markov, a liaison at the Moscow offices of the Israeli Embassy, who in reality worked for Israel Intelligence, was assigned to the case. In the chill of a darkened overcast Moscow morning, he walked briskly past the domes of St. Basil's Cathedral until he reached the banks of the Moscow River. He stopped and stared across the river at the old Stalin-built apartment houses that were the scene of so many killings and terror years before under Stalinist rule.

Markov knew he was being followed, as everyone connected with the diplomatic corps always was. A short, stocky woman passed by him as he leaned against the railing, and he heard the snap of a shutter coming from an opened purse as she passed him.

Markov had instructions from Tel Aviv to use his sources to verify the data that was heard, if possible. He had made a call and arranged to meet Ezra Nikitin, a fifty-five-year-old journalist and ecologist who worked at a foundation based in Moscow, but who had joined the Israeli Secret Service years ago. He had a thick beard now, sprinkled with gray, and his clothes were not of the new Russian fashion--they were simple and showing their age.

As he approached Eli at their meeting location, he smiled at his old friend and Eli greeted him with a hug. "You were followed here, Ezra, but I guess you knew that already," whispered Eli.

Before Nikitin could launch into a diatribe about the intimidation and loss of human rights under the present regime, Markov interrupted, "Ezra, I'd love to continue the discussion of the new fascism in Russia, but I am on a mission and I need your help. The home office has picked up some talk about a terrorist plot that may be in the works, possibly aimed at a location in the States. It could be from Chechnya. We don't think it's a Russian plot--they have their hands full with domestic issues at the moment. But someone must know something about this and we need information quickly. Have you heard anything?"

Nikitin leaned close and told Markov about an ecological conference that took place a few weeks ago. He heard from a source that a group of Chechen terrorists were planning something in the United States. At the conference, a distinguished scholar from Sweden, Doctor Laurent Thieg, spoke about the threat from imminent global warming and the implications to the civilized world. It was a moving presentation. During the coffee break, he approached Nikitin and informed him that it was imperative that Nikitin pass on urgent information.

Thieg told Nikitin that there was a strong al-Qaeda presence in Chechnya and the group had been preparing for some kind of terror strike in America. He believed that some of the nuclear material that was dispersed among Russian-controlled territories after the breakup of the Soviet Union had somehow made its way into the hands of the rebels in Chechnya. Rather than using it against the Russians, they exchanged it with the terrorists for large supplies of tactical field weapons.

Whether they had the technical knowledge to build a device was not known, but Thieg told him that a team was to be set up in the States to do damage in one or more cities. He also heard from an unconfirmed source that the team was to be headed by a trained Chechen who lived in the U.S. That is the conversation that Ezra Nikitin relayed to Eli Markov.

Within an hour of the clandestine meeting, Eli Markov communicated the encoded results of his meeting and assured headquarters that the information was as reliable as could be expected. Now Tel Aviv was faced with the grim reality of a plot of major proportions, and a call was placed to a special branch of the CIA that dealt specifically with major threats. Danny was also put in the loop, and he immediately called David.

Chapter 45

WHILE THE INTELLIGENCE gathering in Tel Aviv and Moscow was taking place, David was in New York. He was sitting in the office of Joseph Ryan, a detective in the 27th Precinct of the New York City Police Department. He had just delivered to Ryan a grainy photograph taken by the branch of the Apple Bank across from David's condo on Seventh Avenue. The manager, whom David had known since the branch opened, was happy to be of assistance once he knew the somber details of David's problem.

The continuously recording camera that photographed activities at the front of the bank also panned out, reaching the location of the transfer of the package of prurient photos of Dianne. It was a long shot, but David knew that Joe Ryan would be willing to attempt to identify the character. Minutes grew to nearly an hour. It was after nine when Ryan came back to his office.

David was already dozing but awoke sharply when the door was closed.

Joe said, "Boy, David, we really struck pay dirt on this one. We got a mug shot of this guy. He's a low-level Russian gofer named Andres Yastrovich who's been involved in everything from extortion and blackmail to assault with a deadly weapon. We can bring him in for questioning, but I doubt that we have enough evidence to hold."

David replied, "No, Joey, I don't want you involved any further. Just tell me where I can reach him and I'll take it from there. You've been a tremendous help. I really owe you one."

"Dave, you and Dianne can take me to my favorite steak house when you're done with him. Happy to help."

David waived down a taxi after ten brutal minutes in the brisk weather, surprisingly cold in Manhattan for this time of year. Compounding the cold, the air rushing through the giant walls of buildings like a wind tunnel created a frigid icebox. David was stressed out and longed for the warmth of his apartment and a large scotch to deal with the fatigue. No more problems to tackle tonight, he thought. He finally had the name and location of the animal that he believed had committed the murders. His plan was to try to get some sleep and get a face-to-face confrontation with Yastrovich early the next day. He would need to pack his Glock, which was in his apartment. But tonight, he mused, he would pick up a couple of sandwiches, go home, pour himself a double shot of single malt, and then get some sleep.

Very early the next day, he would get his private driver to take him to the killer's location in Astoria, and he would do what had to be done to extract the info about who at Black Tech ultimately gave the orders. Once he knew this, he was going to kill Yastrovich and get on a plane to Detroit for the showdown with Edgar Black, who he felt certain was at the bottom of all of this. When he hit the front door of his apartment building, he got a peculiar look from Jose, the doorman. I guess I must look pretty bad, he mused as hit the top-floor button.

Something was wrong. When he tried the key to the door, he found the door unlocked. Damn it, the Glock is in the bedroom and I've got nothing to defend myself with, he thought.

He pushed the door open very slowly and the sight stunned him. Standing in the living area and facing away from him was Dianne, folding some clothes into an open suitcase. He stared at the tall figure he knew so well. She wore black slacks and was in her bare feet. He felt a pounding in his chest as he had not felt in many years. He cleared his throat and it startled her; she turned to face him. His stunning wife looked ten years older--her hair was dark at the roots and grey was showing clearly. Those beautiful thin lines he remembered at the corners of her eyes were more distinct, casting shadows across her face. Her pale-looking lips seemed thinner, and her once-fantastic high cheekbones did not look fantastic. In some way, it was as if a stranger, a tired-looking, sad woman, had entered his apartment.

Nothing was said for what seemed to David to be minutes but was only seconds. Dianne spoke first, "I didn't expect to see you. I just stopped by to pick up some warm clothes and I'll be out of here in ten minutes."

David continued his silence. The conflicting emotions--anger, sadness, longing--flooded him. Finally, he spoke in a quiet tone. "Dianne, I didn't expect to see you either. I got your phone message but I couldn't respond. I wasn't sure how to react. You were, are, the light of my life. We had a trust between us that I believed could not be broken. And now I am just a basket case."

She interrupted, "Please don't, you don't need to explain."

"Could you please be quiet and let me finish," he said with a touch of anger in his voice. "I want you back, but I will never understand why you did it. I can't even say the words. What would have happened if those creeps never photographed you with that kid? Was I not good enough? Please explain it to me."

"David, I'm not sure that I know what I was doing or why. I was lonely, very angry with you for not keeping me in the loop, scared at the prospect of you being hurt or killed and not knowing. Maybe I wanted to get even or just felt so alone that I would do anything to get relief. And as to 'that kid,' you should know that I initiated it; he never came on to me. But regardless, there is no way that I can explain. I left a phone message because everything in my life is over. You, my job, my self-respect--all gone. I called to know if there was some way possible that you could accept me, not excuse what I did. Maybe I could try to rebuild what we had.

"Look at me," she continued. "I'm a shell of what I was. I feel so bad that I would do anything. If you could just give me a chance to show you that I can be trusted, that I can be part of your life again."

The next few moments hung in the air like heavy clouds just before the sky opens. David spoke. "I'm not sure I want to live with you, but I'm not doing too good a job of going on without you." There was a long pause while David sorted his options.

With a serious look, he slowly continued, "Let's give it a try, kiddo. Perfection was never my top priority anyway. Let's try to make it work."

Dianne slowly moved towards him and they stood close, their eyes targeted on each other. David put his arms around her and held her tight. She began to cry bitterly, loudly. Not sobs but vocal, mournful cries. They didn't make love that night. That would have been too much to ask of either of them, but they lay close in bed together most of the night. Sleep came at last for both of them, a deep sleep that neither had enjoyed for some time.

When David awoke at five-thirty, he smelled the wonderful aroma of the strong coffee. They always enjoyed having coffee together. When Dianne sat down on their bed, offering him a cup of the hot brew, David noticed that she had makeup on. She was already dressed and looked refreshed. He yearned for her body but instead kissed her lightly and smelled Dianne, so familiar and comforting to him.

After he showered, they sat in their tasteful kitchen having coffee and bialys with cream cheese, all laid regally on the table.

David explained his plan. Andres Yastrovich would be receiving a visit, and David already had one of the two handguns in the apartment cleaned and holstered.

Dianne moved close to him. "David, I want to go with you; I need to be near you. You know I've been in situations like this with you before, and I can handle it. Please let me do this."

David thought for a moment. He was not thrilled with the idea. There were so many years of working alone, but he spoke. "You know how dangerous this is going to be. I need to know who gave the orders for the damage that's been done, and I'm going to hurt this man. If you agree to follow my directions, get ready. We'll go together."

Chapter 46

DANNY MERKEL SAT at the desk of his hotel room in San Francisco studying maps of the surrounding area and trying to determine where he was going to set up surveillance and obtain photos of Gabriel Koslov and his team. Koslov's offices and manufacturing complex occupied 250,000 square feet in an industrial site outside of San Francisco. Merkel determined that its sophisticated security system was electronically maintained at an off-site location. It would be impossible to breach this without being observed.

An alternative was to set up his equipment near Koslov's imposing and very private home located in the suburban city of Belvedere. However, since the home faced San Francisco Bay on one side and a hilly terrain on the other, it would not be possible to get close enough.

Danny finally decided that his best chance to photograph Koslov and his security team would be on the only public road that led to his office. Lady Luck kissed Danny on this score. Sitting on a hill at a fairly short distance from the entrance to the complex, Danny could, with special equipment, photograph anyone entering or leaving. He planned to set up a maintenance van equipped with the necessary photographic equipment as well as long distance phone and fax capabilities, all supplied by Israeli agents in the area. At this point, American authorities had not been brought into the investigation.

By late afternoon the next day, the van was sitting on the shoulder of the road leading to the Koslov facility. Danny had determined that Koslov punctually left his offices at six, so Danny had all the high-speed equipment trained on the entrance by five. At five minutes after six, three security men emerged from the glass entranceway, followed by Gabriel Koslov. The cameras and video equipment were simultaneously photographing and faxing the images to a tower on a nearby elevation while simultaneously uploading them by satellite to the headquarters of Israeli Special Intelligence. In case of detection, the equipment was set up to show that the faxes were sent to a blogger at a Washington address.

As the darkly tinted limousines passed Danny's van, photographs were already being examined in Tel Aviv and in Moscow. Once he had the images, Danny immediately shut down and dismantled all the equipment. As he returned to the driver's seat of the van, what he saw was not what he expected. One of the limousines had pulled in front of his van and two men in suits were standing on either side of the van with weapons pointed at him. They entered the van, pulled Danny from it, blindfolded him, and transported the contents of the van to a location that Danny guessed was about twenty miles from his original location. He did not believe that Koslov was there.

They were quick and decisive in their questioning. "What were you doing there? Who do you work for? What is all this equipment for?"

Danny had the credentials of a free-lance journalist and responded that he was trying to get a story on Koslov, the successful entrepreneur who might be seeking a seat in Congress or maybe the governor's mansion. He claimed he was faxing photos to a source in DC who was going to sell the photos of Koslov and his family, his facility, and his luxurious mansion. He insisted that his source was waiting for him to call about the material. There was a silence that seemed to take an eternity. Danny then heard footsteps and prepared himself for the final gun, the terminus.

One of them removed the blindfold and said, "You know, my friend, you could get in a lot of trouble by what you did. Mr. Koslov guards his privacy and does not want anyone intruding on it. If he wanted a story done on him, he would have arranged it with the national networks, not some idiot blogger. We spoke to your contact and he wants you to call him. He obviously is upset with the way you went about your business. Your punishment is that you no longer have your equipment. Your van is outside. We suggest you get in it and get back to your home in DC."

When Danny was driving back to his hotel, he called his contact in Tel Aviv, and after relating the story to them, they said, "Your photos were invaluable. When you get to a secure line, we'll outline the next steps."

Chapter 47

IT WAS UNSEASONABLY warm in Israel that evening. The heat came from the south, brought by a searing wind that was fierce, dry, and, to make it more unbearable, accompanied by a sand-like grit. In Tel Aviv, anyone who ventured out clung to the false cool of the shadows. It was night, and most Israelis were asleep, but restless sleeps, always on guard for the strike that might come or for the rockets that might fall. This was part of the culture in Israel.

Captain Ezra Ludkin of the Israeli Special Intelligence Unit was still at work. He worked most of the time. He worked early in the morning and he worked late in the evening. It was Sunday night and he was working counterintelligence. This meant a great many different things, but at this time he was working together with an American, Danny Merkel, who was a spy for Israeli intelligence. He was told to expect and to disseminate any information that Merkel sent on a secure line directly to his group. It was not that Ludkin did not like Merkel; in fact, he had never met him. It was that he believed that Americans that he worked with were not as careful as they needed to be.

As he perused the latest issue of *GQ*, pages started flying from the fax in the center of the offices where small contingents of agents were working. Everyone stopped. Ludkin leaped to his feet and set in motion the capture of the data and subsequent copying. What emerged from a continent away was a series of images, almost twenty, showing a well-dressed, tanned man and three other men, younger and well-muscled in dark suits, clearly a security detail.

When the last image was received, Ludkin followed a well-defined procedure. Despite the late hour, he began calling several other divisions and faxing the material to them. It was as if an alarm clock had awakened the entire second floor of the facility. All Israeli missions were receiving the images, including the Moscow station of Israeli Intelligence.

There were several hours of eerie silence as each agency studied the images, downloaded them into the massive international database, and waited for any recognition. Sleep-starved men and women worked through the night to find any connection between Gabriel Koslov and European terrorists. Nothing seemed to bear any fruit. It was as if this man had appeared from the mystery of the night, emerging as a successful American businessman and a potentially powerful politician in California. All the secret intelligence services were focusing their attention on an attempt to identify Koslov.

After hours of a fruitless search, fortune finally began to shine. A relatively low-level diplomatic agent working in the embassy in Moscow saw something interesting. The agent, currently serving as an assistant adjutant to the Director's administrative staff, recognized one of Koslov's security team from the photos.

After graduating from Hebrew University and prior to enlisting in the intelligence service, Natan Kaminsky joined a United Nations aid group whose mission was to provide economic support in war-torn Chechnya, in particular to the region surrounding Grozny, the capital city. As he stated in the Director's office with all the resident agents either on hand or on a secure line, Kaminsky had come across a small school that was not part of the traditional Chechen educational system.

In this school, there were a handful of young boys who were enrolled in some type of special program. When he made inquiries about the school, he was warned by a school security person to stop his search. The UN general in charge of the aid team, in deference to the complaint made by the school, requested that Kaminsky be reassigned to another mission site. What struck Kaminsky now was that one of Koslov's security team clearly was the security person who had warned him to stay away from that school.

Although the contacts in Moscow had indicated that a Chechen terrorist group might be planning an attack in the U.S., nothing had been verified. Now, however, the focus shifted from Russia to Chechnya based on the first-hand recognition of one of Koslov's security team.

Ludkin made contact with the Swedish government to gain access to the general who had headed the UN aid mission. He was now retired and living in a home just outside Stockholm, and within minutes, Ludkin's group was speaking with him. The general knew details of the school outside of Grozny, but had assumed it was an attempt on the part of the populace to place young children who showed superior intelligence in an environment where they could become part of the new Chechnya. He knew nothing of terrorist links to the school, but he knew where the school was and had recorded a list of the students and their families enrolled during the time he was stationed in Grozny. The UN administrative staff was contacted within hours and Israeli Intelligence had access to the file with the family names.

As soon as this information was received, Israeli-friendly contacts in Grozny were contacting families whose children, now adults, had attended this school. By Monday afternoon, what was left of the Basayev family, Koslov's mother and sister, were shown the photographs taken in California, and despite the years gone by, they were able to identify the photo of Gabriel Koslov as their son, Viktor Basayev.

Now the daunting task of determining the purpose of the deception rose to the highest priority. It became a feeding frenzy; surveillance activity and intelligence forces around the world were secretly examining the school and its trainers, trying to determine their goals and objectives. This was a task that had the full resolve of every agent worldwide--the information provided could hold the key to the threat of a nuclear attack.

A message was also sent to Danny Merkel stating, "We now know whom your Mr. Gabriel Koslov really is."

Chapter 48

At five A.M. in a winter morning's early darkness, a black SUV with darkened windows circled a dismal, run-down block on 31st Street in the Astoria neighborhood in the borough of Queens in New York. The driver finally reached the location given to him. In the gray, dim light, he saw a run-down, wood-framed house with weeds growing wildly in the small fenced-in garden that fronted the house.

The car stopped long enough for its occupants to notice an old Dodge Caravan parked along the side of the house. There were broken screens hanging from the front windows, and the three steps leading to the front door were cracked, with stones missing. The car continued around the corner and its occupants made note of several empty lots behind the house.

David and Dianne Korman sat in the rear of the car as their driver pulled to a stop well clear of the house. "What's the plan, boss?"

David was silent as he sorted out the details, a process that he knew well. He had done this type of operation successfully for many years. "Okay, this is what we'll try. You stay back and wait on your mobile. I'll cross the empty lot and try to get in from the back of the house. Once I determine how I'm going to enter, I'll let you know. Then Jake, you pull up to the front and keep the car running. Dianne, you stay in the car. When I get what I need, we'll move out quickly. I doubt that the Russian expects a visitor but is everyone okay with that?"

Jake and Dianne nodded and David exited the car, quietly closing the rear door. He slipped the nine-millimeter Glock out of its shoulder holster and checked the ten-round magazine. There was enough reflected light for

David to see a back porch with a splintered door exiting to a small dirt-filled yard. He made his way noiselessly through the junk-scattered yard and up the few steps to the back door. After pushing on the door, it gave in easily with some minor noise.

It was dark as he made his way through what David perceived to be a kitchen. He passed a small wooden table and a few cheap chairs. He stopped when he saw a faint light coming from what David took to be a living room.

He quietly made his way, looking in all directions as he crouched along, the weapon at his side. In the faint yellowish glow of an incandescent light, the blue-white blinking of television's images cast eerie shadows on the torn papered walls.

In the room, in what appeared to David to be a lounge chair, lay a dark-looking man with a thick mane hanging down to his shoulders, staring at a cartoon image on the TV screen. He did not seem to be tall, but thick muscles bulged beneath a black, V-necked tee shirt, tattoos running up both forearms. His khaki-colored pants were pulled up to his calves and his bare feet swung aimlessly from the front of the chair. It appeared to David that he was either sleeping or dozing; his eyes seemed to be closed. David quietly moved until he was behind the chair, close to the back of the man's head.

He pushed the gun's barrel against his head and shouted. "Yastrovich, get the fuck up! Come on, get up, now, right now."

The man clumsily leapt to his feet and faced David. It was the face of the man he was hunting, Andres Yastrovich.

"What the fuck do ya want with me, bro? I ain't done shit. Are you the cops, or what?"

David hesitated and said coldly, "I'm not the police but you will soon wish I was. I'm the guy who needs some questions answered very quickly. The way I see it, you are the prick who has to answer for three dead people, and you're the scumbag who took pictures of my wife. You Russian cocksucker, you're not going to walk away from this without giving me what I need."

"What the fuck you talkin' about. You are just fuckin' nuts. Put that piece down, old man, before you shoot yourself in the foot."

David moved closer to him, pushed him back into the chair and pushed the gun into his mouth. "Well, my friend, either you are going to give me what I need, or this piece is going to unload itself in your throat. This way, your brains will fly out the back of your head and miss me totally."

He pulled back on the hammer and the neat, efficient click made Yastrovich freeze. David suddenly heard a dripping sound as urine began to run down the Russian's pants and onto the floor. Yastrovich uttered an almost audible sound as he held his hands up in the air.

David pulled the gun from his mouth and Yastrovich screamed, "I never killed any of those people. I just followed an order and made the connections. Someone wanted those people dead very badly, and I just got paid to set them up. Hey, I didn't even know them. I just followed orders. The photos, hey, I didn't know it was your wife. I just made the call to some guys I know and told them to follow her."

"Who gave the orders, you animal," David shouted at him. "Who told you to do it? Right now, you tell me or I'll spill whatever you have in that sick head all over the floor."

"I never knew who it was," screamed Yastrovich. "I got a call from a Russian who served time with me. He lives in Detroit and took his orders from someone. He said the order came from some broad who lived in Detroit, and she was giving them some kind of information in return. I never knew who it was. He told me he got the names and locations, and that's all. I never knew her name. I swear to God, that's all I know. I found the guys to take care of all this. I'm just the guy in the middle."

Yastrovich's confession echoed in David's brain like a racket ball rebounding across the court. *A woman in Detroit* sent electric shocks through David's body. That could mean only one person as far as he was concerned, and he knew what he must do. But he needed to do first things first.

With all the energy he possessed, he turned the gun over in his hand and began hitting the Russian again and again until his face was just a bloody mess.

Suddenly, David heard a noise behind him and felt a sharp pain at the back of his head echoing through his neck and down his spine. He fell to the ground and momentarily lost consciousness. When he awoke, dazed, two men stood over him as he tried to focus his blurred vision. One was Yastrovich who was wiping the blood from his face with a dirty cloth. The other man was shorter than Yastrovich and was wearing a shirt that hung outside his drooping pants and over his short, fat legs. He was smiling as he looked down at David, who was sprawled on the wooden floor.

The corpulent man approached and, with a broad smile, kicked his shoe hard into David's ribs, sending shocks through his body. After launching another kick, David could not keep the contents of his stomach in and he hurled on himself, retching again and again.

The Russian spoke, "Well, old man, who is going to spill whose brains now? My pal here now wants to kill you a piece at a time but I will get it over real quick. I gotta tell you something before I blow your fuckin' head off. Your wife is some piece of ass, you know? I saw the shots of her blowing that guy, I gotta tell you, I'd let her suck my dick any day. And what a pair of tits, wow. Maybe after you're gone, my bro and I will pay her a condolence visit, what do you say, old man?" They both broke into raucous laughter, and Yastrovich stepped closer and dug his heel into David's face. The blur began again and as he was losing consciousness, he saw the gun pointed at him.

Suddenly, the loud blast of two explosions echoing around him caused David to quiver. One body fell heavily on top of him and he heard the other fall next to his feet. He tried to sit up, but the weight of the man on top of him was too much and all David could do was try to see where the shots came from. Through the fog of his fading consciousness, he saw Dianne standing at the door. She was holding a smoking, snub-nosed Beretta pointed in his direction.

Yastrovich's body was spurting dark fluid all over David. The fat man was lying on his back nearby, his eyes still open and staring into the distance. Dianne stood motionless, staring at David, with the gun still clutched firmly in both hands.

David was finally able to get to his knees, and all he could utter was, "Thanks pal," before he collapsed.

Chapter 49

IT WAS A cold day in the Bay area, Gabriel Koslov was trying to enjoy a tranquil Sunday at home, but a nagging premonition of danger lurked somewhere deep in his mind. He was expecting the arrival of Olga Deripaska, the lead engineer for the project he hoped would bring Chechnya worldwide recognition as a leader in terrorist activity. Koslov hadn't heard from her in a while, and valuable time had gone by since the meeting with Atalo Karamanlis in which Koslov was given the responsibility to build a nuclear bomb and detonate it in the port city of Long Beach, California.

Work had begun slowly under the direction of Olga, a scientist schooled at the Moscow Institute of Physics and Technology, the highest regarded technical university in Russia. Born into a Russian bureaucratic family, she identified herself at an early age with the movement for Chechnya's freedom and was recruited into the cause while attending university. From early on in her training, it was a foregone conclusion by the shadow government in Grozny that she would somehow bring fame for the cause of independence.

Now thirty-eight years old, Olga had spent years researching the capability to successfully build a nuclear weapon. Russian influence in the State Department had gotten her into a special science program at Caltech in Pasadena. While doing pure scientific research there, she secretly organized the manpower necessary to build the weapon. Koslov supplied her with the financial resources and the facilities to start construction.

On a personal level, Olga was unmarried and completely devoted to the cause. Any romantic interests she might have pursued were cast aside long ago. Her dressiest outfit was a pair of Levis, a t-shirt, and flat-heeled shoes. She was a woman who possessed a brilliance totally occupied with thoughts of completing the project. Romantic interludes to Olga consisted of regular masturbation drills, in which she dreamt of sexual fantasies she would never permit to materialize.

At exactly the predetermined time, the doorbell rang, and Koslov invited Dr. Olga Deripaska into his study. They both sat in front of floor-to-ceiling windows overlooking the Bay, he on a soft, leather couch and she on a deeply tufted leather armchair facing him. She sank deeply into the chair, her long legs searching awkwardly for a comfortable position.

"We have not met like this in a long time. So, tell me, Olga, how is it going? Where are you in terms of timing?" he asked.

She began, "Why don't you let me bring you up to the present? The objectives I set from the start were to develop a small but deadly lightweight weapon with maximum efficiency based on the parameters I was given: low cost, low risk of failure, and speed of development. As you know, the design has always depended on the technological and material constraints that I envisioned. Always, the most serious constraint of the project was the acquisition of fissile material. Acquiring the necessary plutonium and delivering it to the construction site has been a very delicate process. Fortunately, we have friends in different parts of the world who have been willing to supply the material to us. Just recently, we completed an arrangement with sources in Pakistan to deliver a small quantity of reactor grade plutonium through Mexico."

She continued, "It was clear to me that what we needed was a weapon that would create a 'small explosion.' I decided upon a yield of ten kilotons, ample for our goal. Remember, this is equivalent to ten thousand tons of dynamite. I'm sure you know, Gabriel, that a yield of this size is absolutely trivial compared to weapons with yields of megatons, but my weapon will be far more dangerous than conventional weapons because of the extremely intense radiation emitted.

"I am working with a projected weapon-size comparable to a large suitcase. This will allow us to move the weapon into its position and detonate it more easily. I hate to use scientific terms to describe the bomb, but let me bore you with my theory.

"In simple terms, we are compressing the fissile core by embedding it in a steel cylinder containing high explosives. The explosive material, exactly

100 pounds of TNT, was easy for us to obtain. The detonation trigger is a high frequency, radio-controlled device I built myself. In simple terms, when the trigger is activated, a small explosion will occur within the steel housing of the weapon. As the detonation proceeds from each direction towards the center core, the material will be squeezed into a critical shape, causing a nuclear chain reaction and then the massive explosion."

After a brief pause, she continued, "As of now, with the help of our staff, we are performing very sophisticated simulation exercises of the entire process including the weapon's detonation. The fact that we didn't require any actual weapon testing will stun the world. By computer testing, we avoid using any of the priceless fissile material. Gabriel, we are very close to the final assembly phase of the weapon."

"Olga, you have surpassed all of our expectations. My goodness, the world will know our strength. What will you need to complete the bomb?" he asked excitedly.

She paused for a moment, re-crossed her long legs and spoke, "When we are ready to completely assemble the weapon, we must have all the ancillary equipment ready to move. There will be little time once compression of the fissile begins. The weapon carrier must be ready to load the weapon into a large case labeled as machine parts for shipment to Bahrain.

"The vehicle's shock system must be carefully designed. A small van like a Ford Econoline should be adequate for shipping to the loading dock. We must time it carefully, so that the case containing the bomb will be in the process of being loaded when we trigger the weapon and the critical mass is obtained. I expect that the explosion will take place when the weapon is about forty feet above ground level. I would have liked a higher level, but we are constrained by the ship's hauling device."

She looked wistfully out of the massive windows to the bay below as she spoke seriously, "You know that once the explosion occurs, the fireball will burn everything within about ten miles of the blast. Immediately following the blast, I would expect hurricane force winds, first outwards from the blast, and then inward to replace the air that was displaced. Temperatures will briefly be in the millions of degrees. Within miles, no one will be left standing. I expect fires from burst fuel tanks, gas mains, and collapsed buildings. The winds will be strong enough to prevent anyone from outrunning the effects of the fire. Widespread contamination will result and everything in the vicinity will be radioactive.

We picked the port area because of its proximity and low security. We are planning to time the explosion when the Santa Ana winds are most likely to occur. This will move the radioactive effects of the blast close to or into the greater L.A. area. That is why I brought a climatologist onto the team. The Santa Ana's will begin sometime this fall, probably in September or October; it's too early to pin it down now. But when these winds, usually upper-level atmospheric winds, spill out of the area between the Sierra Nevada and the Rocky Mountains, they should be propelled northeasterly towards southern California. This will create a windstorm of radioactivity into the Los Angeles area, multiplying the effect of the explosion."

She looked directly into Gabriel's eyes and, with just a hint of sadness, said, "Gabriel, it will be highly unlikely that we will be able to escape the impact and radiation of the explosion. I hope you realize that everyone within miles will either be incinerated by the blast or will suffer massive deadly radiation exposure. I am prepared to deal with my own fate, but I hope that you have taken all of this into consideration."

As she spoke, Koslov knew that he must start planning for his well-deserved vacation this fall. His mind raced quickly and methodically. Alternative passports must be printed for his family, funds must be parked in various locations, and he must, of course, discuss this with his wife, Merrill, who knew nothing of this part of Gabriel's life. He believed, perhaps naively, that she would comply without revealing any information, but he needed a back-up plan in the event that she would not go along willingly.

Olga rose from her chair and they hugged for a longer time than one would expect. Gabriel felt her body against his, and as they silently walked to the door, she spoke, "I'm glad I don't believe in God. It makes it easier this way."

Chapter 50

IT WAS SEVERAL days after the incident in Queens. David was released from Beth Israel Hospital with a few bruised ribs and a sore sixty-five-year-old body. They were at home, David and Dianne, enjoying the little free time they had before they were to fly to Detroit for the confrontation with Edgar Black and the prospect of facing Nicole Lawrence.

Over coffee, sitting on the stylish, leather sofa in front of the massive living-room window in their posh apartment, Dianne spoke first, "I think we need to prepare a plan for this meeting. What do we want to accomplish? David, he's not going to stand up and admit to having people murdered. He has to believe that we have enough to go to the authorities. Even though we're convinced that he and Nicole Lawrence are the thugs who got the contractors to commit the murders, let's have him put the whole ball of wax on her. We need for him to tell us what the motive is--what are they hiding? Black is in the middle of a huge government contract to build some kind of space-age weapon."

David jumped in, "Phillip Courtney moved to Frisco with his laptop but the cops never found it. Ann Reilly was investigating problems at Black Tech and she had an *accident.* I spoke to Harris Malone, and as soon as he was prepared to get me some hard information, he also had an *acciden*t. And as soon as they learned that we were looking into things, they try to shut us up. So, what do you say we lay all of it on the table for Edgar, who probably is the mastermind of this shit, and get him to think we have Nicole's contractor. If he's smart, he'll put it all on her. Maybe then we can take all of this to some authority, probably a federal agency, FBI or something, and get the hell out of it.

If we can do this, he continued, we should go west to help Danny figure out what Koslov is up to. Danny's good at investigating, but this could be a terrorist activity. Israeli security has probably brought the Feds into it, but we know a hell of a lot more than they know. He'll need some support."

Dianne moved close to David and smiled. "Sweetheart, you know what you do to me when you take charge like this; it's a real turn-on. You really are amazing." Dianne softly rubbed the back of David's sore neck while the other hand slid down and quickly created a hard bulge in his slacks.

At that moment, the beacon in David's lighthouse, like a long dormant transmitter buried in his ancient body, was sparking back to life. In places where he ought to be sore and achy, instead he grew hard. David's organ could anticipate what was to come at supersonic speed, leaving his rapidly melting brain to play catch-up.

At the most crucial moment, he could not resist replaying the vision of Dianne, his lovely wife, sucking that young stud's hard staff. Only when he felt her soft lips surrounding his own Mt. Vesuvius did the vision dissolve into oblivion.

Later, David reflected on the power of women to toy with a man's ego. He thought that if the passage of time over generations has taught men one thing, it is that a woman can control the strongest, fiercest man with soft hands that have been genetically altered to raise hard-fast a man's cock. Once hardened, she then can turn him into a soft, mushy pile by merely holding it in her silky fingers. History has also taught us that a woman can put the silliest smile on any man by gently wrapping her lips around his tool.

And so it was in the Korman's living room. The soreness in the lion's body was washed away, leaving him looking like a dish of silly putty.

Chapter 51

Edgar Black was up early. He had been at his desk for several hours, poring over the latest stats on the weapons project, when Leon knocked, drifted in, and sat down on one of the rich, brown, leather side chairs, putting one leg over the arm of the chair and letting his Armani leather loafer wag back and forth lazily. Since the departure of Phillip Courtney, Leon, despite his weak technical knowledge, was put in charge of the development of the weapon, and Edgar was becoming seriously concerned at the lack of progress.

"What the hell is slowing up the prototype, Leon," he bellowed. "The guys at Defense are breaking my balls about the stalling, and the talk on the street is that we are up against a stone wall on the guidance piece. So where the fuck are you?" He stared steely eyed at his son, jaw clenched, ready for war.

Leon was ill prepared for this tirade, although his father was well known for his nasty temper. Edgar was ready to explode and take total control of him. The words that his father said to him made Leon feel as if there were another self, an angry self, inside Edgar. That self seemed ordinarily invisible, but clearly sentient and ready to vent at a moment's notice in the form of violent action independent of his volition. It made Leon wonder who Edgar really was. He had been all consumed with the problems surrounding this project since Phillip Courtney saw it early on.

"Edgar, you know where our effort has gone and which problems remain unsolved. We learned early on that atmospheric conditions can cause the laser beam to break down or to defocus and disperse its energy into the atmosphere. This was evident from the start. Phillip made the decision to use the large mirror that's giving us nightmares. It's supposed to focus the beam on the target. It's one of the key requirements of the system. But that mirror is proving to be fragile, and more often than not, it cracks as the intensity of each phase increases. Phillip knew it and did nothing, and we've been searching for an alternative substance, but are not yet there."

Leon continued, "Frankly, we've tried synthetic materials but they tend to overheat dramatically at power levels consistent with their use. On the good-news side, we have completed the guidance system that pinpoints the target but are still wrestling with the enormous energy requirement of the weapon. We have tried various methods to store energy, but this still remains partially unsolved. We are working on it day and night, but the solution is elusive. The bottom line, Edgar, is we are working as hard as possible to finish and build the prototype, but it's taking more time than anyone expected."

Edgar exploded, "Damn it, you fucking idiot, if I wanted that conclusion, I could have kept Courtney here. I want a timeline for the solution of these issues. Remember what I told you a million times, Leon. You may be poor or you may be loaded, but the one thing nobody can take away from you is the freedom to fuck up your life, in whatever way you want. So how do you want to fuck up your life? Get it?"

At this, Leon saw no point in continuing. Between these huge unsolved laser problems and issues with Nicole, his mind was frazzled. He was sure that Edgar knew about his relationship with her. In Leon's mind, things were just plain fucked-up, as he desperately searched for something to relieve the stress that he was under.

Chapter 52

IT WAS A glorious, early summer afternoon in San Francisco, one of those special cloudless, breezy sun days that glorifies, purifies, and lifts the spirits. In a nondescript suburban café, three men sat under a colorful umbrella eating typical healthy West Coast lunches. One was enjoying an albacore salad, laden with sprouts, seeds, and pineapple. The other two were enjoying toasted focaccias filled with melted asiago, tomato, cucumber, and grilled veggies. Dressed casually in jeans, Izod shirts and sandals, they looked like ordinary guys from one of the many office complexes in the area taking a lunch hour.

Danny Merkel sat with two agents, one with Israeli Special Intelligence and the other a Special Agent with the terrorist section of the Central Intelligence Agency. The topic on the table centered on the recently identified Chechen, Gabriel Koslov, his identity now known.

The problem they were trying to get their arms around was their inability to determine Koslov's goal since he arrived in the States. It was known that he was trained at a special school outside of Grozny for some mission in America. They also knew that the school trained only specially gifted children in a program designed with science and technology as its specialties.

They located several of the graduates in various parts of the world and had them in the loop, but it was clear that Koslov was here for a very specific purpose. They had heard *noise* for some time about a terrorist mission designed to punish the United States for its support of Russia in the century-old struggle against Chechnya's desire for freedom.

They had also learned from a conversation with Manuel Korman that information from an employee of Koslov's company indicated some activity taking place, not related to his company and in a location apart from Koslov's main manufacturing facility. That employee was later killed in what was determined to be an automobile accident.

The three sleuths struggled to make headway. They questioned whether this was a terrorist plot and, if it was, what type of activity and where was it being planned? Koslov had been in the States long enough to develop a successful organization, marry an American woman, raise children, and appear to everyone as an up-and-coming community leader.

Danny expressed his frustration, "Why don't we just pull Koslov in and grill him? We don't have to do it here. We can ship him anywhere and put him through the whole interrogation scheme."

Frank Richelieu of the CIA was the first to respond, "Danny, forget that, will you? If we touch him without knowing where the activity is taking place, whomever he's working with could just implement the plan without him. No, we just need to find the location."

Judah Kassel of Israeli Intelligence added, "I agree with Frank. We need to find the location. The problem we've encountered is that Koslov doesn't go to the location. It's not in his facility. We have all his communication devices tagged, but he has another way of staying in touch. We've gotta find it. He must be delegating to one of his deputies whatever is going to happen; we've been tailing everyone and so far we've come up empty. But there is one potential lead that we should explore."

Kassel continued, "The only solid lead we have is the identification of one of the Chechen special students, who is still in this country. Her name is Olga Deripaska, a real techie whiz. Went on to school in Moscow and, from our intelligence, she's a real brain. She was supposed to be enrolled in a graduate program at Caltech, but the university has no record of any Deripaska ever enrolled. She appears to have disappeared from our radar. We have an older photo of her but that's all. Guys, we need to focus our attention on finding her."

Danny jumped in, "Let me take this one. I know they require a photo ID at Caltech. She probably has a new name, but the photo should be recent enough unless she had a face job, too. But even so, someone should be able to recognize her. Let's make that priority one: find Olga."

They all agreed, and Frank added, "Guys, we need to move on this one. Koslov has had a long time to develop some kind of plan. I'll notify all branches worldwide to accelerate the search, and if you need any help, Danny, yell it out."

Chapter 53

An early summer heat wave in the East brought sweltering temperatures that were already causing some blackouts up and down the Eastern seaboard. The DC area was enduring nineties with humidity near ninety, even into the evenings. That was what it felt like at spy headquarters in the Pentagon. In an out-of-the way area in the basement of the building where air-conditioning barely cooled the air, there was an inconspicuous-looking door with the name "Special Violations Section" stenciled on it. Inside, there was a suite of workstations encircling a conference room. At the far end was the only private office in the section.

Late one afternoon, the suite was empty expect for the eight operatives—six men and two women—who sat around the long, wooden table inside the conference room. Men's jackets were off, collars open, and ties either totally removed or dangling part of the way down their shirts. The women wore shirts open at two buttons, with sleeves rolled halfway to the elbow. The only sound was the hum of the large ceiling fan, whirling overhead at max speed.

They all had dossiers in front of them and were studying their contents, when a tall, thin, older man holding a sealed envelope entered. The completely gray haired man, wearing a vested suit, wore a serious expression on his face. It was obvious that he was the supervisor; he had that tired, hardened-by-years-of-work look. He sat at one end of the table and cleared his throat to announce the start of the meeting.

"We are here because transactions have taken place in the financial markets that have been flagged by SECTAG as suspicious. In front of you are the reports that have been brought to our attention. It involves a public company headquartered in suburban Detroit, Michigan. Its name is Black Technologies, Inc.

"The main sources of revenue of the forenamed company are contracts with several U.S. governmental agencies to produce a new laser-driven weapons system. They have other revenue bases, but their single largest vendor is the Department of Defense. We began to notice unusual financial activity about six months ago, and it has grown materially in the last thirty days. Please turn to pages fifteen through twenty-five where descriptions of the transactions are summarized."

After the page rustling stopped, he continued, "Large sums of money, initially in the ten to twenty million dollar range, were being moved, and after about six months, the amounts increased. The latest tally seems to be in the five hundred million to one billion dollar range. During this time, the funds were kept offshore. Investments in the form of shorting credit-default swaps were being made on Wall Street. We presume that they were using government advances to bet against the housing market. You know the condition of the housing industry and Wall Street's love affair with this kind of 'hocus-pocus' risk-taking.

"More recently, whoever is perpetrating this fraud has begun to unwind the swaps very quickly, and we have calculated profits of at least one billion from these transactions.

"Folks, if these were just transactions involving a domestic corporation's activities, we might flag them, but it would not be within our purview to go any further. But let's not forget that Black is playing the market with advances made by government agencies to finance the development of an extremely important strategic weapons program.

"We looked into the status of the development of the first prototype of a laser weapon by Black and, as you probably can guess, they are struggling and searching for the exotic materials necessary to get the prototype completed. They are substantially behind schedule, and what makes this worse is that several of our elected officials have supported the Black contract over some really heavy, competitive contractors. So, there you have it? Any thoughts as to how to approach the situation?"

From the end of the table, one of the men spoke up, "I think the first thing we need to know is the identity of the individual or individuals involved in this. Who's making the transactions? Does it look like one person or a group effort?"

A short, heavy-set woman in a sleeveless blouse, who was constantly swabbing beads of perspiration with tissues from a large box in front of her, responded, "I think we have a pretty good idea of the perpetrator. The Street is all agog with a broad who seems to be the financial guru for the company. Apparently, she has the looks and brains to pull this off. Her name, at least for now, is Nicole Lawrence.

She continued, "The interesting thing is that eventually the 'profits' from all these deals always end up in Zurich in her name. Some of the paper has another name on it, a guy named Leon Black. He's the son of the founder of the company, Edgar Black, but I think that's a strategy of hers to implicate this dodo in her machinations. She's good, I'll tell you that. She's totally outguessed the market relative to these mortgage-backed bonds. She hasn't made one investment mistake. If it weren't government cash that she was playing with, she'd probably get away with it."

"How did she get past the auditors?" a youngish agent asked.

"My guess is long legs, a pretty face, and phony audit confirmations. So what's the problem here? Why don't we just haul her ass in here and break her down?" asked another agent.

The supervisor took in a deep breath, sighed, and replied, "We have a huge problem. Most of the funds have been returned to the company as she unwinds the remainder of the swaps. She could easily maintain that all she was doing was investing the company's money and creating profits for them. The funds in Swiss accounts could be temporary, which she intended to return as soon as the transactions were complete. Try and explain that to certain congressmen who have been supporting the project from day one. It's clear that they have Black's money in their pockets and don't want to stop the faucet, and they certainly don't want the publicity surrounding circumstantial evidence of fraud. No, this Lawrence broad has covered her bases well; we need to be able to prove that her intent was always to defraud the company and the government."

"What do we know about her?" asked another agent.

The supervisor opened the envelope that he had brought into the meeting, saying, "I had an investigation started on Nicole Lawrence by the

Behavioral Science Section, and I have their opinions. However, I would like to bring in one of their operatives to explain them in detail."

He moved to a phone on a side table, dialed four digits, and requested the presence of an agent. Moments later, as if she had been waiting outside ready to enter, a woman in her forties walked in, dressed conservatively in a white, open-neck blouse and a buttoned suit jacket. She introduced herself and opened a large portfolio.

"My name is Dr. Ruth Landros and I head up a special unit within Behavioral Science. My job is to profile a potential threat, or in this case, someone suspected of fraud.

"Let me talk a bit about Nicole Lawrence or, as she was named, Michelina Aillon, born of immigrant parents in a small, dusty town in Texas. We know that she had smarts as far back as grade school. By the time she reached college, she was extremely attractive and we know that she was sexually active. It was always the cream of the crop that got her attention. Nothing less could get close to her. There is no evidence of a relationship; it always seemed to be how to get what she wanted. She graduated from the University of Texas, majoring in finance and accounting. She tried modeling after graduation and that's when she dumped her past--Michelina from Texas became Nicole Lawrence, the financial whiz."

Dr. Landros continued, "We tracked the progression of jobs that she had before joining Black, and it seems that she always had some romantic connection with her supervisors, all males. After securing an MBA in finance from Temple, she was ready for the big time. We know she met the VP of technical development at Black, a guy named Phillip Courtney, and she immediately started a romance with him, and this time the liaison got her the chief financial officer position at Black. She stayed a while with Courtney until his star started to fade and he got canned. Apparently, he had more on his mind than the weapons development. By the way, after leaving Black and moving to the West Coast for a job, he committed suicide.

"To get back, she needed a new benefactor, so she found Leon Black, the son of Edgar, the founder. So at last, she hit the jackpot. Leon is obviously no match for her, and she was able to take complete control of all administrative activities, including autonomy over the financial structure."

After turning a few pages in the portfolio, Dr. Landros continued, "That brings us up to the present, as far as her history goes, but there are some very interesting pieces to Nicole's personality. All the information we have gathered indicates that she has engaged in numerous romantic relationships but never for any other visible purpose than to achieve some objective. Even early in high school, reports indicate that she had some kind of sex with both the top athletes and the best scholastic students. We believe she acted from a strategy to be associated with *being the best.* At Texas, we dug up info on an advanced financial theory class that, early in the semester, she was clearly doing poorly. Somehow, she ended up with an 'A,' amid students' claims that she was seen more than once driving with her instructor, an older married man. They were convinced that there were no classes held during evenings in a Dodge Dart.

"After graduation," Dr. Landros continued, "she received several promotions at a firm that employed her. Her supervisor seemed to have made routine overtures to several women, but everyone interviewed believed that he scored only with our Michelina. There is no doubt that she got her job at Black as a result of her affair with Phillip Courtney, and when he left, she tuned into Leon Black.

"Let's get to the profile. Here's a woman who has never had a 'normal' relationship. She keeps totally to herself, sharing nothing with any man or woman. She is smart, but lives alone, and is devoid of any outward show of emotion. She uses men and never veers from her objective. The only time we ever found her choosing a friend was in high school when she befriended a girl who was an all-state swimmer and who went on to college on an athletic scholarship. This girl apparently was also attractive and an outstanding scholar. Something caused the relationship to deteriorate; we think Nicole could have been sexually attracted to this girl but that the girl rejected her.

"Nicole will avoid close relationships and clearly uses sex to satisfy a sense of purpose. In this scenario, she will leverage her body, appearance, sex appeal, and sexuality to gain whatever she needs. This leverage props up her self-esteem and regulates her sense of self-worth, which obviously was compromised at a very early age, perhaps by her parents. Finally, we believe Nicole equates intimacy with vulnerability."

The supervisor jumped in at this juncture, "OK, Dr. Landros, I think we get it. We either need to be able to get her in the act of committing a fraudulent activity, or, more remotely, to get her to admit that she had stolen money from her employer and indirectly from the Federal government. Our problem is, what would make her trust when she's been so successful without opening up to anyone?"

Landros responded, "I think she desperately wants to find someone. She has this bottled-up need to interact, to share, to show her skills to someone she can trust. I believe that for whatever reason, she feels hatred towards men, which makes her 'get what she wants' from them through her sexuality. You're not going to like this, but I believe that we can get to her through another woman, a woman like her--smart, attractive, an over-achiever. I believe Nicole Lawrence will allow this woman to enter her head, to show her the brilliance of her achievements. I hate to say it, but you are going to need a lover for your perp."

Silence hung over the room. Nothing was said for several minutes until one agent blurted out, "Marti Glassman." Then the spirited discussion began almost on cue, with each agent firing ideas into space.

After a while, the supervisor turned to Ruth Landros and said, "You know Marti. What's your take? She's been with the Bureau long enough and I know she's gone undercover before."

"She's perfect," replied Landros. "Tall, very attractive, and smart. Just what you need. I'll talk to her and review the situation. We should move quickly."

Chapter 54

NICOLE LIKED TO dine alone, at home. It gave her the opportunity to replay the day's events at her leisure and continually re-plan what had to be completed before she could permanently wrap everything up. Tonight, she was shopping at her favorite supermarket in the west side of suburban Detroit. Her cart was filled as she moved to the end of an aisle. As she turned the corner, she collided with Marti Glassman.

Conveniently, Marti was forced to drop everything as she slipped to one knee in the collision. Nicole quickly helped the woman up and picked up her packages.

"My goodness," claimed the woman. "I'm so careless--I'm sorry. I've been in a board meeting all afternoon and I'm just a bit frazzled."

Nicole smiled as she took in this woman. She had compellingly great looks and was a bit taller than Nicole's five-ten. Slim, she was elegantly dressed in a cashmere blazer over a black sweater, a black skirt and black pumps adorned with small silver buckles. She didn't dress provocatively, but she clearly looked feminine. Nicole took her for mid-forties, maybe 50, and her dark black hair had a fabulously short cut that showed sharp facial features.

"You work for a local company?" Nicole casually asked as she smiled. They both took a moment to straighten themselves out.

"No, I don't," Marti replied, as she extended her hand firmly. Her voice had the same low timbre that obviously commands attention. "My name is Patricia Gilcrist. I'm the president of Statistical Technologies. We have a division here in Detroit, but my home is in Virginia, and I'm just here for a couple of weeks while we're completing an acquisition."

They began to walk together towards the front of the store. Nicole shared her own vitals and they smiled as they both made small talk. As they reached the checkout, Gilcrist said, "Maybe this sounds silly, but look, I really am not in the mood for dinner alone. Why don't you join me tonight?"

For some reason unknown to her at the moment, Nicole eagerly accepted. She enjoyed talking to this smart, attractive woman, and she thought it would be nice to share a meal with her.

As they walked to their cars, Pat, as she liked to be called, asked, "Maybe it sounds odd to bring this up, but are you single?" Nicole responded, "I am."

They met later at a very popular Italian restaurant. Both women ordered martinis and the conversation was breezy; this was followed with two bottles of some Italian whites. Pat said she had been married, but divorced a few years ago, and had no children. She grew up in suburban Philadelphia, the only child of a father who was a banker in Philadelphia and a mother who taught at a day school outside of the city.

Pat was willing to talk about the road she had taken to achieve her current status. An MBA grad from Princeton, she had worked her way up from entry-level banking, struggling up the ladder until she landed a position with her present employer as chief financial officer. Then three years ago, after the chief operating officer retired, she was promoted to president of the privately owned company with revenue of almost two billion.

As they talked casually, friendly, a soft bond began to occur. Pat's features were similar to Nicole in their keenness--she had the architectural style that was completely to Nicole's liking. Nicole stared at her well made-up face. Pat had a high forehead and a shock of dark hair spilling over part of one side of her face. Her great teeth caught Nicole's attention when she smiled. Long sensuous lashes over dark eyes complemented the dark, almost Hispanic tone to her skin. Soft lines were just beginning to show around her eyes and at the corners of her mouth, which tantalized Nicole. Nicole thought Pat was the smartest woman she had ever met and they genuinely enjoyed each other's company.

Another round of drinks and a finely prepared dinner, both were feeling like this was the beginning of a friendship.

Nicole talked about her job and having to deal with a lunatic father and son. She told Pat that she was extremely stressed and had just about had it in her present position. She talked about living in Australia or Argentina, anywhere where she could start anew and build a financial consulting business. She spoke about some of the ideas that she would use in a startup.

Pat carefully spoke about her life as the president of her company. "You know, Nicole, you'd think this was a great opportunity, but I am constantly second-guessed by the board. I fought hard to make this acquisition happen. If it doesn't come off as expected, they will crucify me. Let me tell you something that I hope will go no further." Nicole nodded and her eyes burned with excitement.

Pat spoke confidentially, "I made this acquisition work. The numbers don't fully support the deal, but I made them look good. No one knows how I did it, but I have a feeling that you would understand."

At this revelation, Nicole put her hand over Pat's and smiled. "Pat, I know exactly what you mean. I've done my share of *stuff.* It's what we do to make it happen for us. We need to do it."

They both smiled; the warmth between them was palpable. After a sweet dessert wine, they were feeling ebullient. After Pat picked up the check, they made their way to their respective cars, first to Nicole's. They walked casually through the parking lot, talking about meeting again over the weekend.

Nicole pressed her remote. As she started to open the door, Pat slid her hands out of her coat pockets and touched Nicole's face. Nicole reached for the door but didn't open it. When she turned to face her, Pat leaned in, touched her face again and softly, so very softly, kissed Nicole on her lips, lingering there for a few moments.

Nicole started to draw away, but whatever turns on the hot switch in the human body began to tune to high velocity in Nicole. She felt warmth rush through her as she never had felt before. They stood in the darkened parking lot, first looking into each other's eyes. Then they kissed again, this time long and deep, as Nicole finally was able to release those bottled up emotions, which exploded into a multi-colored, mental fireworks display. They both released their grip and stood in the darkened lot looking into each other's eyes, saying nothing.

Finally, Nicole spoke hesitatingly, "I don't understand what just happened, but I'm totally uncomfortable with it and I need to go."

She moved into her seat, brushed her hair back, and, starting the car, said, "Look, Pat, I enjoyed tonight, you are a great person, but I am not ready to go any further with this, do you understand?"

Pat smiled, did a *360* and walked off to her car without a word. She was talking to herself when she uttered, "*In vino veritas*; I've got her!"

Nicole spent a restless night, reliving what just occurred. The hardest part for her to comprehend was the total release and the exquisite thrill that Pat gave to her. She repeated to herself several times, "This can't be happening. I won't let it happen. I've come too far to get careless now. Put it away. Forget about it."

Two agonizing days passed for Nicole. She feared that she had turned Pat away completely. Finally, during lunch, her cell phone rang. It was Pat, "Hey, how are you? Look, this is nothing serious. I've got two second-row seats to the Detroit Symphony this Saturday night. There's some kind of gala and Joshua Bell is going to play. It should be great. Interested?" Hesitantly, as the wheels turned at max speed, Nicole answered. "Sure, I'd love to. Why don't you pick me up?"

That night, the two gorgeous women, with all eyes on them, entered the Hall. As expected, the seats were sensational and the evening's performance was excellent. Afterwards, hey made small talk, nothing suggestive, as they walked down Woodward Avenue. They were both in a good mood as Pat drove back north towards the burbs.

After a few moments of silence, Pat thought that this was the right time to see if she could get a handle on Nicole's scheme. "I was really moved by what happened the other night. I know this must seem like a bizarre situation, and it is for me as well, but I have to tell you that I haven't been this excited for many years. I have slept with men over time and, to tell the truth, I always enjoyed it. But I must tell you, Nicole, two kisses with you and I was in heaven. I hope you felt that way too and I would like to explore this. But if you really don't want to get to know me better, and all that comes with it, let me know now, and I certainly won't bother you again."

Silence filled the car until Pat pulled up to the front entrance to Nicole's apartment building. Nicole then spoke with resolve, "Pat, drive around to my private garage entrance. I have an extra space."

It really did not take long for the two women, one feigning genuine heat and the other exploding with the emotion of a new-found experience, to rip off their clothes, fling them onto the nearest couch, and begin what would end up as marathon of sexual experimentation. Pat led Nicole carefully through all the orifice journeys, stopping to contain this neophyte nymph as her body heaved convulsively at each stop.

When the trip was over and they lay on the king-sized bed, Pat's arm gently playing with Nicole's hair, Pat softly spoke, "I have never had an experience like this, and I want to see you again. I'd like us to be friends and more, and I know now that you feel the same." She then so very lightly touched the nipple on one of Nicole's exquisitely shaped breasts, and round two of the all-night marathon began.

Chapter 55

THE FLIGHT FROM LaGuardia to Detroit Metro was relatively short, and JetBlue made it as pleasant as possible for David and Dianne Korman. They spent part of the flight finalizing the approach they would take when they faced Edgar Black. For the most part, however, David dozed, aware of the woman seated next to him, the love of his life, who had recently betrayed him. Over and over the visions of Dianne and her lover streamed through his brain. He was silent, knowing that despite their reconnection, he would never lose those images.

He thought back to the first time he saw Dianne at the pool of the luxurious Caribbean resort. He had been airlifted from Tel-Aviv Hospital just weeks before, after nearly being blown to bits by a suicide bomber in Israel. His body, bandaged on one side where bits of steel had torn him open, was covered with a dark-colored robe, an unusual, but essential covering, despite the heat and fierce sun.

His mind drifted to the first sight of Dianne, a tall, tanned, bronze goddess in a two-piece suit. He was immediately taken with her and, as they became acquainted and fell in love, his life began anew. The old images faded as the horror of the photos resurfaced, forcing him to awaken. He didn't talk about what he was experiencing, but he was sure that Dianne knew of his thoughts.

They arrived in Detroit early that evening, and after David rented a car, they headed directly to the offices of Black Technologies where Edgar awaited, alone in the offices of the empire he had built. David was deliberately oblique in his request to see Edgar, but his manner had suggested a sense of urgency and Edgar agreed to meet.

As they pulled into the parking garage, Dianne, for the third time that day, repeated the planned approach. It was as if she was in control of the situation, and she was comfortable with this.

Edgar welcomed them into his office and, as they had mutually agreed, he did not invite Leon or Nicole to join them. They spoke casually for a time. Edgar had not met Dianne before, so there was some small talk before David began.

"Edgar, when I first visited you, I told you that my interest was in satisfying myself about the death of Phillip Courtney. Officially, it was ruled a suicide, but events have taken place that have convinced me he was murdered. Why he was killed remains a mystery, but let me unfold the events surrounding his death and others."

At this point, David, slowly and in meticulous detail, began to describe the murders and all the events surrounding them--the murders themselves, the threats, the beating, the photographs.

"Edgar, do you believe that these are merely coincidences? Dianne is now sufficiently confident to go to the authorities with what we have. What I want to know, what I need to know, is whether you are the kingpin of this horror story, or just a pawn. Someone killed innocent people and hurt my family, and I am prepared to drop you in your tracks, right here in your office."

At this moment, he reached into his waistband, extracted a Beretta, and pointed it at Edgar Black.

Edgar, ashen and shaking, stared at him in total horror. He was not looking at the gun or feeling the fear generated by David's remarks. He stood, pushing his chair back with such power that it toppled over, rolling crazily along the floor.

"Korman, you're nothing but a lying bastard. I built this company with my own two hands. I would never, ever do anything to these people, and I would never sacrifice my company, my entire life's work. Why would I do these things? Take whatever shit you claim to have to any authority--police, FBI, anyone."

As he pounded on his desk with clenched fists, spittle flying from his already-foaming lips, Edgar, the consummate scientist, salesman, and dreamer, was processing the information just revealed to him, and the answer invaded his brain like a fast-moving cancer, eating up all in its way.

Suddenly, he stopped in mid-sentence. He knew the answer to David's questions. He knew it, and it was like an electric shock to the brain as he realized what a fool he had been.

Cash shorts appearing frequently, rumors circulating about information leaking to the competition despite tight security, and now innocent people being murdered--it was all true, his mind concluded.

What David said about the involvement of a woman from Detroit could only mean one person--Lawrence, his private slut, he believed. It must be Nicole Lawrence. So smart, so beautiful. In seconds, it all played out in Edgar's brain.

These horrors couldn't have taken place without Leon knowing about it so he must also be under her thumb. While she was so willingly taking care of him, she could have been doing Leon as well. Anger welled up in his throat.

David and Dianne stood motionless, watching this change in Edgar unfold before their eyes.

Edgar leaned with one hand on his massive desk as he spoke, "David, I am telling you this, and I know you have no reason to believe me, but I swear to you on everything that means anything to me, I had nothing to do with any of this. This company has been my life. I nurtured it, built it. I would do nothing to destroy it. I want to bring this nightmare to an end. I am going to ask something of you now.

"I know the ones who are probably at the bottom of all this, and I desperately need to confront them so that I know the extent of the damage. If all that you revealed to me is tied to some massive undertaking, they may have destroyed my company, my life, and all that it has meant to me. Give me time to find answers. Just twenty-four hours, that's all. I'm not going to run from this, I swear it to you. Come back here tomorrow, and I promise that I either will have the answers, or I will go to the police with you."

David and Dianne studied what was quickly becoming a shell of this all-powerful man, pleading for time. David spoke, "It's late, Edgar. Dianne and I are headed back to our hotel now. But tomorrow morning, by, let's say eight, if we don't hear from you, we will notify the local and federal authorities. Don't try to run. It will get you nowhere."

As they left, they could hear Edgar's throaty response, "Thank you, thank you."

Chapter 56

DANNY MERKEL LEFT the small Pasadena campus of the prestigious California Institute of Technology, with an ID photograph that bore the likeness of Olga Deripaska, but was printed with the name Esther Grodnik on it. He had been successful in getting the office of the Dean to circulate the photo, and someone had recognized her.

Now Danny began the part of his line of work that he enjoyed the most--tracking a suspect. It really didn't matter how well she concealed herself, Danny was sure he could find her. His first stop was the Department of Motor Vehicles, but she apparently either didn't have a license or had one in another name.

He was having a difficult time searching in that geographical area so he decided to take a different tack. Pasadena was in southern California, but Koslov's operations were north, in the San Francisco metro area. He began his search anew. After what seemed to be an eternity for this crack Israeli agent, he decided to return to Motor Vehicles and try a different approach.

After a meeting with the information technology people, they decided to search based on Deripaska's physical characteristics in both registration districts. After narrowing the field down to several thousand names, Danny began the arduous process of sifting through photos, looking for a match based on her Caltech photo. Five hours later, he got a hit.

Edna Drabinsky was living in an apartment in a shabby complex, a short distance from suburban San Francisco. Danny immediately got on the phone, notifying all agencies. Red flags went up globally as preparation for the assault on Olga's residence took shape. No one was to go near the complex until signals were given jointly by the CIA, FBI, and Israeli Intelligence.

Chapter 57

On a late Saturday afternoon in August, Gabriel Koslov was at home reading material from his native Chechnya when the doorbell rang and a courier was ushered into a secretive room at the back of his home.

The message from Olga was brief but to the point, "The project is in its final shake-down. Our climatologists are predicting the onset of storms that will be moving northeast from off the coast. These weather patterns will take the winds just off the Long Beach area within ten days to two weeks, exactly on target. I cleared out of my apartment and moved into the production facility, where I will stay until detonation, to eliminate any chance of identification. We have had rumors that my photo is being shown in the area. Make your plans quickly. There will be only one more message--you will receive it when we begin the loading the cargo. God bless the Republic of Chechnya."

Chapter 58

ON A WARM August afternoon, Agent Marti Glassman, alias Patricia Gilcrist, was sitting on a stone bench near the Joe Louis Memorial in downtown Detroit reading the *Wall Street Journal.* She wore dark glasses and was dressed in jeans and Nikes. She gave all appearances of a local enjoying the sun. After about fifteen minutes, another woman sat on the bench next to her and began feeding a bag of seeds to the crowd of hungry pigeons that soon surrounded her.

Marti spoke, turning to face the woman, "Hi, Jane, how've you been?"

"Just great, but more important, how's your love life?"

"Well, it's been getting hot and heavy. I feel certain that she's taken the bait and I'm ready to spring the trap. I'm scheduled to leave for the home office in Richmond next week. This will be the critical time. Are you ready to set up all the electronic equipment? I'll pick the night in a bit."

Jane said, "Sounds terrific. Everything is totally in place. Please remember, you have to get her tell you what and how she's been managing the dough. It's important that we get a full reading of all her shit. On another matter, we've gotten vibes from Intelligence that the laser project is in a disaster stage and there is talk that some of the detailed specs are leaking. If you can somehow get to this issue, it will be great. We don't know if there is a leak or whether Nicole has anything to do with it, but press her buttons on this."

"I'll tell you, Jane, I ought to get the Medal of Honor for this one. She can go all night. You guys read her perfectly."

They both smiled. Jane emptied the bag of seeds, stood, and walked casually away. Several minutes later, Marti folded the paper, tossed it into the trash backhanded and made her way back to her car. Consuming her thoughts was how and when she was going to get Nicole to reveal her nefarious fraud.

Chapter 59

FOR THE LAST several days, Nicole and Pat had been spending almost every evening together. Tonight Pat reminded Nicole that she would be leaving her Detroit location within the next week, and this put a gloom on the evening.

After a homemade dinner of salad with grilled salmon and a bottle of Pinot Grigio, Pat made her first move. "Nicole, I need to talk to you about us. I am going to be leaving Detroit next week and I want you to come with me. We can figure out how to deal with the future, but I am deeply in love with you, I know that for certain, and I want to spend my life with you. I've got some assets, not a lot, but we're smart enough to figure out how to make it. I'll do anything to be with you."

Nicole thought for a few moments, and then replied, "You really mean everything you said? I'd like to tell you something. I want to be with you as well, but there are things that you don't know about me, but you need to know."

Pat jumped in, "When I say anything, I mean it. I don't care what you've done. Listen, Nicole, I'll tell you something that no one even has the remotest notion that I did. This acquisition we just finished was doomed from the start. The board didn't want to make it, and the numbers were coming up short, but making it meant mega-bucks in stock and cash bonuses for me, so I made the numbers look strong. I tilted the research that our investment banker did on the growth prospects for the company. When I finished with them, they looked like gold and the board was forced to agree. How's that for balls?"

"Pat, I've also done some things that you may not want to be involved in. I've accumulated a shitload of money since I've been at Black. I've invested their cash in some really scary stuff, but everything has come up roses and I'm totally in the clear." Silence as Pat played this piece of her hand.

"Nicole, you are a fucking genius. How the hell did you do it?"

"I did a ton of research into the screwed-up housing market and the worthless bonds that Wall Street was peddling. First, I moved a pile of corporate cash offshore and did a bunch of deals, and then I made some gutsy moves in the bond market. I bet against the market by buying swaps on the shittiest CDO's I could find. Pretty soon, every schmuck on Wall Street was dying to do business with me. Some even tipped me off to the worst packages available. I negotiated my way out of the unwinds with high six figures in my pocket, that is, in a Swiss bank's pockets."

"Unbelievable, my darling. You're the greatest. How the hell could you get away with it? Isn't somebody overseeing the money movement?"

"Well, my sweet Patricia, I have a silent partner in these transactions. At least he thinks he's a partner. Leon Black, the son of the CEO of the company, is in my back pocket. He's like a dog with his tongue hanging out. All I need to do is show him what I've got or grab onto his totem pole, and he is a bowl of Jell-O. He actually believes that I'm going to paradise with him. So, we both know something new about each other. Still interested?"

Pat leaned in to Nicole's face and whispered. "Try and stop me. I still have one question. Black is supposed to be putting together a laser weapons system that the world is talking about, but I hear talk that not only are they in big trouble in the design phase, but there are rumors that the foreign crowd is going to push them out of the picture. I'm amazed that with all this stuff going on, you were still able to move that kind of cash with no one suspecting anything."

"Well Pat, you might as well hear the whole story. I've been leaking some of the details to some outsiders for big cash. Not enough to give them the whole picture, but enough for them to line my pockets."

Pat laughed, "Well, I think I found the perfect woman." She leaned over and planted a large, wet kiss on Nicole. "How are we going to get out of here? Passports are no good. They'll find us as soon as this hits the fan."

"We are going to have to do some quick work, Pat. I have two perfectly forged passports for me. I'll take care of getting some for you. Don't worry, my sweet, I'll take care of all of the nitty-gritty."

As the two women were planning their escape to the Garden of Eden, racing through "Patricia's" mind was her own escape plan from this sordid mess. For her, this evening's planned entertainment was going to be different. Her clothes were casually tossed onto a mauve love seat in Nicole's bedroom, where she had carefully placed an elegant, beaded, Louis Vuitton bag on the corner of the nearby loveseat. Embedded in the inside lining of the purse, with a tiny pinhead hole set into a *bling* on the bag, was a high-tech, digital voice recorder, the latest device in the government's war on crime. It had a recording capacity of 900 hours.

Pat mused to herself that this was more than she needed to crack this case and send the results of the Nicole Lawrence affair up the line, maybe even with a promotion. She knew she had handled herself perfectly, and she couldn't think of any mistakes that she had made. Nicole's trading of information to foreign sources about Black's development in laser technology was not even suspected by the government. Marti Glassman had struck it rich, and she felt as good as she had felt in a long while.

She casually gazed over at the purse where, in a side pocket of the fully zipped bag was her official government ID, badge, and a nine mm, snub-nosed Glock.

At this very moment, Leon, unable to concentrate on the company's problems and enraged at the lack of attention by Nicole, decided to confront her. She had been avoiding him like the plague lately, and whenever he tried to get a date set for their getaway, it was *stall city*. Angry at being brutally manhandled by his father, he globalized his anger and was determined to get to the bottom of Nicole's rejection.

He left the corporate offices early and called her cell phone, hoping for a face-to-face meeting. After calling several times, when all he got was the ubiquitous, *not available-leave a message* crap, he fired a perfect strike with his phone onto the passenger-side window and furiously pounded hard on the steering wheel.

Leon decided to drive to her apartment and, in his imagination, teach her who was really in charge. The anger in Leon's brain was palpable and it demanded reparations.

In bed next to Pat, Nicole glanced at the caller ID on her phone and listened intently to Leon's cell-phone diatribe. Assuring Pat that everything was alright, she put on sexy white mules and a sheer, off-white, silken robe. After tightening the sash, she sat down pensively on the bed.

Minutes later the door buzzer sounded continuously as if someone held a finger on it; Nicole made no attempt to get off the bed.

Within a few moments, the door came crashing open. A painting of wildflowers hanging next to the door fell to the floor. To the racket of shattering glass, a wild tornado stormed into the living area. Seeing nothing, Leon quickly moved to the large bedroom, and what his eyes saw dropped his jaw. There on the bed was Nicole, sitting unemotionally at bedside in a sexy white robe, staring directly at Leon, and next to her was a nude woman, with a sheet hastily pulled up over her. He could scarcely catch his breath at this shocker, but when he did, he began to scream at Nicole.

"You fuckin' fag, you slut. I get it now; you sucked me into a mess. This is where you spend your time. Tell me, whore," as he looked at Pat, "did she promise you a life together in some god-damn foreign country? I got your plan now. I gave you to my father so we would always know what was happening, and all the while you were screwing this dyke. His company is going down the tubes and you're the cause. You had people killed, all on the pretense of setting me up, right?"

He continued to rage, spittle flying wildly from his lips, "You know what I'm going to do to you and your slut?" He began to move to the edge of the bed, fists clenched.

The next moment, all Leon heard was the closing of the night table drawer next to Nicole's bed. The next instant, three successive, closely grouped shots from a thirty-eight caliber Smith and Wesson stopped him in his tracks and dropped him in a heap, spattering a blood trail onto the bed sheets and the white, feathery shoes.

In a moment, after the shock of the scene, Pat, still shaking, screamed at Nicole, "What the hell did you do? Who is this guy? Are you out of your mind?"

"I had to, Pat," she calmly replied. "Who he was is not important now, and the less you know of him the better. I used him, but I never could stand his sweaty hands on me. You saw that he was going to kill me, so I reacted first. Come on, sweetheart, the plan will still work. We just need to get rid of the body and ..."

"I guess I understand," Pat quickly responded, as she moved to the love seat and began to dress. "This whole scene just totally has my head spinning. I've never been involved in a murder." After quickly pulling on her t-shirt and sandals, she reached for her purse and started for the bathroom.

"Nicole, believe me, I'll do whatever needs to be done here, but I just need a minute to get my head together."

Minutes went by before Pat returned to the bedroom. Nicole was standing naked at the side of the bed where she had just pumped three shots into Leon Black, her hands holding the robe that she had removed after the shots were fired.

"Why did you need to go to the john to get yourself together and why did you need to take your purse with you?" questioned a suspicious Nicole. "Let me see your purse, Pat. Toss it over here for a minute."

With a one-handed toss aimed directly at Nicole, Pat raised her right hand producing her government issue Glock, pointed directly at Nicole. "Drop your weapon, Nicole, you're under arrest. I'm with the FBI."

Nicole, ashen-faced, looked at Pat, and coldly fired two shots from the weapon that was hidden under the robe covering her hands. Pat fired, but it was a wild shot and a little too late. Nicole's first shot tore through Pat's cheekbone and the second took its intended route directly through her forehead. As she fell back onto the loveseat, Pat fired several more shots wildly. Blood was spurting from what was once an attractive face as she slid lifelessly onto the floor.

Once her hands had steadied, Nicole poured herself a double Grey Goose, neat, and downed it. She began to move quickly and with purpose. She took Pat's purse and, feeling along the inside lining, extracted the recorder and camera and crushed them with the heel of her shoe, pushing the fragments near Leon's body. She wiped her prints from her own weapon and placed it in Leon's hand. She struggled, but was able to move his body so that it faced Pat's.

She quickly packed what she needed and opened the small floor safe hidden under a corner of the living room carpet. She withdrew the fake passports, about fifty thousand in cash, and Swiss identification documents and stopped to review her plan.

Fuck it, she cursed to herself, as she realized that the flight tickets to Los Angeles and then to Sydney, Australia, and finally a Jetstar commuter flight to New Zealand were in her locked office safe. It was a slip that occurred because she had made the arrangements by cell phone from her office and received the tickets by courier, not wanting anything arriving to her home address. She had carefully studied locations for her new start and determined that Aukland, a city of just over a million residents in the north island of New Zealand, had the requisite infrastructure she would need to thrive and build a new financial consulting practice.

She dressed quickly, and as she reached the door, she looked back at the grotesque scene, then forced the door back onto its hinges and coldly made her way to the garage. The Jaguar XJ roared as she hit the engine button, springing blue and white lights on the dash into motion. She drove carefully for about eight miles to a part of metro Detroit that had economically suffered many years ago and was a ghost town of closed shops and refuse strewn on both walkways and the streets.

She pulled into a self-storage lockup. She parked the Jag, unlocked the grimy handle of the pull-up door, and quickly pulled out into the dark alleyway in an unregistered Chevy Malibu with New Jersey plates. After placing her Jag into the storage unit, she locked the garage and drove the older, black Chevy to her next-to-last destination--Black Technologies' corporate headquarters.

Chapter 60

EDGAR BLACK SAT slumped over his desk, his hands wrapped around his head. Swarming in his now overcharged brain was a recap of all the odd circumstances that occurred in the company since he fired Phillip Courtney--all the "temporary cash shortages," rumors of leaked information, weapons development problems, and the tragic death of Phillip.

With all this swirling through Edgar's head like a tornado, he saw at the vortex the vision of Nicole Lawrence. He saw himself relishing sex with the beautiful young woman, but realized that, as an old man, he was a joke, just a crazy-ass fool.

At this late hour, the offices were entirely deserted. Edgar started by calling Leon's home. Genny hadn't heard from him that day, and she worriedly told her father-in-law that Leon usually called if he was going to be late. Leon's cell produced nothing; Edgar left urgent messages. As he expected, he could only leave a voice message on Nicole's phone, but he didn't even bother.

He poured himself a drink from the familiar black label, neat, and forced it down. As he sat back in his oversized, leather executive chair, the effect of the alcohol and the stress began to take its toll. He soon slumped over his desk waiting to hear from Leon. He wasn't aware of how long he had slept, but he was awakened by a familiar sound, the clack of high heels on the marble office floor. Edgar knew who it had to be. His anger grew quickly into a mental tsunami as he stalked into Nicole Lawrence's office.

The vision he saw was not the sex symbol that he had fantasized about but, to him, an apparition of the devil herself. She was down on both knees, her skirt hiked up almost to her waist, beside her open desk drawer that contained a small safe. Edgar gripped the tufted back of her office chair to keep himself steady as he spoke in a monotone, "I bet you think you're going to get away with all this; killing innocent people, ruining a company that took me a lifetime to build. Tell me, was my son involved in all this with you?"

Startled at first, Nicole kept the safe open as she continued to empty its contents into a large tote.

He continued, "You know you'll never get out of this building alive. Old and stupid, yes I am, but frail, not on your life. A question, for which I guess I now know the answer, was what you expected to get out of your scheme worth all the destruction you caused?"

Still kneeling, Nicole continued her silence and stared at Edgar with a sardonic grin. When she arose, Edgar saw what she had extracted last from the safe. It was a small-barreled weapon that she pointed at Edgar. She wasted no time. Her regimen of weekly target practice was evident as she fired three shots, the first hitting him in his chest and exploding his shirt open, the second entering near his heart, and the third blowing open the bridge of his nose. He stood for a moment, and then fell backwards still holding the chair back as he dropped to the floor.

Nicole wiped the weapon clean with a piece of cloth and dropped it next to the growing mass of blood that was once Edgar Black. She left the offices quickly and pointed the Chevy towards Detroit Metro Airport. As she drove, she opened her Blackberry and confirmed her first-class seat on the red-eye to Los Angeles.

Edgar lay on the bloody carpeted office floor; his breathing was labored in short gasps, but he had enough strength left to take out his cell and dialed the number David had given him. When David answered, the only sound he heard was the gurgling, shallow rasp uttering, "It was her; she's getting away."

David implored for more information, but he heard nothing but the noise of the phone dropping to the floor.

Chapter 61

Danny Merkel drove in an unmarked Ford Fiesta to the apartment complex listed on Edna Drabinsky's driver's license. It was a twenty-minute drive from his office, and he planned to investigate before the troops landed. What faced him when he arrived was a nondescript apartment complex dressed in lumpy, pink stucco, flaking paint on some of the shutters. He estimated twelve units, four flats to a floor divided by a narrow central corridor. Parking was in front of the complex, and there were four cars there. Shredded hedges separated the lot from the units, and Danny could see scattered cans and bottles behind the hedges.

He decided to ring the rusty bell of apartment number one, usually belonging to a manager. A tall woman clearly in her late sixties answered his ring. Puffy face, heavily rouged, she wore her hair, already grey, tied in a bun that looked so tight that it must be painful, thought Danny. She wore a dark crimson kimono dotted with flamingoes and black satin slippers.

After identifying himself with an Israeli intelligence badge, he showed her the photo of Olga. "What brings a Jewish detective to this part of the world," she responded with an accent that hinted of northern Europe. "Ya, I know her. She lives in 2E on the second floor, the end unit," she said. "No need to look for her, she's not there. She always parks near the end stairway, but I haven't seen her car in a while, maybe a week or so. Her mailbox is overflowing with junk; it's becoming a problem. My husband and I, we try to keep this place clean," she defended, as if she were a palatial groundskeeper.

"Do you know what kind of car she drives?" Danny questioned."

"Absolutely, it's an old Honda Civic, dark green. Nobody ever comes to see her. She leaves early and comes home late, but as I said, we haven't seen her in a while. Want her license? We keep a current list of all cars and licenses so no junkers end up in the parking lot. As you can see, we really take care of things here."

Within ten minutes, Olga Deripaska's photo, residence, car, and license were broadcast agency-wide, and within an hour, 2E was being processed for everything. The flat was totally empty of clothing, toiletries, or any evidence that anyone had ever lived there. Prints sent to CIA headquarters quickly revealed her as a Russian, with strong Chechen revolutionary ties. The question left was simply, where was she?

That afternoon, satellites were trained on an area fifty miles in each direction of the apartment. Danny and his team reviewed the photos and found three medium-to-large factory complexes near one another with cars and trucks parked in the communal lots and one large, single-user building approximately fifteen miles from where Olga stayed. That factory seemed deserted; there were no vehicles outside. The completed data was submitted, and a U.S. and Israeli international force, convinced that this was the most likely facility, readied for an assault.

While the assault was beginning, Gabriel Kozlov's throwaway cell purchased that day began its irritating ring. The caller delivered news that Koslov did not expect, and he hurriedly hung up. He immediately dialed Olga and recited the following message, "They know where you are. Move as quickly as possible."

Olga replied calmly, "I was always prepared for something like this. The subject has already been loaded on the truck. We will leave at once."

"Excellent, dear patriot; stay in touch along the way. Remember, no interstate highways. Stay on the local route that we planned."

"Gabriel, I've lived for this almost all my life. I am ready to complete my mission. I must tell you, though, that, in addition to the rapidly pushing Santa Ana winds, there is a prediction for very strong storms approaching the coast imminently. We may be headed for a difficult trip to Long Beach. But don't give it a care; whatever the adversities--this operation will shock the world."

Chapter 62

WITHIN MINUTES, A white, converted Ford Econoline wagon braced with a rigid steel undercarriage holding a modified nuclear device left the San Francisco location heading south. And just as it left, the storm, led by vicious strong winds and heavy rain, began pelting the roads.

The contents of the vehicle weighed about five-hundred pounds, and the detonator for the TNT that would begin the chain reaction was synched to an iPhone, being held by the steady hands of Olga Deripaska, who sat in the passenger seat next to Andrei, the driver. The iPhone, strapped to Olga's wrist with a tight leather bracelet, was pre-programmed to the first seven digits. Only a simple entry of three remaining digits on the cell phone separated California from total devastation.

Determined as she was, Olga was worried about the weather over the nine-hour trip as well as the perceived nearness of her enemy. The night was cast in a shroud of grey. The denseness of the rain, propelled by high winds, was slowing traffic to a crawl. They were committed to staying on local roads, which were becoming paralyzed by the unexpected change in the weather. Within hours, roads, not built for this condition, were becoming flooded, and at intersections, the water was beginning to move rapidly along roadsides, overflowing onto the streets. Driving at night, the water looked black and menacing and the rain pounded the windshield, making vision murky. To Olga and Andrei, it was beginning to look like an end-of-the-world menace. As Andrei drove slowly, desperately trying to avoid already flooded roadways, Olga began to develop an alternate strategy.

Though the five hundred pounds of TNT, plutonium, and other metals were secured into the frame of the truck, Olga and Andrei were becoming fearful that the stress of the vehicle shifting side to side would somehow shift the delicate cargo and prevent detonation. Olga theorized that if the trip to Long Beach became impossible, she had several nearby cities where detonation could take place.

As the truck rumbled slowly towards its destination, a massive military source was attacking the giant factory that was empty, save for equipment and trash scattered throughout. Danny and his team of agents were scouring the building for any evidence of what had been there. Quickly, a Hazmat team was reporting high levels of radioactivity throughout the floor. It was clear that a heavy vehicle had been used; they were able to determine the weight based on impressions left on the factory floor. Trash containers throughout were filled with contaminated radioactive clothing and pieces of dismantled equipment. It was immediately clear that a truck containing some type of hazardous material had left within the last few hours. But where, in which direction, and carrying what type of weapon, was unknown.

The agents in the building were communicating with sources internationally, and roadblocks were being set at main roads in every direction. However, because the vehicle was a common size and because the storm had arrived in full force, the task was becoming impossible.

In thwarting many potential terrorist attacks, it often comes down to a single, isolated piece of information that is obtained purely by chance. Despite all the scientific techniques that agencies have developed, a simple shred of data has often betrayed the perpetrators.

Not seeing anything in the factory that could identify the truck, Danny decided to drive the roads leading from the factory to the main roads. As he reached the stop sign marking the entrance to a main road, he glanced to the left, and what he saw exploded in his brain. There on the corner was a bank, a local bank with a brightly lit ATM facing the road.

He immediately jumped on the phone to headquarters, "There's a bank on the corner. They must have security cameras. Let's get them opened and maybe we get a view of the street. Phone lines buzzed and cars with blinking lights surrounded the bank as the bank manager arrived, leading a parade of armed militia to the room where the video display was housed. They all huddled around the screen where they squinted at a picture cut into four parts. The camera angles not only showed the ATM display clearly, but a longer view that extended obliquely into the street.

They sat silently while the screen was scrolled back sufficiently and stopped at a point about twenty minutes prior. Suddenly, as the timer moved forward, a misty vision appeared--a truck, clearly a white Ford Econoline, stopped at the intersection and turned right onto the main road. Now they had a direction, a recognizable photo, and even a license plate of the vehicle that was shipping its doomsday cargo somewhere.

The relentlessness of the down-pouring rain was getting to Olga. The nonstop torrent never let up, pounding the windshield so hard that even with wipers it was becoming difficult to see. Cars had pulled off onto the shoulders and berms of the road. All Andrei saw as he drove was a red blur from the vehicle in front of him. He feared that if this vehicle pulled over, he would be lost. They knew that, although it could not be seen, there was a rivulet running alongside the road. They heard the noise of rapidly moving water, and Olga feared that rising water would wash out the road at some point.

Andrei directed Olga, "Maybe we should pull off to the side. It's becoming impossible to see what's ahead."

"We don't stop; we stop for nothing. Completion of our mission is too close," exclaimed Olga nervously. Her mind was racing back and forth from her university days, when it became crystal clear that she would be working for the Chechen revolution, to the blur in front of her. When they crossed a small bridge, she could see the torrential walls of water creeping closer to the overpass.

Danny was a passenger in the helicopter that followed a main road south towards Los Angeles. "I don't think they would chance the Interstate," he shouted to the pilot. "They would know that we'd block off all access to those highways. It makes sense that they'd follow this road."

Lights from the chopper bounced along the road, bringing the vision of vehicles parked on the sides, with fewer and fewer attempting to fight through this storm. They saw the river, now clearly crashing at its banks and in places even flooding the road.

The pilot conjectured, "They would be crazy to continue with a truck loaded with some kind of nuke."

"No, they'll continue. They know if they stop, the chances of their plot succeeding would be screwed. They must be heading to L.A. It's the only logical destination. We have to find them, we just have to."

Minutes later, Andrei noticed that there was no longer any traffic in front of him. He was speeding down a road with no forward vision, and the only sounds heard were the water's rapid flow in the river below and rushing sounds of water pouring onto the road. About a hundred yards ahead, there was a sharp right turn, marked by a sign that neither of them was able to see.

Too late, Andrei swerved to make the turn. The truck's rear tires, unwieldy with the large load, skidded onto the berm and immediately caused the front of the truck to slide in a sideways direction. Olga screamed as the truck spun crazily and slid off the road.

Once onto the soft earth soaked with the river overflow, the truck began its descent into the raging waters below. Wheels spinning, the vehicle began to turn upside-down, landing on its side in the current, and quickly becoming part of the flow of the river. Trees smashing into the truck, mud hurled against it, and the overflowing torrent was carrying it on its side, with the precious cargo still holding fast to the frame of the Ford.

In the cab, Olga looked at the figure of Andrei, or what was left of him. His head was pushed forward onto the windshield, blood rushing from a mangled face, as his body lay at an awkward angle flayed by the force of the water filling the cab.

Danny suddenly looked downriver to his right and saw the lights of the truck blinking haphazardly as it spun out of control. "That's got to be it! Get over to the truck; it's fallen into the river. I have to get to it before anything in it detonates."

The chopper turned sharply and followed the flow of the truck as it was carried by the river. "You need to drop me onto the truck. I have to get to whatever is in the cargo. I need to see how the device detonates."

"Are you fuckin' crazy, man? I'm not doin' that. You'll get swept off it as soon as you land on it."

Danny pulled his service revolver and screamed over the sound of the rotors and the raging water. "Do it or I'll put one in your eye and jump myself."

Reluctantly, the pilot maneuvered as best he could. The chopper rocked erratically over the truck as Danny leapt for the side panel that was facing up. He hit the truck hard and held on to the side-view mirror and the truck molding as he steadied himself.

He began to inch his way forward, buffeted by the lashing flow. He was able to pull the passenger door open a crack and push his knee into the cab to keep it open. When he looked up, Danny came face-to-face with the terrified face of Olga Deripaska.

He pulled feverishly on her coat to drag her away from the truck. She fumbled with a revolver in her purse and tried to resist him, but he overpowered her and pulled her out. Just then, they were both hit by a wall of water pushing them away from the truck.

She screamed at him over the din, "We are all going to die. God bless Chechnya!" Then she finally got a firm hold of the phone that, though tethered to her wrist, was being tossed about, slapping at her arm and wrist.

Suddenly, they were separated and Danny could no longer see her in the black water's rush. When he surfaced, he saw Olga ten yards away from him. In the shadowy distance, Danny saw the outline of a bridge crossing the river. Instinctively, he realized that if she could somehow right herself on the concrete supports of the bridge, she could pull the device attached to her wrist with one hand and enter whatever the code was to detonate the weapon in the truck, still only about thirty yards in front of her.

It looked to Danny like the truck was being pulled to one side of the river, which slowed down its forward movement. He judged that there were only minutes until Olga would reach the bridge supports. Danny pushed himself to his physical limit, gaining ground slowly. The chopper stayed close by, spotlighting where she was. Olga went under and, using all her strength, moved towards the bridge, allowing the phone to move in all directions, but still held firmly on her wrist.

Moments later, Danny reached where he thought Olga should be, and he went under, grabbing at her leg. They were both drawn down to the bottom. He opened his eyes, but the churning water was too dark to see through. With all his strength, he drove her flailing body down hard into the river's floor and shifted behind her. With her free hand she was already grasping the phone and appeared to be entering numbers. Danny saw her with the phone tautly held by the strap and starting the code input.

All he could do was grab for her neck and, with all the strength he had left, pull it back, again and again. Her hands broke free of the phone as she tried to pull his death grip from her body. His lungs were burning, and as he gave one last pull, he felt her hands drop from his grip.

Danny released one hand free and pulled the lifeless body to the surface. He desperately needed air, but he also needed the phone attached to Olga's wrist.

Danny was bone weary as he reached the bridge supports and lashed himself to them, still holding the lifeless body in a death grip as the chopper's lights beamed down at him and rescue helicopters began arriving at the scene.

After tethering Olga's body to the lift, they both were raised aloft by the helicopter. Danny looked down at the still raging torrents and the truck carrying the nuclear device hung up on its side on the shallows. Once he was safely brought aboard, he carefully cut the phone away from her body. He quickly opened its back and removed the battery. He leaned back in his seat, totally spent, and just before he drifted away into the unconscious, he caught a glimpse of Olga's face. Her eyes were open and it seemed that she was staring at him.

The next day, the skies cleared and a bright sun shone; the river, though still overflowing its banks, was becoming quiet once again. The military took control of the vehicle and pulled it from the muddy shoal. A dozen men in protective suits were dismantling the nuclear device from the truck.

That morning, a task force raided the Koslov estate. When they arrived, the house was silent. In the magnificent great room, a silent Gabriel Koslov lay back in his chair, blood covering his face, the pistol lying on the carpeted floor alongside him, his mouth twisted in a grimace emblematic of a failed mission. There was no one else in the home.

That same day, Danny Merkel, lying in a hospital bed, was given the details of the device that was intended for mass destruction and was told of the probable targets somewhere in southern California. He closed his eyes and allowed all his emotions to sweep over him. With tears welling in his eyes, he sank into a prescribed sleep. The lifeless face of Olga Deripaska remained staring at him for a moment until he drifted into a peaceful place.

Chapter 63

By early the next morning, Black Technologies' headquarters were abuzz with federal and state officials, investigators, and, of course, David and Dianne Korman. In a separate set of offices, Leon's wife, Genny; Edgar's wife, Veronica; and Marti Glassman's family sat in stunned silence. The FBI's Behavioral Science investigators were at Nicole's apartment examining the gruesome scene.

David was recounting the results of his investigation to the authorities as Nicole Lawrence's profile was being distributed to law-enforcement agencies nationwide. David was able to describe the last meeting he and Dianne had with Edgar and his last gasping words.

Meanwhile airport, train, and bus stations were on high alert; state police were manning all roads connecting to the facility. The lead investigator was an FBI senior executive who had set up headquarters in the company's boardroom. Hours ticked by as preliminary reports were being assembled. The press corps from all the major networks and wire services, hungry for any information, was housed in a room adjoining the factory's distribution center.

A preliminary release was issued confirming the death of an FBI agent and two related parties, but added that more information was to be released on related homicides. The release also described briefly that an undetermined amount of corporate funds was missing, and a woman named Nicole Lawrence was being sought as a party to the crimes. Photos of Lawrence were included.

Chapter 64

On the previous evening, relaxing in her first-class seat, headed for Los Angeles, Nicole's new identity, Laura Benson, finally began to unwind. Now a redhead with preplanned changes in her makeup and eye color, she gulped the ice-filled Grey Goose. The events of the past evening replayed in her mind, especially the destructive end of what she thought might have been a long-term relationship with Patricia, or whatever her real name was. She wondered in amazement how she could have been duped by this federal agent, but she also mused about the realization that she was a lesbian; she really did get it on and feel it for once. All the men she bedded, not caring, not wanting, and finally she knew. Maybe she had known for some time, but the delicious sex with her lover assured her that someday she would be able to seek a relationship with another woman.

As she relaxed, Nicole glanced across the aisle and saw a woman, younger than she, earphones in place, working at a laptop on what Nicole noticed was an Excel spreadsheet. She had reddish brown hair pulled back in a ponytail. Good looking, small frame, Nicole thought. She wore jeans and a long-sleeved, yellow shirt.

By habit, Nicole moved across the aisle. "Getting a lot of work done on a plane; wish I could do that."

The woman hesitated, and then looked up. "Oh, I always have trouble, too, but I have a meeting early tomorrow, and I'm trying to get all the pieces together."

"Well, then don't let me bother you," replied Nicole with an unassuming smile.

"No, I need a break, anyway. Are you going to L.A. for work?" They shook hands and chatted. "Gwen Hansen; I worked for a real estate company in New York, but I left them last month, and I may be moving west. Been interviewed, but you know how long it takes for a large corporation to make a decision."

The conversation was congenial and light. After a while, the banter slowed and the woman returned to her laptop, and Nicole closed her eyes, thinking of the life ahead of her. After several hours, the flight became more and more bumpy, shaking Nicole from sleep. Suddenly, an announcement came from the pilot, "Well, we have some nasty weather in the Los Angeles area. A bunch of storms came in and they want us to wait a while to see if it clears. No need to be concerned. Just stay buckled."

After some nasty air pockets that sent trays sliding, another announcement said, "I'm sorry to tell you this, but Los Angeles is really getting hit by these late summer storms and LAX is closed. We are going to need to land at McCarran in Las Vegas. We will let you off for a while until conditions improve, and then we'll be taking you on to L.A."

Immediate shouting rose up from the masses about the consequences of sitting in Vegas-- late arrivals, missed pickups, and late meetings, as well as every conceivable gripe. Gwen turned to Nicole and said sarcastically, "Boy, this is not going to be my lucky day. I really needed to get to L.A. in the morning. Who knows how long we'll sit in Sin City?"

Nicole was already contemplating how long a layover would she be able to handle before her Air New Zealand flight took off. She was also worried that they would already be looking for her, and that time was working against her.

When the United flight landed, Nicole, the genius mogul, already had a plan for this unexpected disturbance. She stopped a worried Gwen Hansen and offered a proposal. "Hey, Gwen, I've got an idea. It's about a five-hour drive from here to L.A., done it many times. What do you think about renting a car together? We can be out of here quickly, and I can catch my flight to Seattle and you can easily make your meeting."

Gwen came back after a few seconds, "It's a roll of the dice when and if we will get back on. They won't give us any clue how long we'll be holed up here. I'm game for a 50-50 split."

In under an hour, Gwen and Nicole, Starbucks in hand and luggage in tow, were already on the Interstate headed for Los Angeles. Their spirits were up and the conversation upbeat. "Laura, you are terrific. I don't know how you came up with this idea so fast."

Laura, aka Nicole, smiled back and thought, if she had some notion of what I had in mind as soon as we knew we were landing here, she might be a little less buoyant.

The drive through the desert in total darkness, with no cars in either direction, gave the view a phantasmagoric quality. The blue display on the dash added to the dreamlike vision. They spoke about their separate plans for the future, relationships, likes and dislikes. To Gwen it was a really pleasant trip. She thought, this woman is just terrific. She thinks fast and from her clothes, she must be really successful. She'd be a great friend. I really like her.

About two hours into the drive, Nicole looked over at Gwen. "Hey kiddo, do you mind if we stop for a minute. No, don't laugh, I don't need to pee. I just need some open air and to stretch my legs. I'm a little older than you and rigor mortis is setting in."

Gwen laughed, "Sure thing. I'd like to get out, too. Good to stretch."

The side of the road was rocky and it was a bumpy slowdown. They both got out, and Gwen stood leaning against the driver door, looking up at the vastness of the open sky, filling her lungs with the warm, dry air. Nicole walked a bit, bending down to stretch for a minute and then approached her unwitting companion, her heels making crunching sounds on the roadside.

When she reached Gwen, she stood face-to-face, and placed one hand on her shoulder, smiling; Gwen smiled back. The other hand, holding a palm-sized pointy rock, came crashing down onto Gwen's forehead--once, twice, three times, the repeated movements of her hand driving deeply into Gwen's forehead at first, and then, as she began to drop, into the top of her head.

Within minutes, the now lifeless body of Gwen Hansen was rolled off the berm and into a small roadside gully. Next to her was her purse with the driver's license and credit cards of Nicole Lawrence. The newly emerged goddess of evil had thought through her final plan as soon as she knew the flight would be indefinitely detained.

She opened Gwen's small carry-on bag and decided to empty the few things into her own baggage. As she got closer to Los Angeles, she would toss the luggage and all the shredded documents identifying the dead woman onto the road. The plan evolved into perfection; the body of so-called Nicole Lawrence lay in a gully on the side of the road. There probably would not be much of her by the time the desert inhabitants had their meals. Then the new Nicole, with a new identity, a new passport, new driver's license, and a Swiss account number, would be on her way to a new beginning.

For just a moment, she wiped her hands, looked up at the sky, and screamed, "See all you fuckin' Texas hillbillies, I did it!"

Chapter 65

ONE WEEK LATER, all the fireworks began to die down, and the facts were beginning to fall into place. It was clear to all the authorities that Nicole Lawrence was guilty of planning or committing at least six murders. The FBI estimated that she had misappropriated almost a billion dollars, probably hidden in some far-off place. An international manhunt was on for her, but she seemed to have disappeared from the earth. A receiver was appointed to take over the now-bankrupt Black Technologies, and an inquiry was begun in Congress relating to the contract that Black secured for the laser weapons system.

Several high-ranking Department of Defense officials were being questioned and indictments were expected. Some congressmen were facing scrutiny for their lack of judgment in giving the contract to such an uncontrolled entity. The CPA firm that gave an unqualified opinion on the financial statements of the company was under investigation by the Securities and Exchange Commission.

On the other front, Danny Merkel was awarded for his heroism in preventing a nuclear catastrophe. Gabriel Koslov's staff and all the engineers were being held for interrogation in a foreign detention center. The Republic of Chechnya vociferously denied any involvement. The family of the FBI's informant, Marti Glassman, had already secured counsel and was planning to file a lawsuit against the government for negligence in not providing adequate security for their daughter during her relationship with Nicole.

And in New York, David and Dianne Korman took a much-needed quiet time. They had been questioned multiple of times by both federal and state authorities and faced the possibility of action taken against them for not reporting the events earlier. In Boston, Susan continued to rebuild her life as a physician. She and Patty were quietly married with the blessing of David and Dianne. The Korman family attempted to find some explanation for all the events that occurred, and David sought counseling for his continued feelings of distrust and alienation from Dianne.

That fall, on a warm Sunday in Manhattan, the sun was bright and the streets were crowded with New Yorkers who adored being out and enjoying the wonders of the Big Apple. David was finishing the *Sunday Times* and Dianne had just gotten off the phone with the lead federal agent when the phone rang. "Get it, will you," echoed David from the tufted chair facing the east skyline.

She listened quietly, then handed him the phone, a grim look twisting her facial features, and she watched David's reaction. His iterations were simply "Yes," "I see," and "Uh-huh." He continued to listen to the message for a long time, and then replied, "Thank you for the information."

She searched his eyes but saw nothing. He thought for a long moment, and then shared. "They found Nicole or what's left of her body on the Interstate outside of Vegas. The animals had a field day with her. There was very little left of her, but the body seems to indicate a match. All her identification was with her. They are trying to match dental records, but the heat and the desert animals that ate her for dinner are making it difficult. She's got bruises all over her head so they're not ruling out homicide, but there seems to be a real push to identify her as Nicole Lawrence. Danny Merkel feels that the Feds are convinced it's her. They are postulating that she took a flight from Detroit to L.A. under an assumed name. However, the flight was stopped in Vegas because of the bad weather, and it appears she partnered with someone to drive to L.A. They assume whoever it was, knew that she was carrying some dough, and he or she killed her and dumped her off the road, knowing in a few days there would be nothing left. That investigation is continuing."

A smile slowly crept onto Dianne's face and she sat next to David putting her arm on his shoulder. "Well, I guess that's the last piece of the puzzle. That sick bastard finally got what she deserved. What a monster she was."

"I'm sorry, Dianne, but I just don't know. It doesn't seem real. She was such a brilliant psychopath, I wonder if we'll ever know. A monster that had Courtney, Reilly, and Malone killed, had Patty beaten to a pulp, and then killed Leon and Edgar Black and Marti Glassman with her own hand, ends up in a ditch? She stole hundreds of millions from her company, fed classified information to the Russians, and then after all of that, she allows herself to be whacked in the desert just hours before she was leaving the country for somewhere. I dunno, baby, I just think it's a bit far-fetched. In all the years of my career with the Israeli government, I never knew of anything that resembled this creature, and I am wondering if this was part of her plan."

"I know, my darling David, but you have to let go of all of it. It's been so long tracking down this creature, and if she was able to fool the Feds, we'll never find out what really happened."

At that, David Korman, the 65-year-old ex-spy put on his cardigan sweater and took a long walk down Third Avenue, looking in the windows and at people eating at outside cafes, but he saw nothing. The one thought that kept reverberating in his head was that it was better to be by himself than to be alone. This allowed him to return home to Dianne, take her into his arms, and whisper in her ear, "Yes, it's finally over, and my love for you is as strong as ever." She smiled as she guided him into their bedroom and put their entire ordeal to rest.

Chapter 66

AFTER A LONG, tiring trip, Laura Benson's private driver pulled into the modern, one-story home just outside greater metropolitan Aukland, a city on the north island of New Zealand. With her luggage tucked away, Laura, aka Nicole Lawrence, sat on a black leather, Eames chair in her living area and closed her eyes. Events of the past few days danced inside her skull. Moments later, the phone rang. With some nervousness, she held the phone to her ear and a strong female voice said. "Laura, this is Jeanine at the realty office. I am so glad that you are safely ensconced in your new digs. We got you a sensational deal on the house and you'll love New Zealand. How about lunch today, just two single, gorgeous women getting acquainted. OK if I pick you up at one? Great. Bye."

Nicole Lawrence sat back in her chair, wiggled her toes a bit, smiled and contemplated the prospects for her new life.